TREE OF BONE AND MIST

THE SWORD OF RHIANNON: BOOK ONE

MELISSA E. BECKWITH

Tree of Bone and Mist
Book One: The Sword of Rhiannon
© by Melissa E. Beckwith 2016

Cover design, editing, and formatting done by http://fiction-atlas.com
Cover Art by Jackie Felix:
https://jackiefelixart.deviantart.com/
Copy editing done by:
https://facebook.com/WaddellEditingServices/
Map by Cornelia Yoder: www.corneliayoder.com

Woodland Cottage Publications
ISBN: 978-0-692-98131-3

CONTENTS

Before you get lost in the enchanting world of *The Sword of Rhiannon*, pick up the spellbinding prequel to this epic fantasy series for FREE

Click here to get *Flight of the Raven* for FREE:

https://dl.bookfunnel.com/ua8lv3jq3b

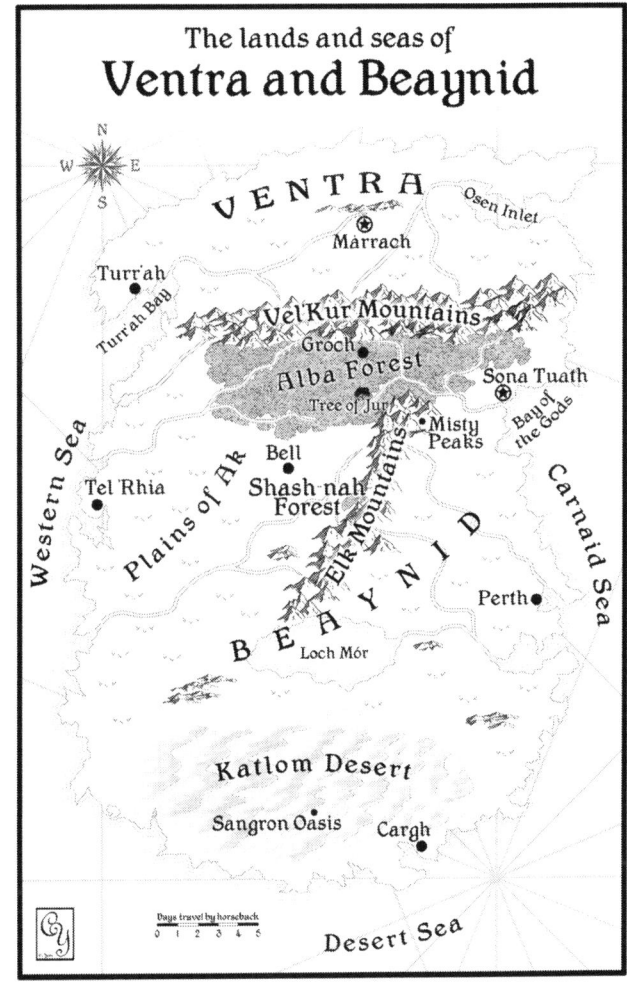

The lands and seas of
Ventra and Beaynid

VENTRA

Osen Inlet

Marrach

Turr'ah

Turr'ah Bay

Vel'Kur Mountains

Groch

Alba Forest

Sona Tuath

Tree of Jur

Bay of the Gods

Misty Peaks

Western Sea

Plains of Ar

Bell

Shash'nah Forest

Tel'Rhia

Elk Mountains

BEAYNID

Carnaid Sea

Perth

Loch Mór

Katlom Desert

Sangron Oasis

Cargh

Days travel by horseback
0 1 2 3 4 5

Desert Sea

To the epic love of my life, my high school sweetheart and husband,
Richard Beckwith
Thank you for believing in me.

PROLOGUE

Through an opening in the trees, the light of an autumn moon illuminated a slim, dark-haired woman kneeling before a swollen stream. She thrust her arms into the icy brook then frantically splashed the water on her face and chest. Her ragged breath and muffled cries echoed off the trees in the center of a dense forest. An occasional spark of lightning jabbed at the darkness that cloaked the land. A cloud drifted over the moon for a moment, then sailed free spilling forth an ethereal light upon the woman. Slowly she held her arms up high, tightly holding a necklace so that it glistened in the moonlight. A loud clap of thunder shook her from her obsessive thoughts.

As if sensing someone was watching her, the woman quickly put the necklace into a pouch and hid it within the folds of her cloak. Still kneeling beside the creek, she looked up at the moon for just a moment and then let out a chilling howl that was carried on the blowing wind as the storm grew closer.

With the singing of the wind and whispers of the ancient trees, the woman's image melted into that of a large black fox. A brilliant green light rose from the animal and with her shape-shift came the smell of damp earth and musty wood. The light dimmed into darkness, and the dull aroma of earth blew away on the wind. Rain started to fall, lightly at first, and then into a driving storm only moments later.

A violent shard of lightning slashed across the blackened sky. The moon once again broke free of the dark shadowy clouds, and the shape-shifter fox darted into the cover of the trees. Through mud and rain and a biting wind, she ran with certainty and determination. Thick trees and soft ferns hailed the fox as she silently sped by.

Finally, she reached a meadow, soaked from the rain, her thick fur sparkling in the silvery moonlight. She collapsed into the tall grass and filled her lungs with the crisp, moist air. The fragrances of sharp pine and cool meadow grass filled her senses and relaxed her body. It was done-she was home. She finally possessed that which she had for so long yearned to hold.

Soon her heart slowed and her breathing became lazy and relaxed. The animal climbed to its feet and looked up to the moon once again. As if coaxed by the soft melody of a night bird the fox's form grew into that of a woman again. Crouched on the ground half hidden in the tall clumps of meadow grass the woman slowly straightened up and stretched her slim arms to the heavens. Her dark skin, slick with rain and mist, glistened in the pale light.

A deer darted into the meadow, sniffed the air, then bolted back into the safety of the forest. Quickly the woman turned and headed off into a dense thicket. So unyielding were the bushes, brambles, and trees that they should have impeded the shape-shifter's progress, yet she melted effort-lessly into the wood. Pulling her cloak tightly around her body, she traveled further and further into the forest until she reached her destination, the Forest Folk village of Ghroc.

Silently the woman made her way down the dark lane. Everyone was peacefully snuggled into their warm beds in a restful slumber. No torches lit up the well-worn paths for all those of the Goyor race could see perfectly even in the blackest of nights. The woman made no sound as she ran down the path to the edge of the village where her cottage sat nestled in the forest.

Hastily she slipped inside. The woman made her way to the cupboards and retrieved a glass. She then went to a worn trunk by the fireplace and opened it slowly. Before reaching in, however, she was stopped by a tinge of guilt followed by a wave of paranoia. Cautiously she looked around the room. Then a thin smile curled across her lips, and she chuckled at herself for she shared the cottage with no one. She pulled out a large glass decanter with a jeweled stopper at the narrow mouth. Amber liquid gurgled as it slipped into a waiting glass. With an unsteady hand, she brought it to her lips and took a long passionate drink. The liquor burned down her throat and set her belly aflame. Her lips curved into a satisfied smile as the warmth rushed through her veins. Her troubles seemed to ease away into a tepid sea of comfort.

She knew she was to bring nothing of the unblessed into Ghroc, especially this intoxicating drink. But she needed it and longed for the sweet release that it whispered into her ears. She did not care for all the rules of Ghroc. She was sure that it was the rules that caused her mother to leave the village so many years ago. The woman sighed and took another drink.

"Did you enjoy your walk?" a deep yet feminine voice called out from the shadows. The woman jumped, surprised by this intrusion and dropped her glass, it shattered on the floor and dark liquor spayed across the hem of her cloak and dress.

An old woman came out of the shadowy recesses into a

shaft of moonlight burning through an uncovered window. Her thick gray hair was left long, so it bushed around her head like a crown held in place by golden combs said to be a gift from Pom-Ni, the god of the Forest Folk. A wreath of dark green Temmer tree leaves encircled her head. Her weathered old face wore no expression at all. "It will be dawn soon, and you have been gone all night." Her voice was as smooth as a frozen lake. "By the way, how is the Empress of Ventra? I am told she is with child." The woman's tone was sarcastic.

"Ventra?" the young woman asked in a shocked voice. "Sun-Song, that is too great a distance for me to walk in one night!" She spoke to the older woman in an unfriendly tone.

"But you saw the empress," Sun-Song accused. "You cannot deny it, Baobh. I saw you arrive at that cottage in the forest." The old woman's hands balled into tight fists at each side of her white robe.

"You must be overly tired. Go back to your cottage." Baobh smiled wickedly and emptied the decanter into another glass dismissing her accusations.

"You are not as secretive as you would like to think. There was a shadow that followed you through meadow, marsh, and forest. I followed you, and I saw what you did to that Archigos woman!" Sun-Song's calm voice cracked escalating into a shout. "You have a murderous heart, Baobh Dark-Water!" she screamed and pointed a long, thin finger at the younger woman.

"Old woman, you are mad." Baobh swept her hand in the air in a rude gesture.

"Deny it! Deny it if you can!" Sun-Song's eyes grew large. "You have brought shame to all Goyor tonight!"

"Go on home, old woman. Go back to your books," Baobh said and turned away from her.

"I saw your unspeakable actions. I saw you strike down the Empress of Ventra!" Sun-Song's voice cracked again.

"I have killed no one. You are just afraid of those heathens!" Baobh turned and looked into the old emissary's eyes. "Now go, I am tired."

"Your persistent hunt of the woman has finally driven you into madness," the old woman whispered. "Is your ambition so great that you murder to feed its hunger?"

Baobh reached into the pouch at her waist and felt the cool, smooth stones of the Necklace of Verna. A smile crossed her thick lips. "My hunger is sated."

"So, you do not deny it?" Sun-Song asked softly.

"Old woman, you need to leave now, or you will greatly regret it."

Sun-Song stiffened, her eyes opened wide. Baobh was not sure if it was anger or fear that caused her to quake. A new confidence started to bubble in the pit of her gut.

"What you have done tonight will spark a war, not only across the land, but also in the realm of the gods!"

"You are a foolish woman," Baobh spat. "I killed the Archigos Empress. She was in possession of something that I had to have." A spark of hunger burned hot in her eyes. "The very instrument I need to take the throne of Sona Tuath-the throne that is rightfully mine!"

Sun-Song looked down searching the worn floorboards as if wrestling with some decision and then finally she looked back up at Baobh. "You are as misguided as your mother, Raven. Hopefully she has finally found peace in death." The younger woman flinched at mention of her poor mother, long dead and buried in a simple grave on a grassy bluff overlooking the Carnaid Sea. The older woman slowly walked up to Baobh. "The Goyor are a peaceful race. We are here to tend to the earth, we are the keepers of the balance between nature and the angry outer world. Your desires are unnatural and disgusting! When you came to us you were a girl and we took you in. Though you had been raised in the world of the unblessed we thought that we could instruct you in the ways of your people. We were terribly wrong!"

She balled her fists again in determination and coldly searched the depths of Baobh's emerald green eyes. "You will accompany me to the elders and await your punishment." Sun-Song grabbed the younger woman's arm.

Baobh tilted her head back and laughed. "You are a foolish woman. You might be of the Emissary Class, but I have the Necklace of Verna!"

Sun-Song's eyes widened in shock, and she pulled her hand away from Baobh's arm as if she had been burned. "The powers of the necklace are not for your use."

"You feeble-witted old woman, did you think I would be content to live here tending the dirt forever?" Baobh's words dripped with disgust as her lips formed the word "dirt."

Sun-Song made a fist and struck Baobh's face with as much force that she could gather. The younger woman landed on the floor with a dull thump. Baobh's hand went to her burning face. She looked up at the woman who was standing over her. Quickly, Baobh grabbed the woman's slim ankle and pulled it from under her causing her to crumple to the ground. She crawled over to the old woman. "Do you really think I would let you strip me of my power as a Goyor and be tried by those worthless Law Keepers?" Baobh whispered into Sun-Song's ear. "I will have more power than you could ever dream of!"

Baobh lifted her head and started to laugh, a wild, demented sound, her voice echoing across the room. Sun-Song's hand carefully curled around a large shard of broken glass lying on the floor. Using all her strength, she slashed the shard across Baobh's bronzed face. She screamed in pain and quickly brought her fingers to her face. She took her hands away, retching at the sight of her own bright, red blood dripping from her curled fingers.

"You stupid woman!" Baobh hissed, then jumped up and took a knife from its wooden block. "I will kill you, Goyor!" Baobh looked down at the old woman on the floor, the pure white robes of the Emissary now stained red with her blood. Then she sliced into the woman's chest in a blind rage, drunk on the promise of power. The Emissary screamed a howling, painful sound of death. Slow, ragged breaths escaped from her dry mouth as tears fell from bloodied cheeks.

Then a small fire of remembrance kindled and burned within the Emissary. She gasped and looked up at the dark figure. "It is you that the prophecy speaks of!" Sun-Song's eye's widened in the horror of this realization. "The ancient prophecy that we have tried in vain to understand, it is clear to me now!"

"The prophecy, ha!" Baobh spat on to the floor next Sun-Song who lay dying.

"You have killed Empress Kossi, but you will not be without judgment," Sun-Song spoke in a harsh voice. "The Leader Kossi has not died without an heir. This prophecy is yours, black-hearted woman: 'Fresh from the womb she will be torn away. An heir will be found among people foreign and unblessed, not knowing the ways of the

ancients. The blood of two nations will burn within her, divided and separate, though she will unite them. She alone will have the power to strike down the child of the earth who has forsaken her position and swims in the blood of innocent ones. This little one will be a leader of many, richly blessed by the Warrior Goddess. With a mighty hand and a pure heart, she will send the Dark One's soul to its death. Betrayed by her own children-one light-one dark, they will rejoice upon her death!' That is how the prophecy was recorded by our people so long ago, and that is how it will be. Now we know of whom it speaks!" The Emissary grew weak but a faint smile crossed her lips, thankful that the mystery of an ancient prophecy had been revealed to her before she was rendered moribund upon her death.

In a rage, Baobh struck Sun-Song one last time. The Emissary sprawled across the floor, her empty eyes staring into the darkness. A rough, ragged scream of rage was torn from Baobh's throat and filled the small cottage. It escaped on a moist breeze down over the village, through the trees, and then out over the fields, where it vanished with the wind. The village of Ghroc was once again in silence.

Knowing the whole village would soon be coming to investigate, Baobh ran from her cottage and left Ghroc as fast as she could. Leaving her life as one of the Forest Folk of Ghroc she fled back into the world of the unblessed where she had been born and spent her youngest years-back to where her ambition and rage drove her.

Once again standing in the meadow that led to the hidden Goyor village, Baobh fell to her knees and began to tremble uncontrollably. A cold gale started to blow from the north, and the moon was soon covered by hostile clouds.

She had killed an Emissary! Sudden realization of what she had just done descended upon her like the slice of a guillotine. Huge, hysterical tears of fear and remorse carved a path through the blood smeared upon her cheeks. She looked up to the moon to ask for forgiveness but was answered with a bitter wind that set her cheeks ablaze and squeezed her heart so tight she thought she might die. Then the wind was gone, the skies fury just a whisper that echoed in the night.

Slowly Baobh lowered her searching eyes and took a deep breath. She slipped her hand into the pouch and brought out the necklace. Her eyes quickly went to the empty socket at the center of the necklace. She gasped at the sight of the missing stone.

"The largest stone is missing!" she cried. "Why did I not see that before?"

For a long time, she looked upon the vacant setting contemplating where the missing stone might be. "It is just one stone," she finally whispered. "The remaining six stones will be enough to guarantee me Sona Tuath and the throne!"

Her sensitive Goyor ears heard the dull thud of quick footfall and recalled her to her senses. She swung around in a panic just as a soft drizzle began to fall, sprinkling the meadow with tiny sparkling drops of starlight. A tall man approached Baobh at a dead run, his face as bright as the moon. It was Eagle Pridecaller, the youngest and newest elder of Ghroc!

CHAPTER ONE

In the forest, you find the light
In the forest, you will have sight

The blood of the stone cries out
The blood within cries of doubt

Green hills, tall mountains, and a river of life
Blurred faces, hard hands and a land of strife

You will find what you most desire
Your life, as payment, it may require

A black spider abides within white walls
With her sticky web and fangs of poison, she calls

She needs to eat of you in the red light of dawn
She needs to stop the Old Word before she is gone

What will you do, oh daughter of the North
Will you take the power from its source

CHAPTER ONE

Can you slay the raven and out of her life bring forth

-Spider Web; author unknown

Like the cry of an angry river the sound of rushing blood filled her ears. As her heart thumped wildly in her chest, a cold mist started to swallow the damp earthen floor. The twisted, gnarled tree trunk began to hum, the still air vibrated with its life song. Her wide black eyes saw the tree start to glow a warm amber color. Brighter and brighter it burned until she was forced to shield her eyes.

A mist engulfed her and filled the air with the dull smell of earth, roots and blood. A voice echoed in the forest. She knew the voice, though she could not ever remember hearing it before. A voice strong and tender all at once. A voice that tickled the edges of her memory. A voice that she knew belonged to her mother. The voice kept crying out to her, yet the words would not be revealed.

She moved closer to the tree, knowing she had no other choice. It could be denied no more than she could refuse her next breath of air. She had to answer its call, for it spoke to her soul. Fear receded into acceptance and wonder into impatience. She crept closer still, never wavering from her course. Aroma and mist swirled around her long black hair as she cut a path to the hollow heart of the tree.

From somewhere deep within the tree she heard another voice. A voice much different from her mother's–his voice. At first, it was as faint as a quickly passing memory, but it grew in both life and color and began to call to her. His voice was like a soothing melody to her ears and tasted of the sweetest golden honey on her tongue. She peered hard into the center of the tree to discern the source of this voice and his form melted subtly from the mist and glowing light. Vague at first,

12

his features began to take shape. His face was obscured as always, leaving her aching to look upon his likeness. Her name floated from unseen lips upon the warm air as he called to her.

Suddenly his form dissipated into the mist and an arm darted from the hollow trunk. It seized her wrist in an angry, demanding embrace and started to pull her into the tree. The feelings of contentment and belonging exploded into fear and repulsion as she tried to rip from her captor. He would not be deprived of his prize though and pulled her even further into the gaping mouth of the tree.

Pain blossomed in her arm as his fingers burned into her skin. Grabbing onto a small branch that grew near the base of the tree, she felt blood dripping from her clasping hand as the sharp, knife-like bark carved through her tender, desperate flesh. She lost her grip, the slickness of her own blood playing traitor, and was quickly pulled into a darkness so bitter it chilled her very bones.

Wakefulness took Rhiannon Kossi so hard and sudden it was like being caught up in a violent churning wind. After she had become aware of her surroundings, she sat up slowly and drew her knees to her chest and buried her face in the soft blanket around her. After a few moments, she slowly crawled out of bed. Her father, Peter, had changed little in her childhood room since she moved out into the main house years before. She sighed and staggered into the central room of the cabin then stopped short. A man sat comfortably on the couch, watching her. The smile on his lips infuriated her.

"What are you doing here?"

"What kind of welcome is that, Peach?"

"The kind a woman gives a man who she finds in her home, uninvited." She eyed him suspiciously.

Matthew Foster laughed. "I see you haven't changed at all

since you've been away." She did not answer. "So, when are ya coming home, hun? You've been away long enough."

"Matt, we've talked about this before." She did not want to have this conversation.

"Okay, okay," he said and stood up. "So ya broke my heart, but that didn't mean ya had to move away. This is just as much ye'r home as it is mine."

She shook her head and started towards the kitchen. "Daddy isn't here Matt." She yawned and poured herself a cup of coffee.

"Where is he?"

"I don't know, but when I find him, I'll tell him you're looking for him."

He walked over to her. "It's our busiest season, for God's sake, where the hell is he?" He leaned on the counter, crossed his arms and smiled broadly at her. "Ye'r welcome for mak'n the coffee."

"Thank you for the coffee," she said finally.

He stayed silent for a long time, and then: "Ya don't know where he went?"

"No Matt, I don't."

"We had two mares foal last night, we've got some sick cattle, and we need to start getting the near fields ready for summer." He shook his head.

"I called him yesterday morning and told him I was coming out. Everything seemed fine then." She shrugged.

"What's this?" He picked up a small dagger that was sitting on the counter and turned it over in his hand examining the knife.

"I'm not sure. I found it on the floor when I got here yesterday. Daddy always picks up weird things here and there."

Matt frowned straining to make out the detailed carvings in the polished ivory handle.

Finally satisfied, he replaced the dagger on the counter. "Well, if ya see him, please tell him I was here." He put on his ragged, brown cowboy hat and started walking towards the front door.

"Matt?"

He turned to look at her. But when she said nothing, he finally left.

Rhiannon stared after Matthew a long time after he was gone. She expected to feel pain, or at least emptiness, but she did not. Again, she was stymied by the numb feeling that had grown over the winter and now seemed to run through her whole body and mind. She tried to pinpoint the exact time when her heart started to harden towards him. She wondered why his touch suddenly turned her cold. As always, she came to the conclusion it was at the advent of the nightmares. It was almost as if she were looking down from a high tree observing her life and having no control over the twists and turns. She sighed and took a long drink of coffee and wondered again where her father had gone off to.

She knew her father was upset when she called yesterday and demanded he tell her, once and for all, what had happened to her mother, Sernia, but she did not expect him to just leave. She felt she was owed some answers and when Rhiannon told Peter about the vivid nightmares she had been having for months, he grew quiet. He finally told her to come to the ranch, and he would tell Rhiannon all about her mother.

All she knew is that she was six when her mother died, and she and Peter came to Daniel Foster's northern Montana ranch twenty-four years earlier, but not much else. She thought it odd that Peter had no pictures of her mother. No pictures of when they were dating, no wedding pictures, no photographs of her of any kind. Throughout her growing years, she would persist with asking questions about her mother, but Peter was stubborn, and her questions went unanswered. This time she would not be put off, but here she was, standing in the kitchen of his empty cabin with a growing uneasy feeling.

Rhiannon looked down at the huge, silver she-wolf that had walked into the room and sat beside her. She patted the wolf's soft head. "Let's go find daddy, Luna."

Quickly, she ate, dressed, and left her father's cabin, and for reasons she did not understand, took the dagger with her at the last moment. She left, determined to get the truth from him even if she had to hunt him down. She went to the stables and saddled her horse and led him out into the bright sunshine. Suddenly she stopped and took the strange dagger from her pocket wanting to look at it one more time. The polished steel tip caught the sun and threw it back into her eyes. Her fingertip mindlessly crossed over the hungry blade. "Ouch!" Tiny crimson beads formed along a small cut across her index finger. Quickly she stuck the injured finger in her mouth. Examining the offending knife, she carefully turned it over in her palm.

An intricate picture of a tiny white castle at the edge of a red ocean was carved into one side of the handle. On the other side, an image of a fierce purple dragon stared out at her. Under the dragon was an inscription that she could not read. The letters looked oddly familiar, yet distant-almost menacing.

Quickly she stuffed the knife in her jacket pocket and hauled herself up onto the back of her stallion she called Zellan. She whistled, and Luna darted from around the corner of her father's cabin. Pulling the reins, she quietly led her horse from the stable and towards the great pastures.

Wind pulled at the thick, black ribbons of her hair. Faster and faster she pushed the large stallion, so shiny and black. On the steed's heels was the enormous form of a she-wolf.

Her tongue hung from her mouth framed with large white fangs. Thick bristly fur danced in rhythm with the wind.

Free as a violent storm that roamed the oceans searching for victims, she crossed the horizon disappearing into the sun. Winter was now taking its last breaths as an early spring began to spread across the never-ending golden fields of the west.

A purple shadow painted the jagged mountains as tawny grass danced across the meadows. As she rode on, she scanned the horizon for any sign of her father. She raced through acres of grazing land that were set aside for the herds of cattle during the winter but were now empty and raw as the day they were first settled.

A sky of the deepest powder blue sat atop the mountains and meadows. A bright yellow sun covered the earth with a warm blanket and seemed to be urging her on as she raced across the land. The air was unusually warm for a spring day, and the smell of pine and grass hung thickly in the air.

A sly fog of exhaustion crept in over her like a spoiled lover. The nightmares had grown steadily worse all winter. Now she pushed the fog aside, discarding it to the warm Montana wind.

At the top of a small rise, she stopped to scan the golden hills that gently rolled out before her. Carefully, she searched the small rocky outcroppings that broke up the grassy land-scape. From the west, a huge black cloud quickly formed in the distance. Where sunshine had been just a short while before, now loomed a billowing, raging storm. Gray sheets of rain fell from its belly, saturating the land. Hot bolts of light-ning struck the earth with deep echoes of might. At this time of year, rain was not uncustomary, but a thunderstorm was very unusual, so she sat and looked at it for a while before she turned her back on it and lopped off towards the mountain.

A brisk wind blew up from behind her as they continued to the base of the mountain, the temperature had dropped quickly. She carefully looked for her father in the shade under huge oaks and between rocky crags.

Cold drops of rain started to fall, drenching horse and rider. Rhiannon turned her face into the rain. She followed a small path that cut into the mountain-a path her father had taken her hundreds of times when she was growing up. Perhaps she would find him here, among the trees, seeking respite from a demanding daughter.

As they rounded a stand of pines on the edge of the small trail, Zellan's ears went back flat against his glossy black head, and he slowed to a walk. All the tiny hairs on Rhiannon's arms stood erect. A strange tingling vibrated through her skin, and everything began to glow an eerie white.

Suddenly an intense flash of light blinded her, instantaneously followed by an earsplitting boom of thunder. A flame shot up where the lightning had struck a tree, and smoke started to drift upwards. The dry smell of burning pine and loud pops of flaming pine cones filled the air. Somewhere an owl screamed out from the trees and fluttered away to safety.

The great stallion reared and shrieked out in fear. He took off at a gallop down the path that led further into the forest, a silvery ghost at his heels. Rhiannon held on to the reins with all her strength. The harder she tugged at the bit, the harder Zellan pulled back. The ground was wet, and the footing treacherous as his sharp hooves slashed through the soft mud. She squeezed her eyes shut and buried her face in his mane, trusting him to bring her to safety.

They reached a small clearing and Zellan finally began to slow; his sleek coat had lathered to a froth. A ray of wet sunshine poked through the black clouds. The thunder had passed on, leaving the lonesome sound of raindrops spattering on fallen pine needles. She stopped at the familiar place she and her father had spent many hours just talking and listening to the whispers of the forest.

"Daddy!" she called, her flat voice dissolving into unyielding trees. She wiped at the raindrops that soaked her face. "Daddy!" she called again.

Luna suddenly started barking and snarling and as Zellan's ears folded back again and he let out a deep warning snort. She followed the wolf's line of vision to a gigantic tree half hidden behind a large oak. Just as suddenly as the wolf had started barking, she abruptly sat down, raised her face to the sky, and gave a long, mournful howl. Zellan sidestepped and neighed, seeming to reprimand the she-wolf. Eeriness lay in the forest like a crouching lion ready to spring.

In the deepest moment of thick silence between Luna's howls, Zellan reared up, and Rhiannon slid from his back. She lay in the mud and looked up at the mighty and proud trees that circled her. As a child the forest had been so peaceful and filled with wonder and possibilities, now it was choked with fear and foreboding. The sky above had cleared a bit, letting a hole of blue show through the blanket of angry gray. All around her, drops of spent rain fell from boughs of sad trees as they reached to the sky in a poetic dance of life. The forest was crying.

Zellan walked up to her and snorted his warm breath in her face as if to apologize. She sat up and patted his inquisitive muzzle. Mud was stuck in her hair and splattered her clothing. "What's the matter with you?"

Luna's plaintive howls once again filled the clearing and echoed through the trees. Zellan nervously sidestepped and shook his massive head. On hands and knees, Rhiannon scampered across the forest floor towards her yowling she-wolf, mud squishing through her fingers as she went. "And what's wrong with you?"

A familiar smell started to fill the air. Rhiannon stopped and closed her eyes tight. The smell of earth and roots and blood wafted across the opening. She opened her eyes and stared at what lay before her: her nightmares realized. The huge tree began to whisper. It was such a faint hum that she was not certain it was there at all. Slowly it became more evident. As if her dreams had been mere rehearsals, her body answered to the call of the tree as it had hundreds of times before.

Slowly she stood before the tree, her eyes were wide, and she began to tremble. She felt Zellan's hot breath on her shoulder and without looking away, reached behind, grabbing tightly onto the reins in a desperate attempt to deny the call she was forced to answer. The stallion proved to be an unwise choice for an anchor, though, for he moved with her, almost pushing her, as they were drawn closer.

The twisted trunk sat in its place as if to mock her and an amber glow started to burn within the tree. The light grew brighter, and a golden mist crawled across the muddy forest floor. Luna pinned her ears back and growled, long sharp fangs framing a feral smile.

The tree began to burn brighter, and she became afraid, but could not move away. Curiosity bade her stay as a familiar feeling sprinkled her soul like an old childhood memory now long forgotten. A heady, dull scent hung in the damp mountain air becoming overpowering as it coated her skin and tongue.

Fear began to recede, replaced by a feeling that this was something she should know, like the words to a well-known song whose name she could not recall. An overwhelming urge to touch the light clawed through her being. Slowly she edged forward, ignoring all rational thought. Like the bitter cold wind calls the winter to come along, Rhiannon continued her path toward an intimate, well-known course.

As though lightning had struck again, she was blinded by a searing light, and a low rumble battered her ears. In an instant, thousands of memories of her life on a Montana cattle ranch exploded in her mind leaving a jumble of brightly colored images swimming within her. Time had stopped, and as each image grew old, she knew they were gone forever.

When all the images were gone, she quietly left that place and flew over the Earth. She was awestruck by its raw beauty and perfectly round shape. As it, too, faded from sight, she drifted farther and farther away into a darkness that could not be explained. She felt as though she were being pulled towards something. A place she could not resist, nor did she wish to.

Onward it drew her into its bosom. And then she saw her: the woman who danced in her dreams. The woman she was convinced was the image of her long-dead mother. "You're almost home, my love," the woman whispered, and then her world went black.

CHAPTER TWO

*"Deep within a man's heart lies a beast or a blessing...'tis only his
mind that can decipher the difference."*
- C. H. Timmon; Modern Philosophies

Voices echoed in her head like rapid footfall in a damp cave.
The abruptness of cool, hard dirt lay dully beneath her sore
body. The prickly scent of pine, and the warm aroma of
horse was all around her.

In the distance, the fierce snarling of a wolf vibrated in
her ears. She took a deep breath and gagged when dirt hit the
back of her throat. Through a veil of pain, she focused on the
foreign words being spoken around her. It sounded familiar
to her, yet she could make no sense of the discussion.

Rhiannon cracked open an eye and saw the rough,
gnarled trunk of a tree-*that* tree! Suddenly remembering
what had befallen her, she opened her eyes a little more to
see if the tree was still glowing and spewing out its earthy-
smelling mist. However, the tree was quiet now. She was
relieved. She let her eyes slide up its trunk with its whirling
knots high up to the sheltering crown of the massive tree.

She almost gasped when she saw hundreds of human bones tied with small ropes swaying in the gentle breeze. Their whiteness shined in the wavering dappled sunlight poking through the leaves.

Before she could think any more about the strange tree of bone and mist, she was roughly flipped over, and a pair of dusty, black boots stood before her. The forms of men in the distance started to come into focus. Trees and horses were not far off. She began to smell meat cooking on a fire, her stomach grumbled in answer.

Suddenly a man's booming voice called out and was answered from a short distance away. Cautiously she looked up at the man, and the light sent a shock of hot pain through her head. Unceremoniously, he thrust his hand through her loose hair and pulled her to her feet. Even at her considerable height of six feet, this man was very large-a good six or seven inches above Rhiannon's head. His face looked like a boiled pig; bloated and pale. His breath reeked of liquor, and he stank like he had not bathed in weeks. His dark blond hair was gray with filth. Bile rose and burned her throat.

Other men had gathered around jeering and laughing. Slowly, she lowered her hands to her thighs and defiantly looked into his bloodshot eyes. He gave a hoot of laughter. "This here girly thinks she is pretty tough," he announced, so heavily accented she could barely make out what he had said.

"This is Daniel Foster's land," she barked. "What are you doing here?" More laughter echoed in the trees. She balled up her fist and smashed the man's face. He yelped in pain and let go of her hair. Crimson blood spilled from his broad pudgy nose, and he quickly covered it with his grimy hands.

"Yer gonna pay for that!" he yelled as blood rolled down into his mouth. He pulled back his arm, and with quickness a man of his size should not have possessed, he slapped her face with the back of his hand. She went spinning off and landed violently on the ground. He brought his booted foot back and kicked her in the stomach. The air was suddenly forced out of her lungs, and she gagged as dirt and pebbles hit her sore face. In the background, she heard Luna viciously snarling and Zellan's furious cries.

Suddenly a loud, raucous voice shouted out over the camp. The men grew silent, and the enormous man quickly snuck off. The crowd parted for a slight man who approached with a steady gait. Defiantly, Rhiannon slowly rose to her feet and with great difficulty and much pain, straightened up-she towered over the dainty man.

White blond hair was pulled back tightly in a small plait at the nape of his neck. His eyes were ringed with blonde eyelashes that were much too long to belong to a man. His skin was red, burned from the sun, and heavily pocked from some long-forgotten childhood sickness.

Rhiannon slowly scanned the men that circled her. Mail armor shone in the warm sunlight, and long swords hung at their hips. Sleeveless tunics of bright yellow and blue with a large crest emblazed across their chests were worn over their mail. An ominous purple dragon stared out at her. She immediately recognized the crest as the same one that was carved into the dagger's handle that she had found in her father's cabin! "Who are you? Does Daniel know you are here?"

"I can see you have many questions," he said, his voice low and calming, "The queen warned me you might have no knowledge of this place."

She gazed out over his head at the massive pine trees ringing the clearing and quickly realized she was not in a place that she recognized. "I see you have met Yaunn." His smile was deceptively warm. "I am sorry, Lady Kossi, he does not know how to treat women of your position."

Rhiannon folded her stiff arms across her chest. "And who are you?"

"I am High Captain Pann Hepin." He flashed a brilliant smile.

"Does Daniel know you are here, on his land?" she demanded, guessing though that they were not on the ranch anymore.

"Look around you!" he offered. "You are not in your world any longer."

She looked around once again, and though it seemed she had been there before, she did not know it. "What have you done with my father?" she finally pleaded.

"He is on his way to Sona Tuath," Captain Hepin answered

"Sona Tuath?" That name sounded oddly familiar to her.

"Your father will be in Sona Tuath *with Queen Baobh*," he clarified. She opened her mouth, as if to speak, but did not know what to say to that. "I see your father has told you nothing of your history, Lady Kossi." Captain Hepin studied Rhiannon's face. "No matter, the queen wants you," he looked towards Luna, "and your familiars, delivered to Sona Tuath immediately and we have a two-week journey ahead of us."

Later that night she watched a brilliant orange sun dip behind the gigantic, primeval mass of pine trees that surrounded her like a deep, endless hole. Rhiannon sat in a dark corner of Hepin's tent as tears rolled down her swollen face. She had thought for sure Matthew would have found her and her father by now.

She recalled the dagger in her pocket, but wanted to wait until the darkest part of night before trying to get free. One excruciating hour after another passed, as she watched the filtered moonbeams slide across the dirt floor.

The shrill call of a night bird floated upon the cold spring night air. Her bound wrists were sore and raw as they lay in her lap and a relentless pain throbbed between her ears with every beat of her heart. With difficulty, she carefully eased the dagger from her pocket keeping her eyes on Hepin's dark figure as he slumbered. Awkwardly, she labored to pull it from her pocket with her hands still bound. Every few moments she would stop and listen to Hepin's breathing, making sure she had not awakened him.

Finally, the severed rope fell to the ground. She gripped the dagger in her hand and slowly started to crawl towards the opening of Hepin's tent. The air outside was cool, but Rhiannon was sweating as she inched closer to the tent flap. Her heart slammed in her chest so loud she was sure it would wake the sleeping man. Her vision narrowed as her only thoughts were of getting free from the tent and out into the open night air.

"Having trouble sleeping, milady? Maybe you would prefer my bed to that dark corner of the tent." His voice was light and fluid, softly caressing her like a playful wisp of smoke. Rhiannon jumped and spun around to see Hepin crouched in front of her like a tightly coiled spring. "'Tis a long way to Sona Tuath, you really should get used to our humble offerings."

The full moon hung overhead and spilled forth its light. She could see in his eyes, which looked dark in the filtered light, that Hepin's ego would not permit him to call out to his men. "I am quite tired tonight, Lady Kossi. Perhaps I shall just tie you to the tree across the way for the remainder of the night. After a night suffering the bites of flesh-ants, I think you will be much happier with my tent tomorrow night." Hepin yawned in a bored fashion. "Or maybe I shall just give you to Yaunn. I am sure by sun up you would have rather had the ants."

Slowly she readied the dagger-her face showed no

emotion. As quickly as she could, Rhiannon leaped forward and crashed down upon Hepin using her weight to grind him into the ground. She held the dagger to his throat. "If you try and yell for your men you will be dead before your breath leaves your throat," she whispered. Her quickness and Hepin's misplaced confidence had worked in her favor.

"Now tell me, very quietly, Captain Hepin, where is my father."

"I have already told you, he is being taken to Sona Tuath," he hissed.

"There is no such place. Tell me where he is, or I will slice your throat open." Her voice sounded foreign and harsh to her ears.

"You ignorant girl, of course there is such a place. The queen is awaiting your arrival."

"What do you want? Do you want a ransom?" Sweat dripped from Rhiannon's brow splattering across Hepin's face. "Who are you with? Why do you want my father?"

"Listen carefully, woman, for I speak the truth. From the Tree, we traveled to your pitiful land and laid hold of your father. Immediately upon our return from the tree, I sent him to Sona Tuath. The queen now awaits my return, with you."

"Why does she want my father?" she finally asked, humoring him.

"Because she knew you would come looking for him. 'tis *you* she wants, Lady Kossi."

"Why?" Rhiannon demanded.

"The prophecy!"

"What are you talking about?" Her whisper was harsh.

"The prophecy," he repeated angrily. "I will tell you no more."

Something started to burn deep within her soul, like a ferocious beast starting to stir. "I am going to ask you one more time, and then I will kill you if you don't tell me where you're holding my father." Rhiannon pushed the blade into Hepin's neck, a tiny sliver of blood formed around the sharp edge. His eyes widened with sudden fear.

"I am telling you the truth. Your father will be in Sona Tuath," he answered quickly.

She held the blade steady against his neck. "Where is Sona Tuath?"

"If you ride with haste, less than a fortnight's journey east of here."

Just then, something moved outside the tent, and Rhiannon turned to look. Hepin heaved Rhiannon from him and onto the floor. In an instant, he was on top of her. "You will be very sorry you dared to put a knife to *my* throat," Hepin breathed through clenched teeth. "As soon as you get to Sona Tuath you and your father will be dead before you can even say your partings," he sneered. "'Tis a good thing the queen wants you alive, or I would kill you where you lay."

A blinding savagery simmered at her spine screaming to be let loose, a ferocity so primal and raw that it threatened to swallow her soul if she did not control it, yet she knew it was already too late.

Calmly she closed her eyes, allowing the power of rage to wash over her. Visions of bloody battles fought by generations of mysterious warriors flashed in her mind as if they were her own memories. They called her to battle. They called her to her destiny. She answered.

With strength she did not know she possessed, Rhiannon positioned her knees under Hepin and pushed with all her might. He flew across the tent and landed with a dull thud. She lunged at him dodging a fist, and without another thought, she carved away his voice, and his life.

She wiped the warm spots of blood from her face as Hepin's eyes widened, then defeated, he died in the moonlight. His shocked eyes peered out at Rhiannon through strands of powdery white hair that looked like orphaned moonbeams in the darkness. His blood burned on her tongue as she turned and vomited.

Quickly she crawled across the dusty floor, carefully stuck her head out of the tent flap and saw a man sitting not too far off keeping watch. A small fire crackled and fluttered in the cool breeze making his pudgy face glow. She did not need a closer look to know that it was Yaunn. He was fast asleep.

She slipped from the tent, quietly crawling towards a large bush. Safely concealed, she sat for a long while and tried to rid her mind of murder, but the memories of Hepin's eyes would not let her go. She looked down at his blood, still covering her hands. Warm tears streamed down her face as she tried to stifle sobs of guilt and confusion. The consuming rage that allowed her to so effortlessly take a man's life was now gone, leaving her cold and empty like a discarded seashell lying on a lonely beach.

The distant screech of an owl pulled her from remorse and reminded her the night was old and would soon give way to dawn. Taking a deep breath, she crawled across the hard earth to her wolf.

She freed both Luna and Zellan, grateful that Zellan had not let anyone close enough to him to unsaddle and bridle him. Knowing she could easily be run down in the unfamiliar forest, she made her way to the soldier's tethered horses. One by one she cut them loose, hoping they would run far away.

As each one was freed, it galloped off into the cool mist, but as she cut through the confines of the last horse, he sidestepped and screamed out nervously, shattering the silence like a crystal vase. From somewhere behind her, she heard a man's voice call out and then another answer.

The horse ran off into the dark cover of the wood. She

jumped up into her saddle, gripped the reins and dug her heels in. Zellan bolted towards the trees with Luna at his side.

A man shouted from behind her and grabbed hold of her hair. She held on to Zellan and pulled against his unyielding grip. She turned around and saw Yaunn. Luna snarled and jumped atop the big man, knocking him to the ground as they disappeared into the darkness.

Zellan quickly found a small path leading away into a dark wood. She looked behind her and could see smudges of fire as torches were being lit, and men entered the forest behind them. The brush was thick and impeded their escape. The trail ended suddenly in a tangle of thorny brush. The shouts echoed across a vast forest as they drew closer.

Bushes gave way as a man pushed through the thicket and ran up to them. Zellan snorted and kicked him, crushing his chest. The huge stallion paced and turned trying to find a way out as the group of men closed in. Zellan reared, reached out with sharp hooves slicing through flesh. Taken by a great fear, they backed away, their torches held high and watched the stallion jump over the vegetation. Horse and woman landed hard on the other side, and as Luna appeared ahead of them, they disappeared into the forest amid the angry screams of men.

CHAPTER THREE

My home is deep within the forest dark.
My playmates are the beaver, the squirrel, and the lark.

My new home is hot but never warm, shady but never cool.
My games are not the ones I knew but now hide a jewel.

I am a shadow now, only a whisper of the goddess's breath.
No one will know me nor even mourn my death.
-Kyia Kossi; Gone

A cheerful sun climbed above the spiked treetops, warming a newborn day. Rhiannon stood on a small rise looking around the hinterland that lay before her. The forest abruptly stopped and gave way to fields, fruit and nut trees and a thick stream flowing merrily over small rocks. A little further away was a large, green meadow that looked as if it were carved right out of the heart of the forest.

She removed Zellan's bridle and saddle and let him drink from the crystal stream and find some tender grass. Exhausted, Rhiannon walked out into the warm rays of sunshine. She warily rubbed her tired, dry eyes and then scanned the peaceful surroundings.

Careful of all her aches and pains she sat down on a big, sun-warmed rock. She hugged her knees tightly and silently wept. She was profoundly tired, and hunger pains stabbed at her belly. She was sure her face was damaged, and the huge dark bruise on her stomach was so very tender. Luna walked over and quietly lay down beside her master offering what comfort she could. Instinctively, Rhiannon laid her head upon her wolf's soft pelt.

"I'm going crazy," she whispered, but her voice was lost in a sea of silvery fur.

After a long while, Rhiannon pulled herself up from the rock and walked down to the stream. As she went, a familiar feeling caught her, as if she had taken each step before. She scanned her surroundings, but once again could not remember a time that she had ever been there. Dismissing the notion, Rhiannon bent down and meticulously washed the blood from her face, hands, and arms. She watched as Hepin's blood was washed down the stream and away from her. Silently, she asked for forgiveness from any god that might listen and then drank from the water that was cold, sweet and pure.

As she bent down for another drink, the waters seemed to still, and instead of seeing her own reflection, she saw that of a little girl staring up at her. Rhiannon gasped and jerked her hands from the water, landing solidly on the ground.

Realization settled hard upon her. She knew that face: the little girl was her! Yearning for understanding she quickly returned to the stream's edge. She peered into the water. However, nothing but her own blurry broken image could be seen this time. Rhiannon splashed the crisp water across her face, letting it drip off her chin and splatter onto her chest.

Slowly she stood and walked back into the sunlight towards the tall meadow grass.

As she entered the small meadow a short distance away, Rhiannon was struck by the awe-inspiring beauty laid out before her and the feeling that she had been here, *often*. An image of the meadow covered in wildflowers flashed across her eyes. Brilliant splashes of blue, purple, red and yellow colored her memories. A figure started to form. Rhiannon blinked, trying to rid herself of the vision. However, it would not be erased.

A beautiful woman materialized carrying a small girl on her hip. They were both laughing as they made their way through tall wildflowers. Flowers hung loosely in their long black hair swimming in the warm, sweet breeze. The sound of their laughter echoed in Rhiannon's ears, making her smile and feel as if she were with them.

The woman, so beautiful and graceful, put the little girl down and she raced off into the glorious carpet of flowers. The woman followed as fast as she could, but was held back by a large belly, ripe with the baby that slept within. Suddenly she looked over to Rhiannon and smiled. "Find me." Though her lips did not move, her whisper was carried on the wind and into Rhiannon's mind.

Suddenly, she was gone, carried on the warm breeze that played to the dancing meadow grass. She looked after them for a long while, but they were not to reappear. As the breeze started to pick up, she slowly walked away toward the water. To her right, across the stream was a large tumble of moss-covered boulders. At the base of the rock pile was a small opening, almost too small for Rhiannon to squeeze through.

Immediately recognizing the stones, she ran to them. In the frenzy to enter the small cave, she scraped up her arms but finally got through. The boulders immediately opened to a minuscule area. She sat in the middle of the small cavity as memories swiftly washed over her. From somewhere in the top of the tiny cave a shaft of bright sunlight cut across the dusty floor.

Her she-wolf squeezed through the opening and came to her. She laid her head down onto Luna's soft fur and took in a deep, dusty breath and started to relax, willing sleep to come. As she carelessly ran her fingers over the loose dirt, her fingers touched something soft. Surprised, she jerked her fingers away and sat up almost cracking her head on the ceiling of the cave. Slowly she reached out to it again and took the small object from the dirt. She held it up in the thin beam of light, so bright in the frigid darkness. A small dirty leather pouch swayed from leather thongs. She immediately recognized the small prize!

Rhiannon gasped for air, the dust in the small cave coated her mouth and throat, making her gag. She held the tiny pouch in her hand reverently stroking its softness. Carefully, she tied the pouch to her belt loop, and exhausted, Rhiannon laid down on the cold dirt to rest. She thought about Hepin's blood staining her hands. She thought about a fairytale her father had told her once, a long time ago. He spoke about the massive, shimmering white stone walls of a faraway castle that sat upon jagged cliffs overlooking a red sea. Then sleep finally came and took her away to a land where warriors and soldiers fought to the death, their bright, red blood spilling onto a thirsty earth.

From that small place in her mind between sleep and wakefulness, Rhiannon heard Zellan's cries of warning and was awakened. Luna jumped to her feet and scrambled out of the hole.

She heard a man's voice, and panic washed over her. She heard Luna's sharp bark, then a cry. Quickly she scrambled from the small cave. Shielding her eyes from the bright sunlight, she stood up trying to focus on what was going on.

Just on the other side of the stream, she saw three men standing over Luna where she lay in the dirt. They were deep in conversation looking down at the wolf and did not notice her standing there. Two of the men were of medium build and height with their hair hanging in long, brown braids halfway down their back. The third man was shorter and stocky and had a mop of blazing red hair that fell to his broad shoulders. His beard was equally as bright and unruly. All three men looked tired and dirty from travel. Their chain mail was dull and scuffed, and their mounts looked weary.

She stood silently at the mouth of the tiny cave with scraped elbows, a bruised dirty face, and dried blood all over her tattered, grimy clothing. Her hand tightly gripped the dagger as her wild, matted hair blew on the warm breeze.

Perched on a low pine tree branch just above her, an annoyed blue jay suspiciously watched her, then upon deciding she was a threat, shrieked out a loud, course warning. All three men looked up from the wolf and stared in shock at what they saw.

"That's my dog!" she called out.

The stocky man stepped forward. "Come here, lass," he ordered.

Rhiannon did not move. "What have you done to my dog?"

"'Tis not a dog, woman, 'tis a beast!" he yelled back.

"What have you done to her?" Rhiannon's voice shook.

"She'll be a'right lass. She's just sleep'n. Come here and see for yer self." His mail sleeves chimed as he motioned her over.

Rhiannon warily crossed the stream and knelt beside her wolf. Luna was indeed still breathing. She bent down and put her ear to Luna's chest and listened to her heart's slow rhythm.

"What is this?" she asked, spotting a large thorn-like dart

sticking out of her rump. Not waiting for an answer, she quickly moved towards it to remove the offending obtrusion.

"Nay lassie, don't touch!" The stocky red man crossed the distance between them and had Rhiannon's wrist within his grip in seconds. Taken by surprise, she quickly spun around and brandished her knife.

"What is it?" she demanded.

"'Tis a wee somethin' ta make the beastie more agreeable."

Furious, Rhiannon ripped her arm from the man's grip and stuck the dagger in front of his face. "What have you done to my dog?" she screamed.

The other two men drew their swords and pointed them at her. Very calmly he spoke to the men in a language Rhiannon did not know. Cautiously, they replaced their swords. "I shot yer she-wolf with a wee bit of the nectar from the Suain-Nimh plant. She'll be wake'n up soon enough, and I'll expect ye ta keep her under control … or I will destroy the beastie."

The man folded his arms across his broad chest. "Now, suppose ye tell me just who ye are."

She lowered the dagger from the red man's face and straightened up as tall as she could; which was a little taller than he.

"My name is Rhiannon Kossi, and I'm on my way to Sona Tuath."

"Oh, yer a Kossi, huh? Well, forgive me, milady. I didn't recognize ye in all yer … uh … splendor." The man made a low, overly gracious bow which sent the other two into hysterical laughter. "I am Teo Jass, son of Holt of Perth, at your service, milady," he stated sarcastically.

Luna started making quiet whining noises, and Rhiannon looked over to where she lay. Teo pulled a leather napkin from a small pouch on his belt and carefully pulled the long thorn from Luna's coat. "Remember lassie, contain yer beastie if ye want ta keep her alive." He turned to the other two men and said something Rhiannon did not understand then turned back to her. "As soon as yer she-wolf is awake, we ride."

Rhiannon stood up again. "I'm not going anywhere with you!" she protested.

"Ye *will* be com'n with us," he restated firmly. "I think Flath would be want'n ta have a wee peek at ye."

"I'm on my way to Sona Tuath to rescue my father!"

Teo laughed again. "Sorry, lass, I must be taken ye back ta the Captain. I think the Archigos just might be interested in what we've found."

"I need to find my father, and then I will be going home!" Her arms were stiff down at her sides, and she tightened the grip on her dagger. "Daniel Foster will have the Sheriff and half the town out looking for us by now."

Teo looked over to the other two men who shrugged, then turned back to Rhiannon. "Well then, they can come retrieve ye from Flath if they so wish."

"I am not leaving with you!"

"Now, ye can either be a nice girly and ride out of here with us, or I will tie ye up like a fat roastin' pig, and ye can leave lay'n across the back of yer yon braw beastie." He pointed to Zellan who was tied to a pine tree.

She knew she must have looked frightened because then Teo quietly stated, "ye mind yer manners lass, and no harm will come ta ye." He directed his gaze to the dagger she still clutched. "Now then, I'll be need'n that weapon of yers, lass."

"You will not take my knife!"

Her protest fell on deaf ears as Teo approached her. "Will ye gut me then, lass?" Teo stuck out his hand for the dagger. Her eyes darted around as she tried to think of what to do. "I have promised ye lass, no harm will be done ta ye," Teo stated again, still holding out his hand.

Resigned, Rhiannon sighed and slapped the dagger's ivory handle in his palm.

He turned it over in his wide hand, inspecting the knife. "This came from a Sona Tuathen Royal Guardsman. Most likely an officer." He looked up at her waiting for an answer.

"I found it," she stated.

"The Captain will have much ta discuss w' ye milady."

She did not want to leave this place for it was a memory she still wanted to explore. She sat down beside Luna and stroked her soft fur looking out over the familiar landscape. She peeked through white-barked trees that seemed to be whispering her name as green leaves rustled in a hushed breeze. Unfathomably, she remembered darting in and out of their skinny shadows, laughing and singing as she went along. Her childish laughter seemed to float on the wind and dance just above the sway of meadow grass, and the gurgling stream was playing a song only heard or understood by her.

As soon as Luna was up and wobbling about they mounted their horses and headed down a faint path so narrow, they rode single file. Teo rode at the front, followed by Jon, Rhiannon with Luna at her side and Bleen at the rear, as Rhiannon learned their names were. A short distance away, they came upon a weathered cabin tucked neatly in sheltering trees and thick brush. There was such an overgrowth of vegetation they almost missed its presence completely.

Teo and Jon swiveled their heads back at Rhiannon's quick indrawn breath. "What is it, lass?" Teo asked.

"Nothing," she replied curtly, staring at the cabin. Teo gave her one last skeptical look and turned his attention to the cabin.

"Looks like someone really wanted to hide tucked back here in the forest," Jon observed.

"Aye, how 'bout ye young'uns go and have a look-see?" Jon and Bleen dismounted, drew their swords and slowly approached the cabin. They hacked their way through twisting vines sending green leaves and pink flowers floating down to the dry earth. They cautiously walked in as Teo watched.

Rhiannon immediately recognized the cabin as a place she had lived before, but did not know when. It was at the very edge of a faint whisper, buried under decades of memories. The memories flashed through her mind like a wild summer storm. Many voices whispered her name and spoke of other things she could not understand. Her heart pounded in her chest, and panic washed over her. She could not stay there any longer. She wheeled Zellan around and darted into the trees. She did not get very far until a sharp, biting pain hit her in the back and things started to grow dim.

CHAPTER FOUR

"There is nothing more prideful or stubborn than the might of a Suen man. What he has his heart set on is where his efforts will lead him despite all good sense. However, the only way a man can reach his goal is with the aid of a strong woman."
-Code of the Feminine; author unknown

Like the ominous rumble of distant thunder, Luna's low persistent growl called her from sleep. Rhiannon lay, eyes closed, not moving except to take deep breaths of air, exploring all the sounds and smells of her dark world. The air was crisp but not frigid, and the aroma of cooking food filled the air, and her stomach grumbled in answer. Horses cheerfully called to each other, their whinnies echoing off trees. Sounds of swordplay and the ring of chain mail echoed across the area. A horse leisurely passed nearby, its large hooves drumming out a slow, dull rhythm, the jangle of reins keeping time. It seemed like she was drowning in a sea of humanity. Voices were both near and distant; sounds both loud and faint, the din of busy men enveloped her.

She carefully massaged her temples and ran her tongue

over the split in her lip. Slowly she opened her eyes to see the pale green ceiling of a tent. Taking in a deep breath of air and rubbing her eyes, she started contemplating the noises outside. That she was in the middle of some huge gathering was obvious, but why and just where, was not immediately evident. Letting her hand fall from the edge of the cot, she carelessly searched around for Luna's big head. The she-wolf stopped growling, but only for a second, then resumed her passive yet persistent vocal complaint.

Abruptly, from a darkened corner of the tent, a man's voice took Rhiannon by surprise. With much difficulty, she sat up. A dirty hand again went to her head in an effort to stop the pain. She strained to see who was speaking, but shadows kept him hidden. Again, the man spoke in a language she did not understand. Finally, a tall blond man walked out of the shadows to the foot of Rhiannon's cot. Luna jumped up and started growling ferociously, hackles up and fangs gleaming white. His face was creased with exhaustion, and his eyes were bloodshot.

He spoke again, but Rhiannon just stared blankly up at him. A golden earring dangled from one ear, and a torque of gold clasped his neck; the ruby eyes of a panther stared out at her. He wore neither mail, nor sword, but looked very dangerous none the less.

"I don't understand," she finally said. He snorted in a dismissing manner and then said something that seemed quite colorful.

She looked down at Luna and softly patted her big head. The man squatted down and looked up into her face and said something in a questioning manner. His face was but a hand span away from Luna, who had resumed her growling, yet he paid no attention to the she-wolf. When she did not answer, he stood up and continued to stare.

She took a deep breath and stood up very slowly. Her

muscles and joints protested as they reluctantly answered her call. Suddenly the tent started spinning, the man's face was getting fuzzy and distorted. Her leg muscles shook, then collapsed under her weight. The man quickly grabbed her and sat her back down on the cot. As Rhiannon sat with her head in her hands trying to stop the room from spinning, he quietly left the tent. Within a few minutes, he had returned with food and water, sitting a plate of food under Luna's nose, as well.

He poured her a cup of water and set the jug on the dirt floor next to the cot. "Thank you," she murmured. He said nothing and left again.

After a while, her strength started to return, and the pounding in her head seemed to have finally stopped. Rhiannon cautiously stood up again and slowly started walking around the large tent. The sun had moved across the sky to illuminate the once shadowed corners. Two tall wooden poles held up the center of the tent, the ceiling being a good seven feet tall and then tapering to about five feet tall in the extreme corners. From both center poles, hung small iron hooks which held two oil-burning lamps now empty and dark.

Off to one side was a rather worn sack with clothes tumbling out of the mouth, and a small table with a large bowl filled with water sitting on top. Next to the bowl was a small, cracked mirror and what looked like a bar of soap and an old razor. In front of her sat a large wooden desk and four chairs. She walked over to the desk and softly ran her fingers over a few large maps that were laid out, stained with age and use, and marked up with ink.

On one of the maps, she could clearly see the words "*Sona Tuath*" written next to a crude picture of a castle on an eastern shore. There were probably a dozen other names carefully written next to their correlating dots spread out over the map ending at the western shoreline with a larger dot and the name "*Tel ˋRhia*." In big block letters stretching all the way across the map was the name "*Beaynid*." To the extreme north was a whole set of pointy upside-down *Ws* that represented a mountain range that ran from east to west splitting the continent. Just above the mountain range, almost off the map, was the name "*Ventra*."

She heard someone step inside the tent and turned around to see a short, plump woman standing near the entrance, eyeing Luna warily. When Luna yawned, curled up on the floor and fell asleep, she smiled warmly at Rhiannon and said something she could not understand.

Rhiannon shrugged apologetically. "I don't understand."

The woman approached her. "I am Laura Felden, Lady Kossi." The woman dipped into a shallow curtsy. "The Captain sent me to see if you needed anything."

"Where am I?"

The woman drew her bushy eyebrows into a confused frown and then spotted the maps that Rhiannon had been looking at on the table. "We are about here," she said, pointing to a blank spot on the map in the north-central part of Beaynid.

Rhiannon sighed deeply and rubbed her temples again, this time in frustration. Laura touched Rhiannon's arm softly. "Milady, I have some salve and tea to help those bruises to heal. Will you accompany me to my tent?" She smiled warmly and motioned for Rhiannon to follow.

A bright noonday sun hung in a blue sky, warming the earth and feeding tiny clover and giant pine alike. Shielding her eyes from the glare, Rhiannon looked out over the massive clearing which was filled with men, horses, armor, wagons and small green tents. Luna lifted her head to the breeze, her moist black nose quivering in the thick trails of aroma. The outskirts of the clearing were ringed by blackened corpses of burned- out trees. Partially burned logs and blackened stumps were sprinkled across the camp.

Rhiannon stopped for a moment and looked around the camp with wide eyes and parted lips. There were thousands of men and horses filling the clearing that stretched on into the distance. In the far distance, she could see where the fire had ended, and the giant pines reclaimed their land. She stared in wonder as reality started crashing in on her.

"Milady, are you alright?" Laura asked.

"What are all these men doing here?" Rhiannon breathed.

"All these men fight for the rebellion, milady." She took Rhiannon's elbow and started pulling her through the crowds. "My husband is one of the surgeons traveling with them. Our tent is right over here."

As they marched through the camp, they were barely noticed as men laughed, ate and drank. She thought they seemed uncharacteristically happy under the circumstances. As they walked, the cheerful sound of a song hung in the air. When they got closer, she could see the tall man that had questioned her earlier playing what she thought, if she could remember from history class, was a lute. The notes were crisp and fast, and he was accompanied by a man sitting beside him playing a small harmonica tapping his foot in time to the music. Then the tall man started to sing. His voice was deep and smooth and captured the attention of everyone near him. The tune was unknown to her as were the expressive words he sung, but the warmth and richness of his voice made the music superfluous. His baritone voice climbed and fell in time to the melody, and she felt herself drawn to him.

"Milady?"

Rhiannon had forgotten all about the woman standing beside her. "I'm sorry," she said bashfully when the woman smiled.

"Has a beautiful voice, that one. Now come on. Let us be making you well."

The surgeon's tent was bright red and stood amid a crowd of noisy men. She slowly entered the tent and was accosted by the still, cool air that was thick with the smells of various herbs and medicines. When her eyes adjusted to the dimness, Rhiannon could see the tent was filled with empty cots, and all had a folded blanket at the foot. Luna quickly ran around the inside of the tent, her nose hovering about the dirt floor.

In the center of the tent was a large table that she guessed was used for surgery. Above the table was strung a cord of rope from one large beam to the next where several sleeping oil lamps hung. Next to the table was a large cabinet with hundreds of bottles and small boxes, baskets, and rags.

Laura guided Rhiannon to a chair next to the cabinet. "You sit here milady, and I will brew you some tea."

As the tea brewed, Laura took a damp cloth and some rather harsh smelling soap and gently cleaned and patted Rhiannon's face dry. She carefully applied a thick, green substance to her cheek and around her swollen eye that smelt like old socks.

As the woman worked in silence, Rhiannon watched her with interest. She thought the woman was in her mid-forties or so. Strands of gray interrupted light brown hair that was tightly pulled back into a large bun resting at the back of her round head. Tiny lines creased the small, close-set green eyes as they smiled up at her. She was wearing a long, brown linen dress, the frills of a chemise poking out from a low neckline, and a cream-colored apron around her thick waist.

"There we go, milady. You will be as good as new!"

"Thank you, Laura, but please, call me Rhiannon."

"Well, I do not know if that would be proper, milady. You

are a Kossi." Laura drew her fleshy face up into a worried look. "You should be awarded the respect due your position."

She looked at Laura in a confused manner, then just smiled and started gazing about the tent. "So, who is this rebellion fighting?"

When Laura did not reply, Rhiannon looked over at her. She was staring suspiciously, a thick brow slightly arched. "The Beaynidan army, of course," she finally answered.

"Oh," Rhiannon smiled, trying to ease the sudden tension. "I guess the rebellion is winning since all these cots are empty."

"We have not seen fighting for about a week now, milady. The queen's army has moved further east, so I expect we will be following them shortly." Laura turned and resumed her preparations.

"The queen? Would that be Queen Baobh?" Rhiannon asked.

"Aye, milady. There are those that say the queen will have Lord Rull's assistance and will not fight against her. Those men are fools!"

"Lord Rull?" Rhiannon asked very curiously.

Laura looked at Rhiannon with what she thought might be confusion, but then she smiled again. "Well, I suppose you do not hear such gossip so far north, 'tis a silly Suen superstition anyway." Rhiannon arched a brow to encourage her to go on. "Some folks say Lord Rull is a god-like man who is at the bidding of the queen. Oh 'tis true, there was a man who rode upon the back of an enormous beast whose Forest Folk men fought with the queen in the Great War. I saw him with my own two eyes! The way I see it, though, he is a man just like the rest."

"So, you don't think this Lord Rull is a god?" Rhiannon leaned forward a bit in her chair looking intently at the plump healer. She recalled the eerie image of a purple dragon on the hilt of the dagger she found in her father's cabin and felt a chill go up her spine.

"Nay, not a god. There were some who got close enough to see him and said he was of the Forest Folk, like the queen —but not so dark skinned—with pointy ears and fine features, very handsome. The way I see it, a man is a man, whether of the Forest Folk kind or of the human kind." She winked knowingly at Rhiannon.

"The queen is an elf?" Rhiannon laughed and sat back in her chair suddenly not so interested; the woman was clearly crazy.

"Do the Archigos not know of this?" She sounded almost incredulous, but then went on when Rhiannon did not offer an answer. "I don't know what an elf is, but Queen Baobh is of the ancient race of people known as the Forest Folk, and I am inclined to believe that this Lord Rull is too, not some silly god." Laura shook her head as if in sympathy for the ignorant Seuns.

"Ah, well, I suppose if I were fighting against someone, I would rather face Forest Folk than a god." Rhiannon realized her tone was a bit too sarcastic when the older woman turned back to face her. She smiled sweetly and decided not to ask any more questions.

When the water had boiled, and tea had steeped long enough, Laura carefully poured the hot, black liquid into a well-used, wooden cup. Rhiannon held it up to her nose, letting the sweet-smelling steam curl around her sore face. The tea was hot and tasted of honey. It instantly warmed her bones and gave her a glowing, relaxed feeling.

"This is delicious, Laura. Thank you so much."

"You are much welcome, milady. It will help you regain your strength and help your abused skin to heal too."

"Too bad I can't soak my entire body in it then."

"Actually, people do! However, we do not have a big

enough tub or enough tea. Supplies are hard to come by as you can guess."

"Are you a surgeon too?" Rhiannon asked.

"Oh no, milady, women cannot obtain the title of surgeon." She cast her eyes downward. "But I am a midwife and considered a healer." She looked back up quickly with a proud smile across her pleasant face.

"Oh." Rhiannon nodded, smiling apologetically.

"In the city of my birth, Tel `Rhia, I was the best healer they had, some of the women even called me a surgeon." Laura went on, sticking out an ample chest then jabbing it with a stubby thumb. "But in Sona Tuath everything was different, you see." Her face clouded over.

"Then why don't you just go back to Tel `Rhia?" Rhiannon asked.

"I am a married woman, milady. I must go where my husband goes."

"And he's from Sona Tuath?"

She nodded sadly. "He had a large surgery within the walls of the city. It was always very busy." An empty, reflective look hollowed her face. "But after the queen is gone, we will be busy again." Laura cocked her head to the side and looked at Rhiannon, her bushy brows knitting together in thought. "Milady, do you mind if I brush out your hair?"

"Uh, no, I don't mind, go ahead. I probably look like a gorilla by now." Rhiannon shrugged and then pushed her matted hair off her face.

"A gorilla?" Laura asked.

"They're like a really big monkey."

"Oh, aye. I have seen a monkey before. It sailed into Tel `Rhia aboard a large ship one year." Laura smiled in recognition. "Funny little creature."

Dismissing talk of monkeys and apes, Laura quickly went to the corner of the tent and rummaged around in a smaller cabinet, finally pulling out a wooden brush. She came back around to Rhiannon and started working on the knots in her long black hair.

As she brushed she talked about her childhood in the port city of Tel `Rhia, all the strange things she had seen coming off the great ships that would dock there. Rhiannon found it completely surreal, but after a while got lost in Laura's musings. Having smelled every inch of the tent, Luna now lay at her feet, curled up and peacefully napping.

Just as Laura finished brushing out Rhiannon's hair a pale, rather thin man walked into the tent. He was wearing a large apron over his crumpled clothing stained with what looked like old blood. He stopped short when he spotted Rhiannon sitting in a chair in the center of the tent. Luna lifted her head, watching the man.

Quickly Laura came around from behind Rhiannon and walked up to him talking once again in that foreign, twisty language. He looked back at Rhiannon and said something rather curt. His face wore an expression of disgust, so she did not need to understand what he said to get the gist of it. His pale skin became reddened with anger, his blue eyes darkening like a cloudy day.

Laura balled her small hands into fists, her right hand still gripping the forgotten brush, and planted them on her round hips. She made a reply to him in an equally colorful manner. Feeling the tension, Luna stood, her ears pointing to straight up. The man roughly pushed Laura aside so that she almost fell to the ground and quickly strode towards Rhiannon who jumped to her feet. Her head started pounding, and she wished she had stayed seated. Luna started growling, and the man backed away guardedly, though no less determined.

"Filthy Archigos whore, why do you not crawl back to your ilk!" he succulently stated with revulsion.

She blinked past the throbbing in her head, trying to

comprehend what was happening. The man was a few inches shorter than her, but his arrogance and pure abhorrence made him seem so tall as to be unreachable.

"Leave my tent!" he ordered, pointing to the entrance. "I hope you suffer and die of whatever disease you might have, savage!"

Luna snarled and lunged; the surgeon backed a little further away.

"Hold your tongue, man!"

Rhiannon looked past the surgeon to see the blonde man from earlier standing in the doorway of the tent. The surgeon and his wife spun around in surprise. The man quickly walked up to the startled surgeon and roughly wrapped a large hand around his skinny bicep.

"I will not have you treat my guest in this manner. She is a Kossi and is due your respect," he said in a low, commanding voice. "If I ever hear you speak to her in that way again, I will sever that wicked, forked tongue from your foul mouth! Do you understand, surgeon?"

The smaller man looked down at his boots, seeming to wither before her eyes, his face ablaze in a red wash of anger and embarrassment. "Aye Captain, my apologies," he replied softly as the larger man let go of his arm. The surgeon grabbed his wife and quickly left the tent.

"Please accept my deepest apologies over that imbecile's remarks," the man spoke softly to Rhiannon. Luna sat silently at her side, watching the man. Rhiannon looked up at him trying to discern his thoughts. He was a lot taller than most men Rhiannon had seen here. He looked almost familiar, yet she knew she had never met him before.

"Who are you?" she finally asked.

"I am Flath," he stated without emotion. "And who are you, *really*?"

Well, that seemed a simple enough question-but what was

the simple answer that went with the simple question-Rhiannon concluded, there was none. She looked down at her riding boots, covered with dust, dried mud and the dark stain of blood, and sighed deeply. Her world was crumbling in all around her, and she did not know how to stop it. Just where had things started to go awry, she could not figure. Perhaps when those dreams started.

She realized it was over the winter that she started suffering from the vivid, colorful nightmares with a huge tree glowing amber in the night sky. Nightmares that seemed to have something to do with her mother, but what, she did not know.

"My name is Rhiannon Kossi. I'm on my way to Sona Tuath to retrieve my father," she finally answered him.

Flath folded his arms across his broad chest. "And just why is your father in Sona Tuath?"

"He was kidnapped."

"Kidnapped?" His brows shot up, disappearing under his pale hair as he quietly studied her for another moment. "The Archigos are not at war, why would anyone dare make off with a Kossi?"

"You know my father?" Rhiannon asked, hopefully.

"No, of course not. I just know it must be a daft man that would take a Kossi and invite the wrath of the Archigos upon him."

"I don't have any idea who these Archigos are you keep mentioning, but I'm not one of them," she finally said. He laughed in a humorless, disbelieving way. His piercing blue eyes stared down at her demanding an answer that he approved of.

"Look, *Flath*, I don't know what you want, but I don't have much time to find my father, so I'm leaving now." She clenched her fists at her sides.

"You told my men you are a Kossi, yet you do not use

your own tongue, and you say you are not an Archigos?" He shifted his weight blocking her view of the tent flap, silently conveying that an escape would not be possible. "I can see you are an Archigos, but why you were wandering around the Alba Forest by yourself and why you insist on using the priest's language and not your own barbaric tongue, I cannot guess."

"Barbaric? You call hauling someone off to God knows where and not letting them leave when they want to, civilized?" Luna started to growl, but he never removed his eyes from Rhiannon. "Barbaric? I'll tell you what barbaric is! Barbaric is kidnapping an old man and taking him away from his home and family! Barbaric is … is … whatever it is you're doing here!" She waved her arms in the air as if she were drowning.

He stood there for a long moment, seeming to be wrestling with a decision or trying to figure out if she was dangerous. He said nothing, just stared. Luna quieted and sat back down at her master's side.

She took the quiet time to study his face. She thought he was young, possibly early twenties, but he looked tired and under much stress. Perhaps, she thought, he might be more around her age-thirty-though she could not be sure. His fair skin was bronzed from the sun, and he had a sprinkling of light freckles across his nose and stubble covering his face. "So, you were on your way to Sona Tuath when my men found you." It was more of a statement than a question.

"Yes. I was told that my father is being held there."

"Why are you traveling alone? Why do you not have the entire nation of Archigos warriors with you, milady?"

"I told you, I don't know the Archigos."

"I think you need some more time to think about answering my questions, Lady Kossi," he said, taking her arm and roughly guiding her out of the surgery and back to her original accommodations. "Please think about your future cooperation, milady," he stated when they got there and left her staring after him as he quickly strode away.

She flopped down on the cot and rubbed her pounding head wondering what she was going to do next. It was as if there was no Montana. No America. No modern world at all! She was completely mystified. Her mind just would not let her believe that she had somehow stumbled into another world. "It's impossible," she whispered to Luna.

CHAPTER FIVE

*"No one knows exactly when the Archigos' goddess, Verna, started
to mark her empresses, or why. Some believe it is to prove which
babe is the most bloodthirsty at birth, thus will be the best leader for
a barbaric society."*
—Customs of Exotics; Lorn VacLell

As the sun started to rise the dim smells of roasting meat
wafted into Rhiannon's cloth cell reminding her that she was
getting hungry again. Except for a quick trip into the forest
with a very stony-faced young soldier, where he gave her
partial privacy to relieve herself, she had been stuck in the
tent all day.

She sat on the dirt floor with her legs folded up under-
neath her and mindlessly stroked Luna's soft fur while
listening to all the different sounds of the busy camp. Off in
the distance, some kind of stringed instrument was being
played along with the abrasive voice of a man trying to sing
along with some unrecognizable song. Finally, she heard
someone entering the tent and hoping she would get a
chance to get out into the air, however briefly, she stood up.

She shook her head when she saw it was Flath. He stood at the entrance of the tent not saying a word and just watched her. Rhiannon took a deep breath and let it out slowly knowing he would start asking her more questions that she did not know or really want the answers to.

"Have you thought about cooperating with me now, milady?" he asked, walking up to her.

"I've only told you the truth," she protested.

"So you are going to stick to that absurd story about your father being kidnapped?" He raised a brow in question.

When she did not answer, he turned to leave. In desperation, she reached out and grabbed his arm. He looked down at her in surprise.

"Please, don't leave me in here any longer. I'm going crazy!" she pleaded. "At least give me a something to drink. Something a little harder than that water."

"Tell me the truth, then."

"I am telling you the truth!" she shouted. Tears started to well in her eyes, and no matter how hard she tried, she could not keep them from spilling down her cheeks. She was embarrassed at her lack of control and grew angry. "My father was missing, so I got worried and went out to look for him," she started. "I didn't find my father, but ended up being accosted by a group of men..."

"You mean the ones who brought you here?"

"No. There were a different group of men in the forest, near the tree..." she thought for a minute, then wiped the tears from her face as she remembered what the tree had been called, "...near the Tree of Jur. There were five of them."

"The Tree of Jur?" he asked, his eyes growing wider. He ran his hand through his hair and looked down at the ground. After a moment, he looked back up at Rhiannon and softly touched her bruised cheek. "I assume they are the ones who did this to you. My men would not have done that," he murmured softly.

"They told me that my father was being held in Sona Tuath. So, that's why I must go there. I don't know anything about these Archigos or anything else about this place because I'm not from here," she stated adamantly.

After a tense moment of contemplation, he said, "The men who brought you here were Teo, Bleen, and Jon. As for whom those other men were, I cannot make a guess."

"They weren't with you?" she asked again, wanting to be certain.

"No."

Finally, she asked, "Do you know a man named Pann Hepin of Sona Tuath?"

He scrubbed a callused palm across his stubbly chin. "I might," he replied, cautiously.

Rhiannon snorted at his ambiguous answer. "Is he friend or foe?"

Flath momentarily looked a bit surprised at her question, but quickly slipped back into an unreadable expression. He must have decided it would do no harm to answer her, so he replied flatly, "a foe."

"Well, in that case, I killed him," Rhiannon whispered.

Flath stared in wonder, and his brows rose. "You killed High Captain Hepin?" Suddenly she was afraid that she had made the wrong choice in telling him. "Are you certain the man you killed was Hepin?" he asked, very seriously.

Rhiannon laughed hollowly. "Certain? I can't be certain of anything anymore. But he did say he was High Captain Pann Hepin of the Sona Tuathan Royal Guard." Rhiannon tried to mimic Hepin's pompous attitude and hacked up accent. "Did you know Captain Hepin?"

"No, not personally." He smiled. Flath happily patted the top of Rhiannon's head like you would a good child and quickly strode to the tent flap, stuck his head out and yelled something she could not understand. Within a short time, Teo entered the tent. "Greannmhor, here," Flath pointed to Rhiannon, "has killed Hepin."

"Captain Hepin?" Teo asked, and then looked at Rhiannon in disbelief.

"Yes!" Rhiannon snapped.

Teo raised his face to the tent ceiling and hooted loudly with laughter and then slapped Flath on the back. He returned his attention to Rhiannon. "And here I was think'n tha she was daft." He laughed out loud again. "Mayhap I'm in serious danger of being replaced by the lass. That is—if the Archigos don't want her back." Teo chuckled and left the tent.

Flath walked back over to Rhiannon. "How long ago did you kill Hepin?"

"That depends," she looked over to the empty cot, "how long was I asleep?"

"Two nights."

"That long?"

"It seems that Teo thought it best to give you a bit of the Suain-Nimh after you tried to run off."

"I thought Suain-Nimh was poison!"

Flath frowned. "Yes, if you are given too much. Do they not teach you that in Ventra?" he asked. "Or are you excluded from such instruction because of being a Kossi?"

"What does being a Kossi have to do with anything?" she finally asked. "And why is everyone always referring to me like I'm some kind of royalty?"

Flath's guarded demeanor changed, and he gave her a puzzled look. "What do you mean?"

"What is so special about my name?"

Flath studied her for a moment. "You are obviously not Empress Shankee, but perhaps a niece or distant cousin or another relative." He shrugged wide shoulders. "In any case, we use the formal title of Lady to show respect for your family's position, as is the custom here in Beaynid."

"What position?" she demanded. "My father is a ranch hand on Daniel Foster's place in Montana. We don't have 'a position' or a pile of money, or anything else!"

Flath regarded her suspiciously. "I have no knowledge of a place called Montana." Flath's expression grew hard again as if his patience grew thin. "It will be much easier on you, Lady Kossi, if you are honest with me while you are a recipient of my hospitality."

"Then you be honest with me!" she snapped. "How do you even know the name Kossi?"

Flath raked a large hand through his hair in exasperation. "The Kossis' have always ruled Ventra, everyone knows that. I am not as inept as you might have first assumed."

Rhiannon shook her head in frustration and thought for a moment. "Okay, let's try another question. Who are you, really, and what's going on here?"

"Do you not know of the rebellion, woman?"

"What rebellion?" Rhiannon recalled what Laura had told her, but needed it confirmed.

"I have never known the Archigos to be so ill-informed." Mindlessly he rubbed his stubbly cheek and stared at the floor. "I knew Empress Shankee was not the most efficient leader, but I have never known the Archigos to be so indifferent as to what is happening in Beaynid." He spoke almost to himself.

Rhiannon's stomach growled again bringing Flath back from his thoughts. "Forgive me Lady Kossi, will you do me the honor to sup with me?" Flath smiled and motioned toward the tent flap, and she let Flath lead her from the tent.

They walked a short distance to where a small fire was burning. Three big logs ringed the fire and served as seating.

Rhiannon saw the stout man with the unruly red hair sitting on a stump engaged in relaxed conversation with Jon and Bleen. On closer inspection, she found that Jon and Bleen were twins.

The air was crisp but not uncomfortable. It was very pleasant out in the open. Flath motioned her to sit on an old charred stump near the fire. Teo continued to talk, but Jon and Bleen turned towards her ever so often with curiosity on their young faces. Flath quickly walked away and disappeared into the crowd.

When he returned, he gave Rhiannon a plate of food and sat another plate on the ground for Luna. Teo stopped talking long enough to pour Rhiannon a cup of ale. She gripped the wooden fork and quickly stuffed a bit into her watering mouth.

Somewhere in the camp, a horse whinnied, and another answered. Rhiannon looked up from her food as she had remembered an important thought. Her eyes were wide and urgent. "Where's my horse?"

"That beast? You call him a horse?" Flath asked.

"Where is my horse?" she repeated.

"I'm sorry, Greannmhor, that beast was implacable. He nearly knocked the head off one of my men and broke the arm of another. Of course, we will replace your horse; after all, he was a beautiful stallion if it had not been for his disposition."

Rhiannon opened her mouth but could not find her voice. "What have you done?" she finally screamed.

"It had to be done. I am truly sorry, Lady Kossi. By the way, did you enjoy your cooked meat?"

Teo and Flath began to laugh while Jon and Bleen watched with wary, uncertain expressions. Rhiannon threw her fork directly at Flath's head, but he quickly dodged the offending wooden utensil. She jumped up and ran towards him, taking him by surprise and knocking him off the log he had been sitting on. They landed in the dirt and dried brush sending dust to the wind. Rhiannon socked his jaw before he could get a hold of her wrists. She twisted and writhed as he tried to get control of her. One of her legs broke free, and she kneed him in the crotch and screamed a wild, tumultuous sound that was quickly absorbed by the noises of the camp. He grunted in pain and threw her off him, and she tumbled across the ground.

"Hold yourself, woman!" he hissed, touching his sore jaw. "Your devil horse is right over there." He pointed to a lone tree on the far side of the camp. Zellan was tied around the neck with a rope, and his saddle had been removed.

"You're lucky he isn't hurt." She frowned as she stood and angrily brushed the dust from her clothes.

"I believe ye are lucky we didn't cook up that beastie. He would have been served for sup on the morrow." Teo laughed as Flath hauled himself up off the dirt.

"Sit back down and mind your manners woman." Flath took her by the arm and roughly pulled her over to the stump and sat her down.

After the snickers had died down, Teo took a big swig of ale and looked at Rhiannon. "How is it that ye have come ta possess the empress' horse?"

"He's my horse," she replied, unconcerned.

"He bears the red mark of the empress." Teo cocked his head to the side in curiosity.

"I don't know what you're talking about. I have had him since he was born. That red mark is just a birthmark."

"Of course it 'tis," Teo said. "All empresses' war horses have the wee diamond mark on their chest, as do Archigos empresses. They share the same mark from birth." Teo smiled proudly at Jon and Bleen at his knowledge of the northern warriors. "My sweet ma told me long stories of the mighty Archigos." Rhiannon swallowed hard, and her hand instinctively went to her chest as if to conceal the mark. She peered into the fire with dull eyes. "Lass, ye don't look so well…"

"I need a moment of privacy if it's okay with you." She looked over to Flath who was studying her with renewed interest. "Terren!" he shouted. A boy appeared at her side. "Please escort Lady Kossi to the edge of camp and give her just a bit of privacy. But watch her, she is dangerous." He gently rubbed his jaw once more.

Terren led her through the throng of men busy in preparation to follow Baobh's retreating army. When they finally reached the far side of the camp, Rhiannon thanked the boy and disappeared into the brush.

She watched him through the thick foliage. He stood like a proud, unmovable sentinel warding off danger from an unknown wilderness. She bent down and searched the forest floor for something she could use as a weapon. The ground was strewn with dull tree leaves in all stages of decomposition. Scraggly bushes pushed their way out of hard dirt and raised their brittle little arms to the sun. Sinewy brown vines wound about bush and tree alike, choking out smaller, less insinuating plant life.

Finally, she found what she had been searching for. Quietly she pushed away a few pine cones and picked up a large, solid branch. The rough bark bit into her hands as she silently approached the oblivious young man. She swung hard, and the thick branch smacked the boy in the back of his head. He fell like a discarded rag. Rhiannon quickly dropped the branch and looked down at the boy. She stepped back and turned to run, but then walked back up to his crumpled form again and felt for a pulse. She exhaled when she found his strong, steady heartbeat. "I'm sorry Terren," she whispered, then turned and ran into the bushes.

Rhiannon stayed amidst the trees circling around to the other side of the camp and made her way to Zellan. Luna lay in the warm sunshine as if keeping the horse company. Nervously her eyes darted around the crowd searching for Flath. Sweaty hands worked at the knot in the rope. Zellan nudged her with his muzzle and stomped his hoof. Finally, the knot came loose and set the rope free to unwind from the tree trunk. Rhiannon grabbed the rope and headed back into the forest. She kept her head down and listened carefully for any quick footfall.

She neared the trees where the camp met the forest's edge. Her heart beat loudly, and her skin became prickly and irritated by the touch of her clothing. Suddenly she heard someone running up from behind her. She immediately froze, not able to move. She wanted to turn around and see her pursuer, but she denied the urge and stayed still as if hoping she would fade from view.

She heard a man call out, but the voice was unfamiliar. Soon he was answered by another voice she did not know. Her heartbeat slowed, and she loosened the strangled grip she had on the rope; her fingers had gone numb. Finally, she turned to see a young soldier running up to an older man who was sitting by a small fire motioning him to sit. Rhiannon took a deep breath and continued towards the tree line in a slow, deliberate manner.

At last, she was in the cover of the trees. She jumped up onto Zellan's back and picked her way through the thick brush of the forest, heading east as far as she could tell. Flath would be missing her by now; she had to make haste. One hand tightly clamped on the rope and the other gripping a handful of Zellan's mane she kneed him into a run and was gone.

CHAPTER SIX

Her boughs stretch wide across the pine-strewn earth, and her head
is held high in the heavens; a crown of needles upon her brow.
She sees all who enter her kingdom; she knows them intimately
before they leave and before her, she makes them bow.
No creature is immune to her stare; no man can resist her lure.
She feeds on blood, bone, and sorrow, giving life to her children
so pure.
Gentle forest breezes sing her praises; upon the dull lips of earth is
her name.
She is the forest; she is the mountain; she is a world that no one
can tame.
-Unyielding Stare; Tamrah Jenn

Within the hour, a thick darkness fell upon the forest. Rhiannon had found a narrow road winding back through the trees and followed it.

She touched her chest, right above her right breast where her birthmark lay concealed. She rode on in deep contemplation, every once in a while patting Zellan's neck reassuring herself that she was not who they said she was. She thought of her mother and the leather pouch she wore on her belt loop. Her hand searched around under her clothing until she felt it. She clenched her jaw and tightened her hold on the reins in utter frustration. Her grip on reality as she knew it was weakening rapidly. Logic was losing the battle to a new understanding of what reality actually was.

Suddenly, for what seemed to be no reason, Luna started growling into the darkness. Zellan's ears went back flat, and he voiced his disapproval. Rhiannon cursed herself for not securing a weapon before she had left. A twig snapped, echoing off the trees and from the corner of her eye, she saw something jump out of the forest onto the path just beside her. Luna snarled and started barking wildly. Zellan reared up and screamed into the once quiet blackness. Rhiannon slid off the back of her horse and landed in the dirt with a thud. She watched as Zellan sprinted away into the trees on the other side of the path. "You cursed animal!" she called after him.

Luna's yelp of pain brought Rhiannon around to see her she-wolf lying on the ground in a pool of blood shimmering under the moonlight. Rhiannon scrambled on her hands and knees to her wolf's side. Luna's whimpering had died down to a soft cry. "No! No … Luna!" Rhiannon cried out taking Luna into her arms, warm blood seeping into her clothes.

From behind her, she could hear men's voices speaking in a language that she could not understand. One of the men approached her. By the tone of his voice, she thought he was ordering her to do something, but she did not understand. Slowly she put Luna's limp body down on the ground and turned around. Still on the ground, she stared up at the stocky man. Four men stood before her. She crouched in the deep shadows of the night. Slowly she moved into a slash of bright moonlight. One of the men slowly approached, and she saw he had a long knife hanging at his belt.

A seething anger consumed her being and like a bright streak of lightning Rhiannon grabbed the long knife from the man's belt and had him spitted on it before any of them knew what was happening. As the dead man's body fell to the ground, the other men gasped and jumped back. Their eyes widened as if what she had just done was inconceivable.

Blood and nervous sweat covered her body. Her hair was tangled and covered with dirt and blood. She dared the men to come closer as her face hardened into a feral expression.

The other three men unsheathed their long machete-like daggers and charged. She took one of the men in the throat and let his body flop to the ground. Before she could spin to kill again, she was knocked to the ground. One of the men forced her to the dirt while the other man wrenched the knife from her hand. A carnal need to kill simmered in her blood as her vision sharpened and her body yearned for the smell of death.

One of the men put his face close, and she could smell his sour breath and heard his indrawn breath when he realized she was a woman. One of the men straddled her legs, and the other held her arms above her head. Quickly one of them started feeling around her clothes. When his hand reached the leather pouch tied to her belt loop, he cut it free and slipped it into a large purse full of absconded booty treasures that he was wearing at his hip. Rhiannon started to struggle as she watched the pouch her mother had given her so long ago disappeared into the bag.

Then the man bent over and shoved his tongue in her mouth. Enraged as his hands groped her breasts, she bit down hard on his tongue. He screamed in agony. She tasted his blood, but still, she would not let go of his vile tasting tongue. Finally, the man struck her jaw, sending shooting pain through her mouth and into her head. She finally let go. He sat up holding his bloody mouth yelping with pain. Rhiannon spit the tip of his tongue out onto the dirt and let out a cool, crazed laugh.

"Keep your tongue to yourself, smelly!" she yelled.

The man reached to his belt and grabbed his knife holding it above his head. Rhiannon could see the moonlight glint off the blade. She thought about her father and where he might be and what would become of him. There was so much she wanted to ask him, and now she would not get the chance. Rhiannon closed her eyes, waiting for the inevitable.

From the chaos of the night, the sound of metal cutting into flesh and hitting bone rang out. When she heard a startled cry of pain, her eyes flew open. The man who had been sitting on her legs only moments before, ready to plunge this knife into her chest, was now lying beside her in the dirt, cut almost in two. When she realized the man that had been holding her arms was now gone also, she sat up and twisted around just in time to see him hit the ground as well.

Standing just beyond the man's lifeless body stood Flath gripping his blood covered sword as it pointed obscenely into the darkness. His mail glistened in the moonlight as his chest heaved. She sat looking at him in disbelief as her blood hunger was sated and then completely drained. She quietly watched him looking down at her. He did not move except to take in large breaths of air. The forest was silent all around them as if the world was afraid to move. No night birds or animals called out or moved through the thick brush of the woodland. The wind was silent. Even the insects were missing. Finally, he wiped the blood from his sword and returned it to its sheath at his waist. He walked over to Rhiannon but still said nothing. Fear, shame, confusion, relief, all fought for position within her.

A tiny whimper broke the silence and then Rhiannon

remembered Luna. She spun around and scampered across the ground to her wolf. "Luna!" she cried, taking the wolf into her arms again.

Flath bent down and cautiously probed for the wound. "She has been cut." He stood up and pulled his mail shirt over his head and dropped it to the ground with a loud clanking noise and took off the overtunic he was wearing. "Wrap this tightly around her wound," he said as he handed her his tunic. She did as he told her while talking soothingly to her she-wolf.

At the sound of horses approaching, she looked up to see Flath standing under the dim moonlight between the questioning gazes of both his horse and Zellan. "I found him wandering around down the road. I thought you might want him back. Crazy beast almost knocked my head off when I tried to grab him." She said nothing but turned her attention back to Luna. "I will have the surgeon look at her when we get back," Flath said.

"Why do you insist on keeping me with you?" Rhiannon finally broke her silence.

"Because, Greannmhor, I am not sure of just who you are. You might give me some bargaining power when I ask the Archigos for their assistance in this war of ours. It just depends on how badly they want you back." Flath handed Rhiannon the rope that still surrounded her mount's dark neck and then carefully took Luna from the blood-soaked dirt and laid her across Zellan's back.

Rhiannon walked up and gripped Flath's arms. "Listen to me very carefully, Flath. I don't know who the Archigos are. They don't know me, so I highly doubt they'll want me at all. I'm not your bargaining chip!"

"You told my men you are a Kossi, yet you tell me you are not an Archigos?" He effortlessly broke away from her grip and then pulled his chain mail shirt over his head.

"I don't know what Kossis' you could possibly be talking about, but I can assure you I am of no relation to them."

"How can that be? My men find you riding around the Alba Forest on the empress's horse, you are obviously of the Archigos race, and you admit to being a Kossi. Yet you are telling me that you are not kin to Empress Shankee?"

"Yes, that's what I'm saying."

"You are a spy, then?"

"A spy?" Rhiannon asked, laughing.

"That would explain why you do not want to go back to Ventra. You know you will be executed for treason."

"I've never even been to Ventra!" Rhiannon stated, harshly. "And who would I be spying for? I've already told you I killed Hepin of Sona Tuath, and I'm certainly not a spy for you, so who would I be spying for?"

"You think I am some simpleton?" Flath asked angrily. "I know the Archigos have had problems with Turr'ah in the past or maybe some nation across the Carnaid Sea who thinks it is strong enough to take the mighty Archigos. I have heard the rumors that even though they wish for Baobh's demise, they will not join in the uprising against the queen because they will not fight with a bunch of untrained farmers and bastards led by a gypsy's son! The Empress could have sent you out here to see how far we have gotten to taking Sona Tuath. She might be thinking of swooping in and taking Beaynid for herself once Baobh is ousted!"

"That's ludicrous!" Rhiannon protested. "If that's so, then why would I not want to return to the Archigos?"

Flath walked closer to Rhiannon and lightly brushed a wisp of her hair from her face. He looked at her hard then his lips curled into a humorless, crooked smile. "You must have done something pretty bad to get sent from the walls of Màrrach, Greannmhor. The empress should have known better than to send out a lone warrioress." He returned his hand to the hilt of his sword; his fingers wrapped idly around the large golden handle in the shape of a panther's head.

"Maybe the Empress knew exactly what she was doing.," he whispered. His eyes showed no expression, and from the light of an almost full moon, she could see a face wearing the effects of sheer exhaustion.

Defiantly Rhiannon took a deep breath and walked over to Luna and tenderly ran fingers through her thick fur. She knew Luna was in serious trouble and Flath's surgeon could help. It was no use stalling any longer; she had to go back with Flath.

"Think whatever you want of me, I don't care," she said. Then she walked over to one of the dead man's bodies, grabbed the bag from his waist, and emptied the contents on the ground. Picking up her small pouch and returning it to her belt loop she walked back over to Flath. "I'll go with you tonight because my wolf needs the care of your surgeon. But know this, Flath, son of a gypsy, I won't be staying with you long." She defiantly stared up into his face. Even in the scarce moonlight, she could see the hurt in his eyes, and she felt a tinge of guilt.

"We need to be on our way, if your wolf is to live," Flath said coolly. Then he turned and mounted his horse, urging it back down the dirt path. Without a glance backward, he disappeared into the velvety curtain of darkness swallowing the world. She looked up at the dark sky as a huge owl flew amidst myriads of twinkling candles. A tear ran down her cheek as she turned towards her horse and injured wolf. Taking in a deep breath, she climbed up on Zellan's back, carefully situating herself behind her she-wolf, and followed Flath back to his camp.

CHAPTER SEVEN

"A good woman will know her place. She will know when to speak and when to remain silent. A man does well if he is diligent in his inspections before he buys cattle or sheep or land. Buying a woman is no different; conscientiousness will gain him peace in his old age."
-A Man's Good Sense; Fif Licnor

"Where is the camp? We should have reached it by now!"

"They have moved further southeast."

"Moved?"

"Aye, 'tis been known to happen. Men have to be moved quickly when at war, milady."

"You think I'm lying to you when I tell you I don't understand all of this, but how do you know that I'm not just telling you the truth?"

"What innocent woman who would knock a man over the head and run like a robber?"

"You left me no choice! Maybe when you find out that I don't bring you any bargaining power with the Archigos, you'll kill me, or maybe just leave me to die in this horrid place." She reined in closer to him. "What will you do with me, Captain?"

He stayed silent, head looking forward as if searching for some unseen creature lurking in the dark.

"Answer me!" she angrily demanded.

As quick as the deadly strike of a serpent Flath reached out and took hold of a mighty fist full of Zellan's onyx mane, stopping both horses in the road.

"You might be accustomed to giving orders, Lady Kossi, but I am not one of your weak, castrate, male Archigos, or one of your palace subjects. I do not take orders from you." Flath's voice was very controlled, though she could clearly see the anger in his eyes.

There was a long moment of silence, and then he spoke softly. "I would never strike down an innocent, especially a woman. However, you are more trouble than you are worth, so I certainly would, in fact, leave you and your menagerie behind." Even in the shadows, she could see a look of contentment on his face when he saw the fear in her eyes. "They should be right over that rise." He pointed to a cleft in between two rolling hills. The night was growing old, and the inevitable glow in the east started to call to the morning.

As they crested the hill, she could see a few tiny fires burning in the valley below. From the early light of predawn, she could see a small number of men and horses hidden amongst the shrubbery surrounding the meadow. The group she had seen earlier numbered well into the thousands, but there were only a few dozen men here. "Where are the rest of the men?" Rhiannon asked.

"As I have told you, they were moved," he said curtly. "These men were held back so that I could chase off after you instead of following my men into battle."

"Is the surgeon here?"

"Aye, milady," he replied shortly.

They rode up to a large, red tent and Flath dismounted handing his reins to a young boy who led his horse away. He reached up and carefully removed Luna from Zellan's back. Rhiannon slid off her horse, and the remaining boy cautiously grabbed the thin rope around Zellan's neck and carefully led him away.

Flath walked into the tent and called loudly, waking the slumbering man. The surgeon sat up scratching his rumpled hair. He blinked like an owl before realizing he had a patient to tend to. Flath laid Luna on a large table in the center of the tent as the surgeon hastily started lighting candles and oil lamps. A large wood burning stove was already lit in the middle of the tent; ribbons of steam were rising from an enormous huge cauldron sitting on top of an old iron grill positioned above the flames. The surgeon pulled an over-tunic over his head and put on an apron to cover his clothing. He moved briskly until he discovered the bundle that Flath had laid on the table was not a person after all. He muttered a few colorful words of which Rhiannon could not understand. Flath answered him in a cool tone and then when the surgeon said nothing else, he spoke a few more words.

Without another word, the surgeon started cleaning the wound. He cut away Luna's fur around the slash, then carefully stitched up the cut. His tools looked archaic and awkward, but they served their purpose.

Flath lowered his voice and asked the surgeon a question. The surgeon's foreign words were flat and emotionless as he answered Flath. The man washed his hands, removed his apron, then shook his head and left the tent.

"What did he say?"

Flath looked like he wanted to say something, but thought better of it. He gently picked Luna up and carried her from the tent. Rhiannon hastily followed him to a tent hidden amongst the trees. Carefully, he lowered the wolf down onto a pile of blankets.

"Flath, what did the surgeon say?" She persisted.

"He said he does not think your wolf will live." The words were like jagged, hungry rocks waiting at the bottom of a pit that she had been hurled into.

"I rescued her as a cub; her eyes barely open. She's been with me for twelve years… she won't die!" Rhiannon took a deep breath as tears welled in her eyes. She fell to her knees and buried her face in Luna's fur.

Flath bent down and placed a gentle hand on Rhiannon's shoulder. "I am sorry, Greannmhor," he whispered and left Rhiannon alone with her dying she-wolf.

Beyond the pain, a tiny spark started to burn in her mind. At first, it was just a tickle at the back of her mind, but then it grew to a nagging cry. Her thoughts gathered around the stone her mother had given her so long ago!

Fumbling through the layers of clothing, her hands reached the leather pouch. She shook the pouch, and a large, dark red stone fell into the palm of her hand. She stared at it not able to move. It had been twenty-four years since her mother removed the silver chain from her neck, pried the largest of the stones loose and handed it to Rhiannon instructing her to hide it in a safe place, for she would need it someday, she said.

Deeply buried memories closed in on her, and she let them wash over her like a turbulent river. Unable to discern the past from the present Rhiannon looked up into her mother's black eyes so full of fear and pain, then looked down at the big blood colored stone, so great and cold in her tiny hands.

"Take this and hide it well, my daughter…"

"Yes, Mommy," she said, not knowing that very night her mother was going to be murdered. Quietly she snuck out the door of the small cabin and crept through the forest to her hideout by the stream.

Memories began to fade like photos left too long in the sun. She was left in the coldness of the tent kneeling over the body of her she-wolf. Carefully, she turned the stone over in her hand searching the depths of the red gem.

A soft tune started to form in her mind. Delicate and slow it danced across her consciousness. But there was something missing. She clamped her eyes tightly shut, trying to sharpen lost memories.

"The words. What were the words of the song?" she whispered. "I have to know the words..."

The tune-filled her mind, but the foreign words eluded her. Desperate and frustrated she looked down at the smooth stone. The depth and beauty were like no other she had ever seen.

"What are the words, Mommy?" Rhiannon cried in a small whispered voice.

Like a sweet fragrance carried on a soft breeze, the words began to form in her mind. Rhiannon mouthed the harsh, solid words of the Archigos nation and then gave them her voice. She sang in a whisper as she held her eyes shut, afraid the words would escape her and would dissolve into nothing but a worn memory. She sang a little louder as the stone in her hands warmed and began to hum.

As her words grew louder so did the singing of the brilliant stone. When she was sure, she could remember all the words she opened her eyes to see the tent glowing in a dark red hue. The light spilled from her closed fingers like ribbons of blood touching Luna's fur. Slowly she opened her hand as she kept singing the newly remembered words.

She placed the warm stone on Luna's chest across the sutured wound. She sang louder, and the stone gave more light and vibrations. The tent was filled with a low steady hum, and the harsh expressive words Rhiannon sung amidst the red glow of sunset.

Finally, the song ended; the words, all spent. The stone fell silent, and the glow died until the stone was once again cold and dark. She felt alone and empty, drowning in a deep need to know where she came from, yet afraid of the answers.

She felt his eyes boring into her back, and she turned around to see Flath standing in the tent behind her. "What are you?" he asked, in shock.

"I don't know," Rhiannon whispered, tears streaming down her face.

Morning crawled over the mountains and hung high in the blueness of the day. Rhiannon awoke to the cheerful songs from dozens of tiny birds happily foraging or building their nests. She looked around and saw Flath sleeping in a clumsy wooden chair near the tent entrance. Quietly she sat up and softly ran her hand over Luna's fur. The she-wolf answered her touch with a warm lick and nudge. "You're a good girl, Luna." Rhiannon wrapped her arms around her neck.

Flath stirred, then yawned and stood. "The gods, and that stone of yours, have smiled upon your wolf." He stretched out cramped legs, and sore muscles then walked over to Luna and patted her fuzzy head. She returned the gesture by licking his hand. "I shall go see what we have in the way of sustenance for the beastie, and us, of course," he said and left the tent.

Rhiannon slowly got up and walked over to a bowl of water. She unzipped her filthy jacket and took it off, letting it fall to the floor. Rubbing the rough bar between her hands, she tried to make something that resembled lather but settled for a thick, goopy substance instead. Gently she rubbed it across her skin, running exploring fingertips over her swollen jaw. She splashed the water across her face, the coldness biting into sore flesh. When she opened her eyes, she saw the bowl ran red with blood.

She stared at the muddied water, drips falling from a newly cleaned chin, remembering how it felt to kill. She recalled the overwhelming need to take life; to smell the heat of spilling blood. Numbly she searched her wet hands for the souls of those she had killed.

* * *

Baobh strolled out onto the sun-bathed terrace. A sweet trade wind swept up from the south carrying the aroma of passion flower. She closed her eyes and tilted her perfectly shaped face into the sun's warm rays. Busy sounds from the courtyard below drifted on the soft breeze to Baobh's ears. Seabirds called to each other as they ravenously looked for food. The whitewashed stone walls of the castle were almost too bright to look at on sunny days like today. The massive structure stood as a pristine, bright sentinel in the white-walled, port city of Sona Tuath.

Sona Tuath was the second biggest seaport in the land, the first being Tel' Rhia on the western coast. Situated on the Bay of the Gods on the Carnaid Sea, its bright walls reached up from the rocky shoreline running inland then circled back around again, ringing the entire city. The magnificent Castle of Sona Tuath sat in the uppermost northeastern corner of the city. It was built right out of the jagged boulder-lined cliffs overlooking the bay to the east and the city to the south and west. Outside the walls were miles of fertile farmland and grazing fields for many livestock. Sona Tuath was truly a great, royal city with a highly trained guard, two-thousand strong. The Beaynidan army was less rigorously trained but made of seasoned fighters just the same.

She scanned the horizon, looking over her domain for any sign of Hepin's returning group of Sona Tuathan Royal

Guardsmen. She balled her fists and set them hard on the wall of her balcony. Hepin was out there somewhere. So was her army. She wondered if they had pushed those inept rebel fighters back to their hovels yet. She would have blood tribute paid for any she even suspected had fought in the rebellion. A slight smile crossed her red lips at the thought of this war being over.

The dark, lithe figure of Eagle walked out onto the terrace and stood next to his queen. He was a muscular man; his dark cocoa colored skin gleamed in the sunlight. Each ear was pointed at the top and studded with a tiny diamond. The small rounded lobes held two loops of gold that glistened in the sun. An elaborate sequence of multi-colored tattoos honoring the god Pom-Ni scrolled across his smooth, broad chest. A strand of onyx Elder Beads hung loosely around his neck, which he had never taken off in the twenty-five years since they both had fled from Ghroc. He wore no shirt, only loose-fitting pants and a brightly colored sash around his narrow waist.

Like all those of the Goyor race, he was dark skinned and perfect in appearance and body tone. They kept their curly black hair cropped shortly to their heads. The Forest Folk were an attractive race, for they were formed from the beauty of the earth, as was the common belief.

"You have been nervous and in a foul mood for days. Do not fret so; your worry will do nothing to speed Captain Hepin's return," he said, trying to soothe her tortured spirit.

"You do not understand the complexity of this situation," Baobh answered. "I must have this woman, or she could bring an end to my rule, to my very life!"

He turned to face her. "You have her father imprisoned as we speak, surely the woman will not be far behind. Your Captain Hepin is the best of the Royal Guard, and he will bring her to you."

Baobh patted Eagle's solid arm, her trepidation slightly faltering. "I am thankful for you, my sweet man. No one can ease my soul the way you do." Placated for the moment, she smiled up into her mate's dark eyes.

Then distracted once again, she looked west at the gentle green rolling hills of White Oak Valley as it stretched out for many miles far out of her keen vision. "They should have returned by now," Baobh stated softly.

Eagle put his large hand on top of Baobh's cold fist resting on the stone balcony wall. The difference between his dark skin and her lighter colored creamy brown hue was ever so apparent in the light of a bright sun. She noticed his comparative stare and smiled to herself; it was quite evident she was not full-blooded Goyor, and for that she was proud.

"You have the promised aid of Lord Rull. He helped you take the throne of Sona Tuath; he will help you keep it. Moreover, you have the necklace, my Queen. What can harm you?" He tried again to soothe her.

Baobh's small hand went to the ornate silver necklace at her throat. Her delicate fingers ran over the smooth, blood-red stones pulled from the very mines of Del Nort far to the north in Ventra. A confident, warm expression spread over her face. However, when her fingers moved over the empty spot in the center of the necklace, her mood dimmed once again, for the biggest stone was missing. "Yes, I have the Necklace of Verna, but I am missing the most powerful of the stones of the necklace," she said solemnly.

"Have you not held power over Beaynid all these long years? Even when the Archigos came up against you, they could not defeat you!"

She looked over to him, and for a brief moment, she felt as vulnerable as a child, but then the moment passed, and she was a strong, ruthless queen once more.

"I must have this Kossi woman before the Archigos discover she lives and before she finds the lost stone…"

From behind an immense purple curtain, a young soldier stepped out onto the balcony, a worried looking castle servant standing behind him. "M-many pardons, my gracious Queen. I am a messenger for High Captain Hepin's party. I have ridden with much haste." Baobh spun around to look at the apprehensive young man drawn with almost unbearable fatigue.

"He has the woman then?" Baobh arched a brow in question.

"N-no Your Greatness." The pale-skinned, white-blonde haired young man stuttered.

"Where is Captain Hepin?" Baobh screamed, her shrill voice carrying out into the courtyard.

The servant jumped and started to tremble. He looked to Eagle with pleading eyes and then back to Baobh. "He was killed by the Archigos woman. She escaped m- my Queen." He added quickly, hoping to defuse her anger, "We managed to track her to the rebellion army where she is being held captive, your Majesty."

She lifted her head to the stone ceiling and let out the terrifying enraged howl of a great beast. Her wail carried on the warm breeze to descend upon the inhabitance of Sona Tuath. Once again, they were reminded of the razor-sharp edge they all walked with an angry, dangerous queen sitting on the dais of Beaynid.

CHAPTER EIGHT

Sing you little bird who sits upon the tree,
Sing the song of Jur.
Burdened his people were, but who now are free,
Sing the song of Jur.
On azure wings from heaven came his loving decree,
Sing the song of Jur.

*Sing the song of Jur, you little bird, sing of all the things you've
heard, sing of the glory of our God you little bird, sing of all the
things you've heard.*

Delivered from the land of darkness into the light,
Sing the song of Jur.
He heard their mournful outcries and turned towards their plight,
Sing the song of Jur.
Once from pain and sorrow, he's now given them much delight,
Sing the song of Jur.

Sing the song of Jur you little bird, sing of all the things you've heard, sing of the glory of our God you little bird, sing of all the things you've heard.

- Song of Jur; author unknown

Tiny twirling sunbursts danced across the insides of her closed eyelids. She melted into the earth as though she were water being hungrily swallowed up by dry mouths. Her breaths were long and slow as she felt the unobtrusive power of nature vibrate through her body. The warm sun baked down upon her, darkening her skin and setting her hair ablaze in a deep purple-black fire. Beside her lay her constant companion; a child of the wilderness whose heart beat to the rhythm of the tides and whose blood flowed as the mighty rivers of the land. The wolf: majestic and fierce; poetic and unknowable; mighty and soft.

Now she lay quietly in a small meadow listening to the sounds of the wood. There were always the voices of men and the sounds of swordplay along with the neighs and whinnies of horses. However, she was accustomed to shutting those noises out now and listening to the earth: the shift and groan of giant trees swaying in the hot, southern wind; the bray of angry jays hopping about within the dense cover of the trees; even the busy rummaging of hungry field mice.

She heard the dull thump of footfall and knew he was coming to her, as he always did. She wondered if he would ask more questions, but realized she did not care. She could feel him staring at her; his gaze hotter than any day. She stayed quiet a little while longer, hoping he would think she was asleep and leave. But she knew he could tell she lay awake, lost in deep pools of memory and the dark uncertainty of the future.

"She looks much better today," he said.

Rhiannon sat up slowly and looked over at him as he sat

next to her she-wolf. "A lot better than I thought she would in only a few weeks' time." Flath ran his hand over Luna's thick coat, loose fur catching the wind and floating away. "The next time I suffer an injury I will come straight to you, Greannmhor, and bypass the surgeon altogether." She smiled but stayed silent. "Are you sure you do not know what kind of stone that is?"

"I told you, I just found it. I have no idea what it is." she lied. Telling him that her mother had given it to her would just make things complicated. She could not even explain to herself how she knew the words to the song that coaxed the stone to life.

She looked away toward a pair of fighting squirrels running through the trees, and then turned back to him when he said nothing. His pale hair ruffled ion the hot wind sending his earring spinning around like a kite in heavy wind. As always, his face was tired and carried sorrow and contemplativeness. It made him look older, yet she knew he was still too young for the heavy responsibility that he carried. He was always weighted down with it; like a stone around his neck pulling him deeper into the depths of a bottomless ocean.

He pulled a small yellow flower from a weed that was growing near his hand. As he studied the intricacies of the flower, she studied the intricacies of the man. "How's your war going, Captain?" She had seen the messenger ride into camp earlier.

"My men are pushing further south towards the Elk Mountains." He threw the flower down and looked over to her. "With any luck, we will drive them further from Sona Tuath and maybe cut off their supply route."

"Why aren't you following after them?" She watched as Luna got up slowly and trotted off into the bushes with barely a limp.

"I am still trying to decide what to do with you, milady."

"Don't let me hold you up, Captain." He kept staring, and she wondered what he was thinking.

"We will leave in the morning and join up with my men," he nonchalantly replied and looked away.

"You're always so serious, Flath. You need a vacation," she offered.

"A vacation?" he asked, curiously.

"Some time off to relax," she answered.

"I shall have plenty of time to relax-as you put it-after the war is over, and Baobh is dead." He looked over to an unusually intense sword match between two rather large soldiers.

"So, what *do* you plan on doing with me?" she asked when the noise died down.

"I do not know. Maybe I will just give you a sword, and you can fight right alongside of us." He raked his hand through his hair.

"And what makes you so sure I won't just take your head off with it?" she asked, without humor.

At that, he laughed. "You could try, Greannmhor." She snorted in offense, but knew he was right. She watched a large flock of geese lazily float by on a hurrying breeze. "When we reach the others I will be leaving you for a while. You are undoubtedly tired of roving about. You will have time to rest and—," he hesitated, "to have a bath."

She looked over at Flath. "Are you trying to tell me I stink?

"Men fresh from battle smell less offensive than you."

"Maybe I won't bathe then and just continue to torment you with my noxious stench."

"Then I shall have to throw you in the water and scrub the smell away myself!"

She gave him a sideways glance. "You could try, Captain."

At that, a soldier yelled something at Flath while holding

his sword up in the air. Flath pulled himself up from the ground and walked over to the man.

Losing interest, Rhiannon began to think about home. She thought about the Sheriff looking through her father's cabin and a search team combing the mountain for them. But they would not be found. She thought of how hurt Daniel and Matthew would be with their disappearance. Matthew had been very hurt when she gave him back her engagement ring. She remembered the confused look on his face as he held the diamond ring, still warm from her finger.

Anything to do with Daniel Foster, owner of the largest cattle ranch in the state, made headlines. So, his son's engagement party had been the social event of the county and newspapers around the state announced Matthew Foster's fall from the ranks of the most eligible bachelors. She imagined the headlines from those same newspapers now screaming out about the two souls who simply vanished from the earth. She wondered if they would come across that old tree-the one in her dreams-the one that somehow swallowed her into the pit of this nightmare. She rubbed her sore jaw and ran a finger over where the split in her lip used to be. She wondered how bruised her face still was.

The loud ringing of clashing swords pulled her from her thoughts. She looked over to see Flath and another man engaged in what seemed to be a heated sword fight. Sweat dripped from both men's faces as they danced around in a circle, each gripping his weapon with skill and determination. The man brought down a hard blow, but Flath deflected it and dodged sideways. Grunts filled the warm air as did cheering from a few younger men who had gathered. The soldier kept trying to knock Flath's sword from his hand with powerful swings, only to be completely dodged or stopped mid-swing with a counter blow.

They filled their lungs as fast as they could as they

continued their violent dance that was not quite graceful, but not clumsy either. Both men were intent on the other's moves and searching for that one weakness that would end the fight. Finally, the man brought his sword down hard, but Flath deftly missed the blow, twirled around and with the tip of his sword, flipped the man's weapon from his hand

The spectators erupted with laughter and cheers as the losing man went to retrieve his sword. Flath handed the sword back to the young soldier he had borrowed it from and tried to catch his breath. He walked over to his opponent and slapped him on his back. They laughed and traded some colorful expressions. Flath looked over to Rhiannon and waved. She just snorted and looked away. "Show off," she said to no one in particular.

After a while, Flath appeared at her side again. He had cleaned up a bit and was wearing a fresh shirt. "Come, Greannmhor, let us see if Cook has food ready." He held out a calloused hand to help her from the ground, and he pulled her up to stand next to him. Stiff muscles protested, and joints popped.

The warm air was cooling a bit as the sun started its descent. They made their way through the small camp to where several men were already sitting around a fire. Small tendrils of white smoke drifted up from the fire and then disappeared in an ochre sky.

She sat on a log near the fire flames, and Flath took a seat next to her. "Why don't you have a last name?" she asked out of the blue.

"A last name?"

"You know, a family name, like mine, is Kossi."

"Gypsies have no family names," he replied quietly and looked down into the fire.

"How do you know where you come from, then?"

"We come from the wind. The wind has no name-neither

first nor last." The setting sun caught one of the ruby eyes of the panther he wore at his neck and sent a red star out into a world awash in golden light. "There are no boundaries to gypsies. There are no social classes and few enough rules as to say we have none."

"Where is your family now?"

"Roving about the countryside, I suppose. I have not seen them for many years." His eyes took on the color of the dancing flames.

Rhiannon frowned. "Don't you miss them?"

"No," he stated flatly.

There was a long silence, and Rhiannon knew she had gone as far as she could on the subject. After a while, she spotted Cook marching in long strides towards them. A stout man with a shiny bald head and a golden hoop earring in each ear stopped in front of them and handed her a wooden plate piled high with food. He was wearing a large apron stained with the smudges of many suppers. He had soft hands, kind eyes, and a friendly smile. He said something she thought she recognized but couldn't be sure.

"Thank you," she replied, not knowing if he could speak English.

"Ah, the beautiful girl speaks Jurian. In that case, you are welcome, milady." His mouth spread into a warm smile, devoid of most of his teeth. "If there is anything at all that you wish, I will make it for you!" he pronounced happily and then turned and walked away.

Flath put a plate at Luna's feet then sat down next to Rhiannon with his own food. "Cook likes you," he said, regaining his cheerfulness. "'Tis good to be Cook's friend around here, you are sure to get the best food."

"Food is food," Rhiannon said picking up the meat with her fingers and stuffing it in her mouth.

"Hunting is still good right now; you will be happy to be friends with Cook when winter hits."

"You think I'll be staying with you that long?" she asked.

"That depends."

"On what?"

"On whether or not you eventually tell me the truth about who you are." He spoke without looking and her.

"Not that again." Rhiannon heaved an audible sigh. "I've told you the truth from the beginning; you're just too stubborn to accept it."

"I beg your pardon, milady, but the truth as you speak it is quite unbelievable." This time he did look over at her.

"I know it's unbelievable. I don't even believe it myself, but it's the truth just the same." She held his gaze. "I must get to Sona Tuath to free my father before it's too late. He's an old man, and I'm worried for his safety. I can't stay here with you."

"If what you say is true and the queen does have your father, then he is most likely already dead, milady," Flath spoke softly, but the words cut just the same. She put her plate aside, got up and slowly walked a short distance away. Tears streamed down her face as she thought of the hopelessness of the situation. She could hear him approach and quickly wiped the tears from her cheek. "I am sorry Greannmhor, but if you are being truthful with me, you must face the fact that your father…" he paused and gently put his hand on Rhiannon's shoulder, "might already be dead."

She could not stop the tears, nor hide her pain. She turned to him. "Then what am I to do? Should I just leave him to rot in the dungeons of Sona Tuath?" Those words sounded ludicrous to her. It seemed her old world was completely lost to her now.

Taking a deep breath, he watched the sun dip behind

darkened trees. Finally, he spoke again. "Why do you speak Jurian?"

Rhiannon sniffed and wiped her wet cheeks with the back of her hand. "I don't know what Jurian is."

Flath looked back over at her. "Jurian is the tongue of the Priests of Jur," he said as if she should know.

"Where is Jur?"

He frowned. "Jur is not a place; he is a god!" She shook her head. "The priests of Jur are the traveling messengers of the god, Jur. They travel all around the countryside paying no attention to borders or various clan or tribal battles and skirmishes that often plague the land."

"And they speak the same language I do?"

"Aye. Now, can we finish this conversation closer to the food, I am hungry, woman." Flath walked back to the hollow log near the fire with their forgotten food and Rhiannon slowly followed. She stirred the food around on her plate but had lost her appetite. After eating a few bites, Flath went on. "When I was young my family encountered one such group of priests. Since we were also traveling, we shared camps and meals. During the evening we would all gather around the fire and listen to the priests tell us the ancient stories of Jur."

Flath looked into the flames of the campfire and smiled as he spoke, "The fire would crackle and hiss and give an eerie, ochre glow to their faces. We kids were so frightened, but we could not look away. They told us of a great war that broke out all over the land. Many people died of hunger or disease or were killed by the armies of different lands.

"The legend told of a small group of men, women, and children that escaped their burning village and hid in a nearby cave. They prayed through the night not to be found and to be delivered through this hardship. Sometime in the middle of the night, a drawing depicting a large tree on the wall of the cave started to glow a bright golden color. The people were frightened, and the children began crying. Suddenly a black opening appeared in the center of this cave etching. The men decided that this was a sign from God and that they must go through the opening."

"An opening in a drawing of a tree?" Rhiannon's hands shook slightly, and perspiration picked at her armpits.

"Aye." He looked at her suspiciously. When she said nothing further, he turned back to his plate and went on. "The men gathered their families and one by one they stepped into this black opening. On the other side, they found themselves stepping from the hollowed trunk of a large tree that looked just like the drawing in the cave."

After eating a few bites of his food, Flath continued with the story. "The small group of families immediately started giving thanks to whatever god it was that delivered them from harm. The priests then said a bright blue songbird descended from the branches of the tree and told them it was Jur who brought them to his world. The bird then told them they were Jur's people now and that they should tell everyone they encountered about the kindness of Jur. The men named that old oak, Tree of Jur, gathered up their families and started traveling around the land expounding upon the greatness of Jur. It is said that the priests of Jur are the descendants of those saved families."

Rhiannon stared down at her filthy riding boots and began to tremble. She gripped her wooden spoon in an effort to stop the shaking.

"A lot of people know how to speak Jurian because of the traveling priests, but the only ones who actually use the language exclusively are the priests and priestess of Jur. That is why I am disconcerted at your constant use of the tongue. You obviously are not a priestess of Jur. Why do you speak only Jurian?"

"That's the language I was taught as a child."

"How is that possible? The Archigos consider the priests of Jur to be half-wits, and nothing more than superstitious storytellers who live like leeches off of people stupid enough to listen to their jabber. I have heard that most Archigos do know the language, though they refuse to use it, so I think you are being untruthful with me when you tell me it is your native tongue."

Ignoring the accusation, Rhiannon asked, "Tell me again about the cave and where these people came from." Her voice was urgent and insistent.

Flath hesitated a moment but then continued. "The way the priests tell it, they came from another world, a place that had suffered many wars and injustices. I am inclined to believe them because I have actually seen the Tree of Jur and I felt a peculiar power radiating from the tree."

"So, you're telling me there is this other world out there somewhere, and occasionally people just pop out of this tree trying to escape their homeland?" Rhiannon's heart pounded in her ears.

"Those families, the first priests of Jur, are the only ones known to have actually come through the tree," he answered in a calm voice, brows drawn together in contemplation.

Rhiannon silently looked out over the small camp. Flath scratched his head and resumed eating, and after a while, Rhiannon also started eating again. They sat, not saying a word for a long time. The sounds of the camp encircled them and became intrusive. Flath finally asked.

"What does the queen want with your father?"

"Hepin said she was holding him prisoner, waiting for me to come to her."

"That is very unusual, Greannmhor," he said. She looked up at him with a question in her eyes, but he remained silent.

"Who is this Queen Baobh, anyway?" Rhiannon asked

91

after a while. "Why is the rebellion fighting against her?" she asked.

"Of course, you should already know all of this, but I'll humor you. She is an evil woman of a race of Forest Folk called Goyors."

"Forest Folk?" Rhiannon asked sarcastically. She remembered back to the conversation that she had had earlier with the healer woman Laura. She suddenly became very wary because though she did not fully trust this man, she did not think he was crazy either.

He looked at her strangely, as if she had something stuck on the end of her nose. "Aye, Forest Folk." His tone was flat and almost daring her to contradict his statement.

When she did not reply, he finally went on. "She is uncaring and vicious to the people of Beaynid. She taxes the people into exhaustion and then when they cannot pay, she takes their possessions or their land. She needs to be stopped before many more people die."

"If she's such a horrible ruler then why did the people of Sona Tuath allow her to become queen?"

"You really do not know?" Flath asked.

"I told you, Flath, I don't know anything about this place."

He stared at her again. "When I was but a babe, Baobh entered the castle undetected by the Royal Guard, and killed King Basilias and all the royal family. She took control of the Royal Guard and then the whole Beaynidan army."

"How could one woman do such a thing?" Rhiannon asked.

"She had the help of the one they call Lord Rull and his army from some far-off land, and she is of the Goyor race, they have certain powers." He was quiet for a moment. "She also has the Necklace of Verna."

Rhiannon gasped at the mention of a name she recognized. Her mother's necklace! Flath looked over at Rhiannon and frowned. "Where did you come from Rhiannon Kossi?"

Lost in long forgotten memories, she almost did not hear him. Finally, she looked up at him as he turned towards her in realization that she had heard his question. "I'm from the other side of that tree," she said just as quietly.

CHAPTER NINE

"Many strange creatures make the forests and woods of Beaynid their home. Among them is a rather peculiar species of large cat. It is known as Pax. This feline is quite different from the alley cats of Sona Tuath in that it has large wings that can carry the seemingly insignificant weight of the cat easily. An additional unusual feature is the cat's enormous, globe-like eyes, though it does not appear the Pax can see any better than any other cat. Strangely, there seems to be some superstition surrounding this animal. The local folk are quite provincial in their beliefs and have expressed some trepidation about the Pax."
-Field Guide of Beaynid; Myrin Zantroc

The small caravan clamored up the long, windy path towards the rebel fighters who were most likely on the other side of the Elk Mountains by now, provided they were traveling quickly. The air was increasingly becoming colder as the gentle rolling hills of Sorrel Valley disappeared behind tall pines. Like insistent fingers, small shafts of warm sunlight clawed their way through the conifers but were soon lost to a thick canopy.

"Why does the queen want you?" Flath asked.

"I don't know." Rhiannon shifted in her saddle trying to find a more comfortable position.

"Did Hepin tell you anything?"

"Not really." She shrugged and swatted a fly who was curiously buzzing around her head. "He did say something about a prophecy."

"A prophecy?" Flath looked out over the mountain pass. "Interesting," he said contemplatively.

"I think he was crazy, or lying," Rhiannon quickly interjected.

"How can you be certain you are not part of a prophecy?"

Rhiannon shook her head. "None of this is real, and I'm going to wake up very soon now," she mumbled under her breath. "I guess I can't be certain, then," she said a little louder.

The sun had fully disappeared behind dark trees, and the once sweet breeze turned into a cool wind. The birds were quiet, and the only sounds besides the wind were from the wagons and horses as they traveled the road. Creaks and jangles and whinnies and thumping hooves all echoed off the tall pine trees and hills that were quickly turning into mountains as they climbed up and into the wilderness. "Teo's mother is a Prophecy Keeper. We will pay her a visit and see if she has knowledge of this prophecy."

"It's probably nothing," she said unconcerned.

"Maybe so, Greannmhor, but if it is true, would you not want to know?"

She looked over at the tall, fair-haired man riding next to her and wondered again if this was all some coma-induced hallucination. She did not answer him.

They traveled on through the day, climbing higher up the mountain pass. Finally, as night blanketed the ancient pine trees, they made camp for the night. They laid out their sleeping bundles and slept under the protective boughs of the trees. With Flath sleeping a short distance away on one side of her and Luna snuggled up on the other side, she looked up at the undersides of the trees and shimmering stars that peeked through the branches. She fell asleep thinking about her father, wondering if he still lived.

At dawn the next morning they were traveling again and reached the crest of the trail by midmorning. Just below them lay Faerie Lake. Its serene waters reflected a bright early May sun. Small rounded waves bounced from one shore to the next in a never-ending cycle of motion. They descended the trail carefully and skirted the lake for the rest of the day. During the next day, they traveled further back down the other side of the mountain. The road was steeper and more treacherous than the path leading up the other side, so they traveled much slower. Wagons creaked, and their load swayed in the chilly wind. The horses were tired and unhappy about the rocky path they were forced to follow.

That night, under cover of darkness, they were met by scouts patrolling the area. A bright half-moon hung in the starry sky but proved to be impotent under the thick umbrella of the vast pines. Four men melted out of the darkness appearing from behind the trees. Quickly they surrounded Flath and Rhiannon, and Luna started growling. Steel sword tips gleamed in a lost moonbeam as one of the men barked out an order. Flath replied.

With their arrows returned to their quivers, four archers dropped from their hidden bough and joined the scouts below. Their swords were quickly put away, and they began talking. Rhiannon thought she understood some of the words, but the gist of what they were saying was lost to her. A restless cloud moved over the moon and threw the forest into complete darkness-the voices seemed to be coming from nowhere. The opaque cloud finally sailed free from the moon, and she spread her soft glow over the mountain again.

A short while later they rode into the camp. No fires burned and only whispered voices could be heard. Night birds and insects sang their music into the chilly night air having no idea that men were so close. Upon closer inspection, Rhiannon found small tents hidden in between bushes and trees. She figured the horses and equipment must have been hidden under the trees as well.

As they dismounted, a handful of grooms approached out of the darkness and led the horses away. Rhiannon thought Zellan must have gotten used to all of their new acquaintances as he did not put up a fight.

Two men quickly walked up to Flath, both were talking quickly and with much animation. The candles they held in their hands gave out the smallest bit of light, but to eyes that had been used to the complete darkness, the light was sufficient enough. One of the men was carrying a rolled-up parchment of some kind. Flath pointed east and asked a question. Both of the men answered in unison. Flath shook his head and ran his hand through his hair.

Finally, Flath turned to one of the young men who had appeared as they road up. "Show Lady Kossi to an empty tent near mine and bring her and the wolf some food." He spoke Jurian to the young man who quickly looked at Rhiannon straining to see her through the darkness. Upon discovering she was a woman, his eyes widened with shock.

Flath snickered. "Things are not always as they seem, young Tim.

Rhiannon looked up at Flath and wrinkled her nose at him in distaste. "Have a good evening, Captain," she said and started walking into the darkness with Tim following close behind.

Rhiannon was led to a small tent where she and Luna

were given plates of food. A tiny lantern cast a weak yellow glow as it sat atop a very small wooden table. A cot with three folded blankets sat beside the table. After washing her hands in a small clay basin of water, she ate her meal in silence, thinking about her father and how much she missed him. She must find her father, and she made up her mind that if Flath would not help her, she would have to try and sneak away again.

Rhiannon eased herself down onto the cot and let out a long sigh. Dozens of night birds softly serenaded the forest. Croaking frogs and chirping insects announced their presence, too. It was a very relaxing symphony harmonized by a soft easterly breeze. Finally, Rhiannon fell asleep, burrowed under scratchy wool blankets with pictures of her father in her head. An equal number of bright, vivid pictures of her mother, also floated through her dreams. She finally let go of the world around her and retreated to a softer, warmer world within.

The next morning, on the orders of his Captain, a young, fully armed soldier stood at attention outside Rhiannon's tent ready to defend his spirited charge. "Who the heck are you?" Rhiannon asked as she was stopped just outside of her tent. The early morning sun painted the sky in bright orange streaks as it chased away a few twinkling stars left from the night before.

"Tim, from last night, milady. Do you not recognize me?"

Rhiannon rubbed the sleep from her eyes and blinked a few times before she looked back over at the redheaded young man barring her passage from the tent. "Oh yeah. Good morning Tim, now get out of my way, nature calls."

"Well, uh, I have strict orders to not let you from your tent until Flath arrives." Tim stuttered nervously. Rhiannon quickly pushed past Tim in an unconcerned manner and walked into the bushes. "Lady Kossi, please wait, the Captain gave me strict orders not to let you from your tent!" In a blur, Luna tore out of the tent and jumped on top of Tim sending him to the damp ground with a thud. Tim's eyes grew wide, and he did not move.

"Tell Flath I'll come and go as I please," she called as she disappeared into the thick brush. After Rhiannon had relieved herself, she walked further through the dense vegetation and inhaled the sweetly fragrant bushes. Birds called to one another far up in the treetops, their music so soft and expressive its likeness she had not heard before.

Somewhere off in the distance a kind of mewling-growling sound drifted on a soft breeze. Just as soon as it was there, it was gone and was replaced with croaking frogs belching out their love songs to uninterested females. A soft trickling sound like the gentle rings of a small bell became louder as she moved towards it.

Rhiannon followed the gurgling sound of water to a small stream. She knelt down beside the water and scooped up the icy cold liquid in her cupped hands. She vigorously scrubbed her face, then slowly drank her fill of the sweet water.

For a good long while, Rhiannon sat on a rock hugging her knees to her chest. She mindlessly watched tiny leaves being swiftly carried down the stream in a bumpy ride to an unknown destination. Every so often a giant green frog would hop into view, croak a few times and then hop back into hiding. She picked up a twig, tossed it into the stream and sighed as she watched it float away.

The sound of beating wings and the feel of soft wind on her hair startled her. She looked up at the tall pines and searched the exposed branches but saw no bird. After a while, she grew bored and continued to survey her surroundings.

Her vision came across a bright ribbon of golden sunshine that had found a void in the canopy and shone down to the damp earth below. Standing in the middle of the light was a small creature. Rhiannon strained to see what kind of creature it was. Very slowly she crawled on her hands and knees closer to the animal. She tried not to make too much sound. The animal looked up at her, but then unconcerned started grooming its coat.

She gazed at its beauty and graceful features. It glowed in the golden sunshine. The animal looked very similar to a young cougar in shape and coloring. The cat's tawny and white coat was speckled with darker spots, making it almost indistinguishable in the dimness of the forest. On both sides of its shoulders sprung large fawn colored wings that were tipped in a deep black. Its feathers were iridescent and shimmered in the light as the cat moved.

Suddenly it looked up at Rhiannon. She gasped and fell back at the sight of its haunting eyes. The enormous eyes were overly large for the cat's face, making it look almost comical. In the center of each eye were two onyx slits set in one huge, amber iris. Frightened, but overwhelmed with a need to get closer, Rhiannon slowly crawled up closer to the animal. They stared at one another not moving as everything else in the forest melted away-just the small beast and a woman.

Not quite quickly, yet not slowly either, the center pupils started to open up. Wider and wider they grew until they swallowed the entire eye in deep blackness. The cat's eyes grew even larger, so they covered most of its face. Suddenly a small figure started to appear in each eye. It gradually came into focus until the image of a small dark-haired little girl shined in the eyes of the animal.

Rhiannon's heart thundered in her chest and sweat beaded and dripped from her forehead. She leaned in closer to the animal trying to get a better look at the child held within the wide orbs. Suddenly she knew who the child was.

She began to shake as a feeling of foreboding gripped her chest so tight she could not breathe.

"No..." she whispered as she watched herself, as a child, screaming over the body of her mother lying in a pool of blood steam rising into the cold night air.

In an instant, the image was gone; the animal's eyes shrunk, and its dual pupils returned to the tiny slits of a cat. Rhiannon fell to the dirt and rolled onto her back. She stared up at the pine trees, so thick and tall. Slowly, her breathing and heart gradually picked out a more comfortable rhythm, and her shaking subsided. The sound of rushing blood was replaced with the splashing water, happy birds and singing frogs and the loudest purring she had ever heard.

Soft, silky fur rubbed up against her arm, she flinched, but the little cat rubbed up against her again. Rhiannon sat up, and the animal crawled up into her lap, purring away and fell asleep. Her lap was not big enough to serve as much of a bed, but the cat slept on. She stroked the soft fur on the back of the cat's wide head and started humming a familiar lullaby. A twig snapped, and she looked up to see Luna and Flath standing in the trees.

"What in the name of the gods have you done?" he asked softly as he removed his dagger from the sheath at his waist. Luna, sensing Flath's trepidation, started to growl.

"What?" she asked, confused.

He slowly approached her with his dagger drawn and pointed the tip at the cat who was now awake and no longer purring. "Do not move Rhiannon..." he ordered, softly.

"Flath, what do you think you're going to do to this animal?" she asked, unsure of either the cat or the man. Luna stared at the winged beast and growled a low, threatening warning.

He and the wolf-dog moved closer. "Do not worry; I will not let the beast hurt you."

"What are talking about?" she asked, becoming a little wary of the animal. Just as Flath got into striking distance, the great cat opened its wings, and in a flutter of soft feathers, it took to the air with a loud screech and growl.

"Are you all right, Greannmhor?"

I'm fine," she said, fully annoyed. She stood up and began searching the trees for the cat. "Why did you scare it away?" she asked.

"Do you not know what that was?"

"No, and I probably never will, now," she said sourly, still scanning the trees.

"It was a pax," he said calmly. "That animal could have taken your head off with one swing of its paw."

Rhiannon turned her gaze to Flath. "It seemed very nice; quite tame if you ask me."

"That is because it was young. If it had been grown, it would have eaten you before you had even taken your last breath!" Flath looked up to the trees and made a quick search of the area.

"Have you ever seen one up close? It had the most beautiful eyes..." Rhiannon said as she peered into thick branches.

"I have not gotten close enough to one, but I have heard of the power those beasts have." Flath grabbed Rhiannon's arm. "They are dangerous. And I gave orders that you were not allowed out of your tent until I came to retrieve you."

"Orders?" She yanked her arm out of his grip and stood glaring at him. Luna yawned and trotted back towards the camp. Rhiannon watched Luna's fluffy silver and white tail disappear into the trees and felt deserted. Remembering what Flath had said two weeks earlier, she turned it back on him. "Well, I am not one of your pathetic, subjugated, weak women that you can order around!" She looked at him defiantly, ready for a fight. Flath grabbed her upper arms and pulled her towards him so close she could feel his breath on her cheek.

"Listen to me, Rhiannon Kossi, it is not safe for you to be wandering around here by yourself. The queen wants you very badly, and I am sure it is not to make you her heir. Furthermore, I cannot trust all the men in my command. I need soldiers, and I must accept any that show up to fight for our side. Some of them might not be as loyal to the cause as they seem. You may have a large price on your head, and many are most -likely looking for you."

"I told you, I can take care of myself!" she snapped and tried to pull free. He tightened his grip around her arms, and she winced.

"Despite what you want to believe, you are vulnerable and naive and could very easily be picked off like some dinner fowl in a hunter's backyard." He looked deeply into her eyes and seemed to be struggling with some indefinable emotion.

Her brow wrinkled abruptly. "You have one blue eye and one green," she said matter-of-factly, completely changing the subject.

"... Rhiannon, are you listening to me?" he demanded, losing patience, not bothering to acknowledge her discovery.

"Yes, I can hear you," she snapped, pulling her arms out of his loosening grip.

"That animal was very dangerous; it could have killed you. The forest is full of dangers that you are not aware of. If you insist on disregarding the protection I am offering, something bad will happen to you."

"What did you say was the name of that animal?" she asked, looking into the tree canopy.

"It is a pax." He took a deep breath and knew he had lost her attention. "They are not usually this far southeast, that one must have been lost. They devastate cattle and other herding animals, so the farmers have killed most of them."

"That one didn't seem like a ferocious killing beast," she argued.

"Wait until you come across a full- grown male. Then we shall see who is right." He searched the undersides of dark trees. "If there was a cub around, its mother is not far away. We must leave." He grabbed her arm again and pulled her back towards camp. "Let us see if Cook has something to break our fast."

"Men! They're always thinking of their bellies."

CHAPTER TEN

"With his armor gleaming in the light the brave knight rode his mighty steed into war.
At his sight, men quaked with fear as he fought valiantly and many fell to his sword.
The fighting was heavy; many were slain, and upon the fields, their blood did pour.
The knight looked out at his slain fellows and enemies alike, never to fight anymore.

They said he was from a country farm in the green, green land of bliss.
To his god and king, he swore an oath always to protect in faithfulness.
With his golden hair and comely face, from the maidens, he was assured a kiss.

He smote his enemy upon the battlefield; his might was beyond compare.
Tales of his bravery and prowess filled the land, and against him, no man would dare.

*One day he spied a shiny black steed and upon its back rode a
maiden so fair.
In that instant, he gave his heart as he watched the wind blow
through her raven hair.*

*They said he was from a country farm in the green, green land
of bliss.
To his god and king, he swore an oath always to protect in
faithfulness.
With his golden hair and comely face, from the maidens, he was
assured a kiss.*

*That was the last day anyone saw the brave, shining knight.
The king searched near and far, but the knight was kept from
his sight.
Some say she was a spirit or a fairy that lead him to his doom
before she took flight.
'Tis said that if the moon is full, you can see him riding high on his
steed in the moonlight.
They said he was from a country farm in the green, green land
of bliss.
To his god and king, he swore an oath always to protect in
faithfulness.
With his golden hair and comely face, from the black maid did he
receive his last kiss."
-The Knight and Raven-Haired Maid; G. L. Niv*

As night crept across the forest, Flath took his men and
melted into the darkness towards the rest of the army. He left
a cook, a surgeon, six armed men, and Tim behind. He said
nothing to her before he left, just gave her a wave as he rode
away. She looked after him for a long time, much longer than
the waxing moonlight afforded her. She felt a sudden tinge of
what she thought was loss, followed by worry. A messenger

had galloped into camp only hours ago with a report that the fighting had increased. Because of familiar terrain, the rebel fighters had a small advantage over the Beaynidan soldiers, though that gap was diminishing.

Flath rode out to war and the thought he might not return unsettled her more than she would admit. She wiped her nervous palms down the legs of her borrowed pants, retreated into her tent and fell asleep with a frown on her brow.

The sluggish sun crawled up a sleepy pink sky. The days were growing longer and the breeze warmer. The forest seemed an inviting retreat from insurmountable worries. "Walk with me, Tim." She held out her elbow, and Tim reluctantly hooked his arm in hers. She found a meandering deer path that cut across giant lacy ferns that towered over her head. The ground was spongy with mounds of moss in gray, green, yellow, and black. Luna walked on ahead, taking small stops to sniff at bushes.

"How old are you, Tim?" Rhiannon asked as she looked down at the fair-skinned young man. Tim straightened up, stuck out his chest and a youthful smile spread across his face. "I am going to be ten and three, milady," he announced cheerfully. Rhiannon looked him over a little closer and decided he would be a tall and strong man someday—provided he survived. "Uh, ten and two is awfully young to be fighting in a war," she said reluctantly.

"I will be ten and three in just a few days Lady Kossi. I am no child," he stated boldly.

At the offended tone of his voice, she quickly looked over at him again and smiled sweetly. "Of course you're not a child Tim, I was just thinking of how hard it must have been for your mother to send you off to war." They followed the path into a small gully and carefully stepped over an excited stream that paid no mind as it hurried into a lush green symphony of moss covered rocks, ferns, and tall trees proudly standing like sentinels in a shadowy wood.

"My mother passed over a few years ago, milady. Father sent me to Flath. He told me I would come back a man."

Rhiannon smiled. "He must be very proud of you."

"Aye, milady, he is indeed!" Tim's freckled face turned rosy, and his smile broadened. "He says me and Flath will save all of Beaynid from Queen Baobh."

"You're very brave, Tim." She smiled warmly at her young attendant. "I feel safe with you escorting me on this walk." Rhiannon looked up the path a bit to see Luna lope off after a small brown rabbit.

"Thank you, milady. I was instructed to protect you with my life; I will gladly do my duty for you and Flath." He smiled up at her, and his cheeks reddened.

"You seem to be very fond of Flath. Is he a friend of your father's?"

"Aye, milady. In my village, Flath is a hero. Almost all the men of fighting age have left the village to join the rebellion."

"I guess that doesn't make the women of your village very happy," Rhiannon replied as they ducked to avoid a low branch.

"Most of the women of Bell have died, milady. Only a few survived," he said somberly.

Rhiannon stopped abruptly. "What happened to them?"

Tim did not talk for a long moment but softly began to recount the story. "The women of Bell were known for their talent in weaving tapestries of unsurpassed beauty, milady. The tapestries were woven from the soft, fine, brightly colored wool of our own Ppie sheep." Tim's eyes grew wide when he spoke of home and the famed sheep of Bell. "'Tis said that the Goddess Penelope created the soft, fuzzy Ppie sheep so the women of Bell could create beautiful things.

The wise women say the tapestries of Bell are blessed by the very hand of the Goddess Penelope."

Rhiannon looked into Tim's bright blue eyes, so full of wonder and still holding fast to boyhood pride and the dreams they are made of. "A few years ago, Queen Baobh came to Bell and told the women that she had heard of their beautiful tapestries. The queen said she wanted the women of Bell to make a large number of tapestries them for the castle at Sona Tuath. Well, the women were brave and told the queen that because she had proven to be an evil leader who misgoverned Beaynid and mistreated her people, they would not make anything for her!"

"They told Baobh that?" Rhiannon asked with an arched brow.

"Aye! The women of Bell were very brave, and they could blister your ear with nothing more than a single word."

"I would have liked to meet your women of Bell, Tim."

"My mother would have loved you!" Tim said excitedly. "She was always toward the Archigos."

"I know what Flath must have told you, but I'm not an Archigos, Tim. I have never met one either."

Tim looked perplexed. "Milady, I-"

"And I'm not royalty either. I don't care what Flath told you. I'm just a regular person like everyone else." She took a deep breath. "Now, tell me the rest of the story. What did Baobh do?"

Tim looked up at her, his brows drawn together, but left the subject and continued relating the story of the women of Bell.

"She was furious, as you can imagine," he resumed. "She said we would all be very sorry for refusing our queen. She said that instead of just having us all killed, she would do something worse, something that would cause even more pain. And then she left."

A golden shaft of sunlight poked its way through a lazy bough and shown down on Tim's vibrant, red hair. Pieces of shiny hair fell in his eyes, and he brushed at them with his free hand. "Then what happened?" Rhiannon gently prodded.

"The women started dying off very quickly. They would get sick for a few days and then the next word we would get is news of their passing over. My older sister was one of the first to pass. She was so beautiful-as lovely as you, milady!" Rhiannon smiled at the boy. "In just a fortnight's time, she was to be wed to the blacksmith's son, Almed. When the poor man heard of my sister's passing over, he went into the hills and killed himself."

Tim and Rhiannon were both quiet for a while. It was an awkward moment of mournful tranquility that Rhiannon silently dedicated to the memory of Tim's sister and her heart broken beau. Rhiannon softly pulled at Tim's arm, and they started walking down the path again.

"All the women of breeding years died within a year. Not only the women, but the adult female sheep died as well. None could reckon what it was that had killed them all until a small boy came to my father and told him he saw the queen throw a tiny purple pouch into the well by the big olive tree. He had been too afraid of the Queen to come forward earlier, but his mother and two older sisters had succumbed to Baobh's curse, and it eventually compelled him to relate what he witnessed.

"Immediately all the men of Bell shoveled in that well and completely buried it. We had to carry water from a half a day's ride away until we finally dug a new well."

"So, no more women died after the well was buried?"

"Just my friend Hun's older sister, but she was already sick. The boy was right about the well-water, but it was already too late. Only a few of the old, wise women were left, and maybe ten and five little girls. Everyone's wives and mothers were dead. Our once sunny pastures are now full of headstones with the names of the famed women of Bell."

"Did any of the little girl's mothers teach them how to create the tapestries?"

"Sure! Little girls were taught from the time they were in the cradle to handle the soft Ppie wool and how to twist and spin it into brilliant, poetic images or an old story of the past." Another silence and then, "But the girls are too frightened to go near the spinning wheels or the looms. They fear it was the tapestries themselves that took away their mothers."

"But it's a tradition the little girls must restore! The men should tell their daughters it was Baobh who killed their mothers and sisters, not the tapestries!"

"I reckon the men just do not care anymore. Everything they had was ripped from their hearts, and they could do naught to stop it."

"Oh, Tim I'm so sorry. When this war is over, will you take me to Bell?"

"I will be happy to, milady!" My father would love to meet you!"

She smiled at Tim and ruffled his bright hair. Tim's face immediately burned red. "Lady Kossi, 'tis not proper to muss the hair of a soldier, especially one who will be a knight someday, or maybe even the Captain of the Guard!"

"Oh, okay. I beg your pardon, Tim. This will have to do then." Rhiannon bent down and planted a quick kiss on Tim's cheek. He blushed even brighter.

Suddenly the cool quiet was broken by a low scream. In the distance, Luna began to growl and snarl. Quickly Tim dropped Rhiannon's arm and unsheathed his sword. Tim jumped in front of Rhiannon and held out his arm, motioning her to stay behind him, sunlight glinted on his blade.

"That's my wolf!" she yelled and sprinted down the tiny path around Tim.

"Milady stop, please!" Tim called, but Rhiannon disappeared behind a stand of pine trees. Tim followed after her as swiftly as possible, but the sword was still too heavy for him to run with very quickly. As Rhiannon reached a small clearing, she could see Luna standing by a small stream. Her hackles stood high, and her tail was bristled to twice its size. She followed Luna's line of vision to the same young cat she had seen earlier. It sat just on the other side of the stream; its wing was bloodied and hanging at an unnatural angle.

"Gods, 'tis a pax!" Tim breathed. The pax's haunting eyes slid over to Tim and Rhiannon, and it let out a loud scream. "Lady Kossi take your wolf and go back to camp. I will rid the earth of this vile creature."

She placed a soft hand on Tim's shoulder. She could see he was trembling, trying to be brave. "It's okay Tim. I know this pax. We met earlier." She hoped the animal would remember her and realize she was not a foe.

"But milady, these animals are killers. I cannot let you near it."

"Tim please, trust me. If the pax starts to show aggression, I'll back away, and I promise I will leave with you."

"But milady, you must not go, they ... they have special powers from the god of the underworld."

"That's superstitious nonsense. That animal will not hurt me." She moved forward, and Tim held out his arm to stop her.

"My father told me all about pax and the powers they have from the God of the Dark World. They are his pets."

"I know it's hard to believe, but on occasion, you'll find your father isn't always right." Rhiannon looked past Tim at the animal. Her brow furrowed in concern.

"I'm sorry Lady Kossi, I cannot let you go to that animal. I have orders from the Captain to keep you safe."

Rhiannon took a deep breath and let it out loudly. Mindful of young Tim's sword and as gently and quickly as possible, Rhiannon darted past the boy. "I'm sorry Tim!" she cried as she moved to the edge of the stream. She folded her trouser legs above her knees and stepped through the stream to the other side. Luna ran to her.

"Luna go!" she admonished. Still, the wolf would not move. "Go, now!" Luna looked up at her in confusion, but slowly retreated to the other side of the stream and stood by Tim who was now just at the stream's pebbly bank.

"Please Lady Kossi, come back you're not safe!"

"I'll be all right," she said as she made her way to the bleeding animal talking to it softly. Her calm murmuring lulled the pax into a relative peacefulness, and it allowed her to approach; its raspy growl died on the pine-scented breeze.

She moved closer and sat beside the injured animal and started to sing, gently stroking its fawn colored head. The pax started to purr, first very quietly, but the rough sound grew louder as the animal relaxed. Rhiannon moved one of her hands to the creature's wing that looked like it had been shot by a hunter's arrow. The right side of its body was covered in dried blood. When Rhiannon tried to pull the wing out to see the extent of damage, the pax yowled in pain. She jumped, but then started stroking the cat's head once more.

"Tim, do you have any Suain-Nimh with you?"

"What do you want with that, it's very poisonous and not for a lady to handle."

She looked over at him and smiled. "You're right," she said sweetly. "That's why *you* have to do it."

Tim's face grew even more concerned. "Do what, milady?"

"I want you to calmly and quietly shoot this animal with a

very small amount of Suain-Nimh so we can take it back to camp and have the surgeon look at it."

"We can't bring a pax into camp!" he stated incredulously. "It's bad luck. The men will … they will…"

"They'll do nothing, or they will have Flath to answer to!" Rhiannon snapped. When Tim did not reply she looked over to him. His eyes were downcast, and his sword tip rested in the dirt. "I'm sorry Tim; I'm just very worried about this animal. It needs to be seen by the surgeon."

"As you wish, milady." Tim fingered around his belt pouch and pulled out a small tube and an even smaller pouch. He pulled out a tiny dart, careful to not touch the tip, which had been laced with the drug. He inserted it into the tip of the tube and instructed Rhiannon to move back. He put his mouth to the tube, and in a blur, the dart was shot into the neck of the cat. It yowled in surprise and jumped to its feet. It looked around nervously and started to walk towards a thicket of trees, wobbling as it went. Rhiannon followed it closely until it fell to the ground.

"I will do no such thing! Do not bring that demon beast into my tent!" the surgeon yelled at Tim a short time later as Rhiannon stood at the flap of the healer's tent. Warily he looked over at Rhiannon. She clenched her fists and stepped up to him. "You will tend to this animal's wounds, or you'll have to answer to the Captain." She stood erect and folded her arms across her chest. "Flath knows I have this cat," she lied. Tim looked over at her but did not say a word.

"Lady Kossi, this is a cursed animal, it will bring much bad luck. We should not even have it in the camp at all."

"I'm fully aware of your superstitions, good surgeon, but this animal needs medical attention immediately." Rhiannon gave the surgeon a stern look. "Milady, if the men find out you have brought a pax into the camp, they will…they will..." He shrugged boney shoulders and looked at her pleadingly.

"The men won't find out if you do your job quickly." Rhiannon looked up to the man and gave him a smile. "I only come to you because I need your services as a surgeon. I don't want to bring you any bad luck or trouble." She knew she could not use the stone without detection—if she could even get it to work again—and did not want to have to try and explain *that* bit of 'magic" to the already skittish soldiers.

The surgeon let out a long sigh. "Please," she finally begged.

"Hurry." He pointed to a small table in the middle of the tent. Tim walked to it quickly and carefully laid the pax down. The surgeon slipped on his large green apron and gathered some tools.

After the surgeon was done cleaning and treating the wound, Tim warily picked the pax up and quietly left the tent. Rhiannon laid a hand on the man's shoulder. "Thank you, good surgeon." She could feel the ripples of surprise run through his awkward body. He quickly moved away from her and busied himself with cleaning his tools. She sighed and followed Tim out of the tent.

While the men were quietly sitting around a small fire, complaining about being left behind when their companions were at war, Rhiannon and Tim snuck the pax into her tent. Rhiannon grabbed two blankets from her cot and laid them out on the floor. Tim gently lowered the drowsy pax onto the blankets. "Milady, Flath will be most disappointed in me for allowing you to bring this pax back to camp," Tim said nervously.

Rhiannon put her hands on his shoulders and smiled at him. "Young Tim, you've proven yourself a good and loyal friend of mine. I will make sure Flath knows how hard you tried to keep me from bringing the pax here." Tim smiled, but said nothing and quietly walked out of her tent.

As the days passed the temperature began to warm. The

nights were still chilly, but the frostiness of a woodland spring night was gone. The songs of birds seemed less clamorous and more at ease. The calls of lonely woodland creatures died on warmer winds and days filled with lustrous sunshine.

The pax recovered its strength quickly, and as the sun melted into spiked treetops, the cat ventured out into the forest once again, always returning to Rhiannon's tent at the birth of dawn. Every night as Rhiannon lay waiting for sleep to come she thought about Flath and whether or not she would see him again. No word had come to inform them of how the battle faired, so tensions were strained as imaginations ran with abandon.

One night, in the gray light of predawn, Flath finally returned, eight days after his departure. Wearily he dismounted, and a man led his horse away. He spoke in hushed tones to a man who had come up to him. Finally, he walked over to Tim, who stood as Flath approached.

Rhiannon had heard him ride in with a few other men and now lay awake wishing to go to him, but refraining out of the uncertainty of her emotions. She heard him walk up to Tim and listened to him speak.

"You did what?" Flath hissed. She did not hear Tim reply but knew they spoke of the pax.

"It was injured, sir. Lady Kossi wanted to make sure it recovered," Tim stammered.

She heard Flath wearily let out a long breath and knew he was no longer angry at the boy. From the shadows of the moon, she saw him remove his gloves and mail shirt and hand them to Tim. His darkened silhouette approached and moved to her side. She sat up, and he sat beside her. The moon cast long shadows across his face so that she could not see him plainly. "I didn't know if you would come back," she said softly.

"Neither did I, Greannmhor." He brushed away a raven lock of hair from her face. "You were concerned for me?" he asked playfully.

"Yes," she whispered.

He said nothing but sighed in the darkness. Softly Flath ran his fingers over Rhiannon's cheek and down to the point of her chin. "Tomorrow we must travel to Perth, sleep for now." He kissed her solidly on her lips then he left the tent.

CHAPTER ELEVEN

"A society's Prophecy Keepers are one of its most important assets.
They are the lay historians-the people's historians. Often it is they
who hold the real truth of the matter-a "truth" that either gets
much distorted in the ballads of the minstrels or buried under
centuries of callous fact as it sits in dusty, unread tomes.
In past times the Prophecy Keepers have been regarded with
suspicion and even outright hostility. In the Dark Years of
mankind's Middle History, many Prophecy Keepers were beaten
and burned, and even educated historians were sometimes dealt
with harshly. No one knows what first ignited the Culling, but it
has been said that if the Prophecy Keepers had been men their
plight would have been different."
-Middle History: Prophecy Keepers; Thomas Thunn

Sparkling like tiny gems in drops of dew, sunshine poked
through stubborn tree boughs and threw splotches of white
light on the shadowed ground. The pax had returned hours
before and was sleeping on top of a pile of blankets in Rhiannon's tent. "Remember Tim, do not let anyone know she's
in there."

"I should be going with you and the Captain instead of waiting here like a child," Tim complained.

"You are not a child, but a fighter for the rebellion," Flath said as he walked up. "You must keep this camp." Dejected, Tim looked down at his boots. "You will be in charge while I am away."

Tim quickly looked back up and smiled. "Will I?"

"Aye, Tim. You must watch over the cook and surgeon and the men that I am leaving behind." He leaned in close to Tim. "And that blasted little beast Lady Kossi insisted on bringing into camp."

Tim's smile widened. "Thank you, Captain. I will not disappoint you."

"I know you will not, Tim, that's why I have chosen you to be in charge while I am away."

"Are you ready man?" Teo called out from the back of his horse. Jon and Bleen were also mounted waiting to be on their way.

"We will catch up, go on!" Flath called out and waved them on. He bent down and pulled a large knife from his bootleg and handed it to Rhiannon. "You might need to protect yourself while on this journey, Greannmhor."

She eyed the knife with suspicion and looked back up at him. "Where did you say we're going?"

"Perth. It is a fishing village on the coast about a week's ride southeast from here."

"Are you expecting trouble?" she said as she slid the bone-handled knife into her riding boot.

"I am not sure; however, many things can come to pass in a week."

By nightfall, they had completely left the Elk Mountains and its surrounding forest and camped in a sloping area that would lead them into the valley below. The night sky opened up so wide and black it seemed you could touch the stars, moon, space, and even time. Bright stars sputtered and flickered against a backdrop so huge its ending could never be found. The incandescent orb of a full moon rose silently, illuminating the valley below.

Rhiannon could see each hollow on the moon's somber face. It was as if giant raindrops had fallen to the moon and left dimples across its powdery expanse. Dark, geometric shapes fell across the moon's face tricking the eye into seeing what was not there.

The travelers moved on in the soft light of dawn. They descended into a green grassy valley with gentle hills and shady trees spread unevenly across the land. White Oak Valley was a long, wide valley that began south of Perth at the lapping tongue of the sea and swept north, past Sona Tuath all the way to Alba Forest. Its soil was black with organic life and was fed from hundreds of streams and rivers that originated from Faerie Lake, up high in the Elk Mountains, and Fellk Lake, nestled in the Chyro Hills situated in the middle of the valley. They rode southeast across the valley, making their own path as they went along.

Finally, at the end of a week, as a sleepy orange sun fell into the horizon splashing the world with pinks and reds, they pushed their way across East Beaver River and camped in the shadow of Chyro Hills.

With the moon lighting her way, Rhiannon moved down to the banks of the river. She melted behind a rock for privacy and slipped off her clothes. The water was like ice, and her teeth chattered to the sound of rushing water. She washed with a dwindling bar of course soap, then walked out of the river, slipping on small smooth stones then quickly dried off. Luna came up from behind her, sniffed around and not finding anything interesting trotted off into the darkness. Rhiannon pulled on a clean shirt that she had gotten from Flath and a pair of trousers Tim had given her before she left.

She went back to the mouth of the river and began cleaning the dusty clothes she had worn for the past two days. She heard him coming up behind her, and he sat down beside her in the sand. "Did you enjoy your bath?" he asked.

"No. It was freezing, and this bar of soap is so rough it scrubs my skin off!" He laughed and looked up at the night sky. The moon was so bright it lit up the hills and rocks and trees. Only the deep ravines which slashed into the hills remained in the shadows.

When she was done with her washing, she laid her newly cleaned clothes on a large boulder hoping they would still be there in the morning. She sat down next to Flath and dug her wet feet into the coarse river sand. She looked up at him but did not speak. His face looked sharp in the gray shadows of the moon. His hair was pulled back, and his gold earring gleamed in the light. He unlaced the leather bracers he wore on his forearms, rolled up onto his knees and dipped his wide hands into the hurried river. He splashed the water on his face and shook his head like a dog would, sending icy drips of water disappearing into the darkness. When he was done, he sat back down and wiped the water from his stubbled chin.

Finally, he looked over to her. "Rhiannon, I need you to be completely truthful with me." He brushed back a wet piece of hair that had come loose from its binding at the back of his neck. "Tomorrow we will reach Perth, and we will be visiting Teo's mother. As I have told you before, she is a Prophecy Keeper. She knows much of the old way and can read things about people that are hidden or long forgotten. If the claim Hepin made regarding a prophecy involving you and the queen was truthful Maggie will know. I do not want to be taken by surprise." His eyes were hidden in shadows, but she could feel his gaze. "I need you be honest about who you are. If what you have told me is the truth, then I owe you a sincere apology. However, if there is something you have kept hidden from me, I ask you to tell me now."

She stayed silent balling sand up in her hands and then letting it slide through her fingers. Her mind drifted to her birthmark and the stone that she remembered her mother giving her when she was a child. She closed her eyes, and the vision of her mother's lifeless body lying in cooling blood washed over her. Her eyes opened, and her lips moved, but she could not say what was in her heart-she could not tell him the truth.

The next morning Rhiannon sat on Zellan's back and looked down at the busy city from a hilltop. Perth was a fairly large seaport village. Teo, Jon, and Bleen had already started down the wide dirt path that led into town. "C'mon boys me family awaits!" Teo yelled as he kneed his horse on faster.

"Teo's wife Shawna and their four children live here as well," Flath explained, and Rhiannon nodded her head not really listening. "He has not seen them in months." He looked over at Rhiannon. "He has given up much to fight for the cause."

"As you have, I'm sure," Rhiannon said, brushing the hair from her eyes. He just smiled hollowly.

The ocean breeze was cool and salty and heavy with the smell of fish. The deep red waters of the Carnaid Sea lapped at the edge of a giant pier where several ships were docked. The violent crimson waves crashed onto a sandy beach covered with fisherman's nets that were drying in the sun. Seabirds called out to one another as they tried their best to steal from the fishermen's nets as the nets were hauled up onto small boats far from the shore.

Flath and Rhiannon left the hills and followed the road to

town. Excited though she was with a plethora of new aromas, Luna stayed a few paces ahead of them her nose hovering the ground. The laughter of children and braying of donkeys floated on the air. Chicken, geese, goats, sheep, and dogs all walked along the wide cobblestone streets. Zellan neighed and was answered immediately by two donkeys that looked at him amorously as he passed.

They turned off the main road and followed a sandy path towards Teo's mother's home. She lived in a pleasant cottage situated on a bluff overlooking the sea.

A fat black and white cat was lazily sprawled out across the cold stone pathway that led to the front door. Her tail jumped and curled every so often snaking out a slow, methodical rhythm. Bright red flowers growing out of white sand danced in the ocean breeze. A fat mother hen followed by a handful of fluffy yellow chicks appeared from a tuft of wavering sea oat grass. They carelessly pecked at the ground, then walked a few steps and pecked some more until they were out of sight.

After a short while, Teo emerged from the cottage, said a few words to Flath in a language Rhiannon learned was called Ska, then quickly rode off to see his family. Jon and Bleen left to secure rooms at one of the inns that were spread across the coastal village.

"Flath, me boy, come here and give me a hug!" called a short, round woman that stood in the doorway. Brassy red-orange hair was tightly pulled back in a sunset-colored bun. Her apron was stained with flour and other baking supplies, and the smell of bread followed her out of a quaint, wooden door. Fat under her chin and plump jowls shook as she talked.

Flath slid from his horse and tied the reins to a hitching post, and Rhiannon did the same. Flath quickly went over to the woman and wrapped her in his thick arms.

"Maggie, I've missed you," Flath said to the short woman.

"I've missed ya too, lad! Have ya been good ta me Teo?" She rolled up on her toes and delicately placed a kiss on Flath's cheek.

"Ha! I have gotten him out of more tavern brawls and paid for more of his gambling debts than I would like to admit. Maybe Shawna can knock some sense into her husband this time."

"Let's hope so," the woman said as a giant curving smile spread across her rosy colored face. She turned to Rhiannon and took the younger woman's hand. "So this is the lassie Teo told me about?"

"Aye, this is Lady Rhiannon Kossi."

"A Lady! Weel, I've never entertained royalty before, you'll have ta e'cuse me manners, lass." The woman quickly did an awkward curtsy.

Rhiannon shot Flath an evil look. "Ma'am, I'm not a lady…"

"Ha, that is the first truthful thing you have said all day!" Flath said, snickering.

Rhiannon scowled at him and looked back at Maggie. "I'm not royalty," she said flatly, wanting to conclude their visit as soon as possible.

"I think what Lady Kossi is trying to say is, she does not know who she is. That is why we need your help, Maggie."

Maggie smiled at Rhiannon warmly and opened her door wide. "Weel, come in, then." Luna calmly started in the door, and Maggie jumped. "Is that yer beastie, malady?"

"Yes, ma'am," Rhiannon replied nervously.

"Ye travel with a wolf?"

"Well, she's actually more like a dog. I've had her since she was a pup." Rhiannon patted Luna's giant head in a convincing way and smiled at the woman apologetically.

After a moment, she finally said, "Very weel then, come inside." She stepped aside and motioned for them to enter.

The cottage was warm and bright. Sunshine bathed a wooden floor covered with several woven rugs. A few plants grew in containers here and there, and light-colored wood furniture filled the room. Two bright tapestries hung on her walls, one picturing the ocean and surrounding rolling hills, the other was decorated with intricately knotted streams of color and rune symbols surrounding a tree. Her thoughts went to Tim, and she hoped he was safe with the pax.

"Come an' sit down, lassie." The woman motioned and pointed to a pillow-covered chair. "Me name is Maggie, since the big buffoon didn't bother ta introduce us proper-like." She pointed a stubby thumb at Flath and smirked at him. Rhiannon smiled and nodded as she sat down in one of the chairs ringing a large round dining table. "I'll be right back wi somethin' ta wet yer whistle," Maggie said, as she parted a curtain of brightly colored glass beads and tiny shells that swayed and clinked together as she swished passed them and disappeared into the kitchen.

"Are you nervous?" Flath asked.

"No, I'm not, and I think you're wasting your time," she replied, unconcerned, belying the quaking fear that was growing deep inside.

"Maggie Jass is one of only a very few women left who are Prophecy Keepers." Rhiannon stayed silent but kept his hardened gaze. She could see that he plainly did not believe that she had told him everything she knew. Finally, she looked away, afraid he could read her thoughts through her dark eyes.

Maggie entered the room again, carrying a tightly woven tray painstakingly constructed with wisps of oat grass. She handed them all delicate porcelain teacups with tiny painted flowers and tendrils of transparent steam rising from gold painted rims. Rhiannon readily took her cup and warmed her cold, sore hands. Flath awkwardly grabbed the cup, clearly too tiny for his large hands.

Under the intense stare of the woman, Rhiannon shifted in her chair nervously. Maggie's brow knotted as she narrowed her gaze into Rhiannon's black eyes. Rhiannon wanted to look away, but could not.

Finally, the woman spoke in low tones. "Teo tells me ye are from the Tree of Jur, and someone has spoken of a prophecy that concerns Queen Baobh, is this right?"

"Yes," Rhiannon said quietly, suddenly afraid of the woman.

Maggie took a long sip, inhaling the aroma and lazily closed her eyes. "I see a lot of confusion and fear in yer eyes, Rhiannon," she finally said after swallowing her tea. "Ye are afraid of what ye already know." Maggie nodded and set the cup down onto the table and studied her again. "I also see a bright light in yer deep eyes. A light I have not seen in many a year. You've the protection of a goddess, Rhiannon Kossi, and since ye are clearly an Archigos I'm bet'n 'tis the Goddess Verna who's blessed ye," she pronounced somberly.

After a while, Rhiannon found her voice, though it was shaky and uncertain. "You're ruled by superstitions that I don't believe in. I'm not who you say…" Her voice trailed off, dying on the salty breeze and the sound of relentless waves pounding a solid shoreline.

"Ye have the mark, don't ye lass?" the woman cautiously prodded.

She began to tremble and looked quickly to Flath. She knew that he had already guessed. Finally, she turned back to Maggie, suddenly angry. "I don't know what you're talking about, old woman!" she snapped.

"The mark is clear ta yer heart, ye can't hide it forever, love."

In a whoosh of determined movement, Flath took hold of her shirt and ripped it open sending wooden buttons bouncing noisily on the floor then rolling under furniture or resting on sleeping rugs. Rhiannon gasped and jumped up from her chair as her cup fell to the floor and shattered into tiny shards at her feet. He rose from his chair also, and she could see he looked upon the red diamond burned into her chest from birth. "You *are* the Empress," he breathed.

"Listen carefully to your prophecy, Empress Kossi. 'Tis one I was taught many years ago by me old ma before the queen had her killed. 'Tis because of this prophecy that most of the Prophecy Keepers are dead and gone now." Rhiannon's eyes slid over to the old woman's face, dark with sorrow and emotion. She took a deep breath and closed her eyes as if reading from an unseen scroll.

Very quietly she started to speak. "'Fresh from the womb, she will be torn away," she recited, careful to enunciate the words as they were scribed so many years before. "An heir will be found among people foreign and unblessed, not knowing the ways of the ancients. The blood of two nations will burn within her-divided and separate-though she will unite them. She alone will have the power to strike down the child of the earth who has forsaken her position and swims in the blood of innocent ones. This little one will be a leader of many, richly blessed by the Warrior Goddess. With a mighty hand and a pure heart, she will send the Dark One's soul to its death. Betrayed by her own children-one light-one dark-they will rejoice upon her death!'" Maggie swallowed a dry breath. "'Tis yer future that I speak, Empress Kossi,"

"No! This can't be possible!" Rhiannon yelled as tears streamed down her face.

CHAPTER TWELVE

*"A woman's intuition should always be followed, for her body is of
the earth, her blood of the cool oceans and her spirit of the wild
moon. Her logic and instinct are undeniable, and to her
premonitions, attention should always be given."*
-Code of the Feminine; author unknown

A cool, salty breeze set lace curtains fluttering like the skirt
of a dancing girl. The wind was bitter, as was everything
around Rhiannon. Paint curled and lifted on the windowsill
painted as white as the stretch of crushed seashell beach. The
wind blew west off the vast Carnaid Sea. Rhiannon searched
its breadth watching great ships appear on the horizon
carried along on an ever-present wind.

The pounding of the waves sung a sweet melodic cadence
to Rhiannon. It sang of things she could never have expected.
It sang of her mother, Sernia and her father, Peter. It sang of
bedtime fairy tales long thought to be only fiction, but now
were as real to Rhiannon as the headache that squeezed her
mind like wrung out laundry.

Jon and Bleen had found them rooms at the Rusty Mug

Inn. Luna was not allowed to stay, so she was banished to the stables with Zellan and the rest of the horses. Flath had left for his own room immediately after depositing Rhiannon in hers and posted a man at her door making sure she did not try and leave. He had not said one word to her after they left Maggie's cottage. It pained and frustrated her to think she was once again a bargaining chip to use as he pleased.

He turned icy and distant when he saw the diamond birthmark over her heart. He was once again the towering, stolid figure she had first met in that tent so many weeks ago.

She renewed her vow to escape and find her way to Sona Tuath and her father who was the key to answering her questions. She had to find out the truth now. She had to peer into the secrets of her origin no matter what the cost.

Soon evening turned to night as the brume crept from the watery blackness to swallow the village. Lanterns swayed from posts on either side of the streets, offering unsteady light. The small bay and the ocean beyond were nothing but an oily blackness. Were it not for the salty wind and constant roar of foamy waves; no one would even know the sea loomed so closely. It was as if the world had stopped just past the frail lantern lights.

Rhiannon stood, stretching stiff muscles that had been idle for too long. She opened the window further and peered out into the darkness. It was late, and people were safely tucked into their warm beds. She looked down, trying to judge how far of a fall she would have to make if she crawled out of the window and dropped to the ground below.

Looking around the outside of the window, she discovered an eave for the window right below hers. Carefully Rhiannon eased herself out of the window and hung from the sill trying to feel the roof of the eave with the toe of her boot. As hard as she tried, she could not reach the eave, so she looked down to see how far she was from the ledge. She was only a few feet, so she let go and landed with a thud. Immediately she crouched in the shadows and held her breath to see if anyone had heard.

No one moved, and the only sounds were from the sea calling her to freedom. Rhiannon slid off the eave and onto the soft dirt. The misty fog left her moist as she strained to see. She kept to the shadows of the building making her way to the stables.

As she reached the stables Luna came out to greet her, her lolling tongue and wagging tail was a welcome sight, easing her loneliness. She slipped into the stables and found her way to Zellan trying to decide what she should do next. She knew if she followed the coast north it would take her to Sona Tuath, but what would she do once she got there? It seemed hopeless.

"How long are you going to run from the truth, Rhiannon?" A deep voice asked from the shadows.

Rhiannon jumped and caught her breath. She spun around and peered into the darkness. She could not see his face in the dark, but knew his voice and saw the glint of his earring caught in the wavering glow of a lamp. "What are you doing here?" she asked enraged.

He laughed a deep humorless sound. "Empress Kossi, you were not thinking of running away from me again, were you?"

Rhiannon spun and dashed out the door, the cobblestones under her feet were slick with dew as she darted into the complete darkness towards the beach. A cold wind peppered her face, leaving a salty fish taste in her mouth. Wind whipped her hair into her eyes as she ran on. Her muscles burned as she trudged through the sand, her legs were heavy with exhaustion. She became lost in the thunder of violent waves and throb of her own heart. The chilly, salty air coated her face and turned it to ice as the dim light of Perth disappeared altogether, leaving her running into an abyss. She could not hear or sense his presences behind her, and she hoped she had somehow lost him in the night.

Suddenly a hand of steel reached out from the darkness and clamped onto her arm in an unbreakable hold. She was pulled from her feet and promptly fell to the sand. "Let me go!" she screamed, kicking her legs and flailing her arms. He took hold of both her arms, pinning her beneath him. "Let me go, Flath!" She continued to scream and squirm until she was too tired to move, and then she lay there catching her breath. "Flath, why don't you just let me go?" she cried.

"I cannot," he replied.

"Why not? Why can't you just let me be?"

"You are so hardheaded! Can you not see that you are a part of something much bigger than yourself?"

"I'm a part of nothing. That old woman is crazy; she doesn't know what she's talking about!" She tried to push him off, but he would not budge. "Damn you! Let go of me!" Rhiannon could feel the tears threatening to spill from her eyes.

"What shall it take to make you believe? After Baobh has murdered you and your father, will you believe then?" Flath angrily asked her. Tears started running down Rhiannon's cheeks spilling into the thirsty sand. Finally, he sat up, and he took her into his arms. She began to tremble and sob. "You have much to experience-some of which will be pleasant-however, most will not. You have a responsibility that you cannot abnegate. Do not fear, Greannmhor. Your people will guide you down the paths you must take."

"I don't want to go to my people," she said weakly.

"You must, Rhiannon."

"Why? Why can't I stay with you?" she pleaded. Flath did not answer for a long time as though he too pondered the possibility. He sighed deeply and looked up to the stars penetrating the mist, winking in the black sky.

"You must go to your people," he finally said, burying his face in her soft hair. "You are a part of the prophecy that will bring an end to Baobh. I cannot train you in the ways of the Archigos. They must be the ones to train you as an empress."

"I'm not an empress, Flath. There's been some horrible mistake. "

Gently he lifted her face up to meet his. "Oh Rhiannon, my sweet Greannmhor. How hard it will be for me to give you up," he whispered

He gently cradled her in his arms, rocking back and forth as if she were an infant. Finally, he started to sing, softly at first, but then with more certainty. She did not know the words, but the slow melody relaxed her, and she felt safe as if nothing else in the world mattered at that moment. The song he sang was long and melancholy, and when it finished, she felt suddenly exposed to the world again, bereft of the comfort of his deep, smooth voice. She held on to the echo of his song in her head.

* * *

The journey back to camp was long and arduous. Not so much because of the terrain, but because a burgeoning realization of what must come. The mood was made even bleaker by gathering storm clouds and the relentless rain that followed. It soaked clothes, chilled the skin, and set teeth to chatter. It continued to rain as they traveled through the Elk Mountains causing leaves to trickle and bark to turn black. Animals hid in dens and birds did not sing. The only sound was the rhythmic beat of horse hooves and cold rain.

A week from their departure from Perth the weary travelers gratefully reached the camp, and Tim's beaming face was as bright as the reborn sun peeking through damp tree boughs. Rhiannon gave him a big hug and asked how the pax was fairing. "The beast is well, Lady Kossi," he said, and he winked. Rhiannon looked to Flath as he slowly led his horse away, his head down searching the drying earth.

As Rhiannon lay on her cot that night, she thought of her mother Sernia Kossi, a mother she had only in memories. A mother she had been forced to grow up without. It was ludicrous to think that she had been a powerful empress of a mighty race of warriors. And that now she was expected to take her place. "This can't be happening!" she whispered into the cold night.

She knew it was just a matter of time before Flath would take her to the Archigos. It frightened her that he was planning on just leaving her with people she did not know. From what she had heard of the Archigos, they were an arrogant, proud race of powerful, bloodthirsty warriors. Would they even accept her? If not, would they kill her for trying to impersonate an empress? And if they did accept her, the only life she had known would be gone like a wisp of smoke caught on a turbulent wind. She closed her eyes and eventually fell asleep.

The next afternoon Rhiannon sat at the edge of a stream and watched the clear water rush by as if it were late for an appointment. The pax lay beside her in a shaft of warm sunshine; its purr lost on a pine-scented forest breeze. She sorrowfully wondered if she would ever see her father again and left a question in her mind whether or not he was even from the world she had grown up in and if not, where had he come from? She got none of his fine, pale features, in fact, she looked nothing like her father, Peter. Suddenly she wondered if he was even her father at all.

Deep in thought, she did not notice Flath walking through the trees until he sat beside her. Neither spoke for a while, just listened to the water and the birds singing and the harshness of the pax's purr. "A messenger has arrived," he said softly, almost afraid to break the sounds of the forest. "I must leave at once. The Beaynidan Army has marched within a mile of my men." She did not speak but looked to the trees for answers.

"When will you take me to the Archigos?" she asked in a hard tone.

"I have not decided as of yet."

"Then you've made up your mind to take me?"

"I have no choice, Greannmhor. You must return to the Archigos to fulfill the prophecy."

She finally looked up at him. "Then what do you fight for if I'm the only one that can bring an end to Baobh?"

"I have pondered over the futility of the war we now fight since I first heard that prophecy. But it is like a great movement of much earth rumbling down the side of a steep mountain slope. Once it has started to tumble down the mountain, it cannot be stopped until it has reached the bottom." He took her hand into his. "We have fought this war for over a year and cannot stop the avalanche that we have begun. My hope is that we can distract, and hopefully whittle down their numbers until you are ready to finally put an end to this madness." She said nothing but looked into his mismatched eyes. The snake that hung from his ear winked in the breeze and sunlight. He softly kissed the palm of her hand. "I will see you when I can, Lady Kossi." He stood up and walked back into the trees.

CHAPTER THIRTEEN

"Men fight wars because they cannot, or more truthfully, will not find a way to avoid a bloody fight. As the more aggressive of sexes, men will rather run to a battle than from one."
-Code of the Feminine; author unknown

The sky was barely growing lighter as night gave way to dawn. A faint whitish yellow color crept over the horizon as Flath rode down into the fringes of White Oak Valley and into the large war camp. The mist that had clung to him like slick, cold skin started dissipating as the light burned it away.

"Flath, it is good to see you, man," a friendly voice called to him as he rode into camp and dismounted, stretching stiff muscles.

"I wish I could say it is good to be back, Adam." He smirked and clapped the older man on the back. "I hope we can push them even further back to Sona Tuath."

"How was your trip to Perth?"

"It went well, and I saw none of Beaynid's army. They must have still been recuperating from the losses they suffered." He smiled.

"Too bad we did not send more of them to their grave!" Adam proclaimed and thrust his arm into the air eliciting a few cheers from nearby men. Like most of the men of the rebellion, Adam had been inexperienced in any kind of warfare when he joined Flath and Teo in organizing a rebellion against Baobh a year before. Now he was a commander of a small regiment of archers.

The two men entered a large tent at the edge of camp. Teo, who rode straight to camp from Perth, was sitting in front of a huge map laying open on a table lit with four lamps to supplement the diffused sunlight.

"Do you have a count of our dead?" Flath asked Adam.

"We lost one hundred and sixty-two men," Adam said and shook his head.

"And how many did they lose?"

"We gathered up four hundred and eighty-eight bodies belonging to their army."

Flath leaned over the map and studied it for a while. "A heavy loss for them."

"Aye, 'tis why we are sup'rised they are ready'n fer battle so soon," Teo said looking up from the map. "There's been rumor of Yellow Island join'n Sona Tuath to fight against us," he said seriously.

"I have also heard the talk in Perth, and I think 'tis true." Flath ran his fingers over the spot on the map that showed Yellow Island. "They have always been an ally to Beaynid. We cannot discount them merely because a Basilias does not hold the throne any longer. Maggie said she saw a Beaynidan warship leave a month past. I think Baobh has finally asked King Umar for his help."

A scuffle outside the tent made the men look up as two soldiers came in pushing a young man in front of them who crumpled at their feet. His light blonde hair shone in the lamplight as he defiantly jumped to his feet. "Some of the men were out hunting, and they found this little toad hiding in the bushes," one of the soldiers said, pointing to the young man.

Flath slowly walked around the younger man quietly assessing him. The young man did not say a word but followed Flath with eyes that burned with bold defiance.

"You are Seun, are you from Sona Tuath then?" Flath asked, still circling the young man. The younger man said nothing. "Do you know there is a war going on, and it is not safe to be hiding in the bushes, boy?"

"I am not a boy!" he snapped.

"So, you can talk." Flath stopped and faced the young man. "What were you doing in the bushes?"

"I came to fight for the rebellion," he said, proudly puffing out his chest like a bullfrog. "I am looking for the man they call Flath, the leader of the fight for Beaynid's freedom!" Teo leaned back in his chair and snickered.

"Well, you have found him." The boy looked closer, carefully scrutinizing the tall, broad man that stood before him. "Not what you were expecting?" Flath arched a brow and could not hide a lopsided smile.

The boy stood up tall and proudly faced the leader of the rebel army. "Not as impressive as what I envisioned, but I suppose you will do." Flath's eyes widened, and his smile broadened. Teo and Adam found the statement quite amusing and laughed loudly.

"Now tell me who you are."

"I am Ian, and I am here to fight for you, Captain."

"If you were here to fight for me why did my men find you hiding in the bushes?"

"I … I was not hiding." The young man looked down at his muddy boots. "I was afraid they would mistake me for one of the queen's men and kill me on sight." Flath looked up at the soldiers standing behind Ian, and they both shrugged.

"Because I am from Sona Tuath," he said softly. "But I want to fight for the rebellion!" he stated, much louder.

"How old are you, Ian?" Flath asked the boy, who had clearly left childhood and now stood on the edge of manhood.

"I am ten and seven, sir."

"Do your parents know you are here?" The boy was silent. "Answer me! Do your parents know you are here?"

"I have no father. My mother is a whore in Nabb who I have not seen in several years." Ian looked up into Flath's mismatched eyes. The younger man's face was awash in humiliation and pain.

Flath was shocked but masked his expression as a cord of understanding struck Flath deep within him. He wanted to trust the young man, yet he had an uneasy feeling about him. At four -thousand men, outnumbered by nearly two to one by the Beaynidan Army, Flath was in no position to refuse men who wished to fight for the rebellion.

He took a deep breath and ran his hand through his hair. "Take him to Jon and Bleen and tell them I wish this man to be trained in warfare." A look of relieved caution flashed through Ian's ice blue eyes then he thanked Flath and left with the two soldiers.

Flath looked over to Teo and Adam. "What do you think of young Ian?"

"I don't ken," Teo said, shrugging, his red hair looking bronze in the lamplight.

"Could be a spy, though I highly doubt it," Adam said.

"Nay, not a spy, but I am hav'n a wary feel'n about ta lad."

"As do I. Let us keep an eye on him," Flath said.

The hot June day began to fade as the coolness of night crept over the valley. Three days of fighting had pushed the Beaynidan Army further east towards Sona Tuath, however not by much. The rebellion army had an advantage over the paid company soldiers whose only concern was staying alive long enough to collect their pay. The rebels were fighting for their sweet freedom. Freedom from stifling oppression that had progressively gripped all of Beaynid during Baobh's twenty-four- year reign.

The bodies of dead Beaynidan soldiers burned in a great fire, sending harsh arms of white hot flames reaching up into the darkening night. It was a psychological ploy that struck repulsion and fear into the hearts of the other army. The smell of sizzling flesh blew northeast away from the rebellion army, working in their favor. The heavy stench added to the vision of their fallen men being consumed in pillars of mocking flame and was devastating to the living. The battlefield looked black now in the graying light of the receding sun. Soldiers of both camps slipped and faltered in the blood of slain friends and foes alike as it soaked into the trampled earth. The stench of congealing blood filled the air, turning the stomach to bile.

Flath looked towards the surgeon's tents knowing they were full with men dead or dying. Though greatly outnumbered, the other army's body count was much higher than the rebels. However, they too suffered a loss of many men. Flath felt that one man's spent life was too much. The past year had taken a toll on so many; rebels as well as Seun soldiers.

Just before he reached the warmth of his tent, Teo stepped out of the darkness. "The scouts have returned," he said solemnly.

"What is the word?"

There was a pause, then: "'Tis Yellow Island's army; they've massed tagether on both our north and south sides."

Flath scrubbed his hand through blood-spattered hair and looked out into the dark trees. "How many?"

"Mayhap twenty thousand men in each camp," Teo answered darkly.

"How far?"

"Two days," he speculated. Flath blew out a desperate sigh. He turned his face skyward and searched the stars for an answer to his predicament, but they stayed silent, the great moon herself said nothing.

"We cannot stand against so many," Flath breathed. Teo nodded but did not offer anything further. "Do we retreat and hide amongst the forest, or do we stand and fight, knowing we are doomed?" Flath shifted his weight, the gravel under his boots crushing into a dry earth. "There will be so many that will not return to their families..." his tired voice trailed off on a cool breeze.

"'Tis war, lad. There will always be death."

"Will it ever end? Will Baobh ever be stopped?"

"Aye, she'll be stopped, don't worry 'bout that."

The next morning Flath stood high on a rocky bluff that looked out over the distant valley as it stretched out of his view. Beaynid's army had disappeared during the night, probably meeting up with Yellow Island's forces.

He looked back towards his men. They would follow their leader into a doomed battle. They were an army of nearly eight -thousand men ready to fight to the death if need be-an army of men who were led by nothing more than a gypsy. He sighed and swallowed a dry lump in his throat that turned to bile in his stomach.

Should they stay and fight a battle they could not win, or should they flee while there was still time? Indecision and anxiety lay hold of him. He had been eaten whole by doubt that now lay rotting in his belly.

If he had been older, more experienced, he was sure he would have had the answer. Perhaps it was the gypsy's blood that ran through his veins like a poison that rendered him moribund. The day was turning hot as the sun sleepily crept higher in the azure sky. Flath turned back around and faced east, straining to see anything moving on the grassy horizon, but all remained lost to his view.

"It seems we have scared them away." A voice behind Flath tore him from his morbid thoughts and made him jump. He spun around quickly to see Ian standing before him.

"You should not sneak up behind people like that." Flath scolded the younger man.

"I did not sneak; you just did not hear me," he protested. "So where is everyone?" he asked, changing the subject.

"Regrouping with Yellow Island's army," Flath said smoothly.

"Yellow Island?" Ian asked, his bright blue eyes widening. "I've heard they have an army that no man can number!"

"Not quite that big, but almost," Flath said, then once again turned to watch the horizon. Ian came to stand next to Flath. "I see they gave you your own sword." Flath eyed the dull handle of a purely utilitarian weapon lacking in any design, so different from the glistening panther head hilt of his own sword.

"Yes, and Bleen said he would let me fight when next we meet the enemy," Ian proclaimed.

"Why are you so anxious to fight when it could be your last day alive?"

The young man looked up at Flath. "I am a man, and I know what is right and wrong. I know that Queen Baobh is wrong." Emotions were building in his voice.

Flath did not know why he got such an uneasy feeling about the young man. He certainly seemed loyal to the rebellion. But he just could not shake his apprehension towards him. "You say you have no father?" Flath probed.

"No, I do not." He looked away quickly. "Or rather, I do

not know who he could be. When your mother is a whore, your father could be anyone." Ian shot Flath a look under hooded eyes, then turned and walked away.

"We might need ta think of another plan," Teo finally offered. "We are quite outnumbered," he offered, later that day.

"I cannot shake the feeling we are sitting here just waiting to be ambushed," Adam said from a chair in the corner of the tent.

"I agree," Teo offered. "I feel too exposed here."

"Maybe we should move to a more concealed location," Adam said.

Flath looked over at the tall, thin man sitting in the corner. His shoulder length brown hair was tied in a queue at the nape of his neck. He was in his early forties, a sheep raiser by trade, as were most of the men from Bell. He was also an expert tracker. It seemed the famed sheep of Bell often wandered into the surrounding wilderness. Adam was a good man who Flath trusted implicitly.

"We shall move west, back into the cover of the forest. We will have the advantage of higher ground and more knowledge of the land. Tell the men to move as quickly as possible." Adam got up, nodded, and quickly left the tent.

"I feel as though someth'n terrible is 'bout ta happen, laddie. We must be careful," Teo said after Adam left, his face dark with concern.

"Maybe there is more of your mother in you than you would like to admit, my friend."

"I've had a bad feel'n all day." Teo pulled at his bright red beard.

Flath eyed his friend warily. "We will move back into the forest where open battle will be impossible. We will set traps with deep ditches and have Adam hide his archers in the trees, and whatever else we can think of. There has to be a way to win this fight, or the rebellion will fail."

Two hours later the men were moving west, up into the cover of the Elk Mountains. Lightning cut through an angry sky and a sticky, wet early summer rain drizzled down upon them making for a miserable trek through mud and unlevel ground.

The terrain grew steeper, and brush became too thick to ride, so those with horses dismounted and lead the nervous beasts higher up the mountain, as they melted into the forest. Flath had sent four scouts ahead of them to look for signs that one of the armies had cut off their escape. He had yet to hear back from them and hoped their silence meant a clear path.

Flath and a few men had gone ahead of the rest hoping to find an appropriate spot to take a stand. Walking beside Teo, Flath was lost deep in thought as they led the horses down a small deer path that cut up a relatively level rise. Jon, Bleen, and Ian followed silently along while five more young men trudged behind pulling their stubborn horses along. Adam was a little farther behind, not too far from his lithe archers as they crept through the shadows.

A hard rain began pouring down, and an unusually cold wind started to howl through the trees. Teo anxiously looked around searching for any sign of an ambush. "The wind warns us of somthin, lad. We must take care if we go further," Teo warned.

Flath stopped and looked around. "'Tis not a good spot to stop, my friend. We must find a more appropriate area to make a stand." Flath wiped the cold rain from his eyes and continued towards a small, flat clearing.

Just as they reached the muddied clearing, Adam ran up beside Flath. "I have found tracks of many men. I think we are heading for a trap, man." Flath's horse nervously sidestepped and pawed at the ground. Teo looked behind them forebodingly searching the wet trees. If there were archers in the trees or soldiers creeping through the brush, they could not be differentiated from the dark colors of the wood.

Suddenly a crowd of men emerged from the bushes and trees, completely surrounding them. Dull brown cloaks where thrown to the ground, revealing the bright yellow and blue tunics of the Sona Tuathan Royal Guard. It was then Flath saw the dead bodies of the four scouts. The Royal Guard rushed them as Flath, and his men pulled swords from sheaths, and metal began to clash. Forgotten horses ran for the safety of the trees.

As soon as Flath lifted his sword two men were immediately upon him. Hastily, Flath swung through the air cutting one man down and severing the arm of the other. As he turned around three more men slashed at him with blades gleaming red with blood. Three of the men he had brought with him lay on the ground in a macabre stare into the gray sky.

Flath quickly went to Teo as sharp swords overtook the stout man. Teo swung around and quickly dispatched one of the men while Flath deflected a blow then cut through a charging soldier. As they hacked their way through men who were nothing more than yellow and blue blurs in a gray forest, they moved to Jon's side cutting down all who approached.

Anxiously Flath looked around for Ian but did not see him. The rain softened to small whispers as they fell to the wet ground. Blood mixed with mud and men faltered as swords clashed.

Flath's sword was slippery in his hand, and his fingers were numb, but his grip remained tight. Suddenly he felt a sharp burning pain in his thigh. He swung around to find a tall, blonde Guardsman pointing a sword at his chest. He looked down and could feel rather than see, his warm blood seeping through his rain-soaked breeches.

Flath almost cried out with relief when he saw Ian standing behind the man with his newly acquired long sword ready to split the man's head in two. As Ian approached the man, he stepped a branch that cracked under the weight of his boot. The man snapped his head around and looked at Ian standing only inches from him. "Ian?" the man asked, taken by surprise.

Flath lifted his sword to dispatch the distracted man and then suddenly Flath's world went dark. He was hit on the head with the hilt of a sword and crumpled to the ground. Ian looked over at Flath with wide, frightened eyes and then fled into the forest.

* * *

As the last of the bodies fell, Teo searched the littered clearing for Flath. He did not find him amongst the dead and so stood in the middle of the clearing intently searching the trees that seemed to be hiding a dark secret. He looked about and found Bleen, Jon, and Adam, sword tips lost in the muddy dirt, staring at the carnage.

Adam then took notice of Teo and ran up to him. "They took Flath! They have him!"

Teo's eyes grew wide with fear. "Are ye sure?"

"I saw them hit him over the head!" Adam cried. "It was Ian. I saw the little bastard betray our commander to the enemy!"

"That cannot be true! Are you sure it was Ian?" Bleen asked, his face smeared with blood as rain dripped down the long spikes of his dark hair.

"Yes! I saw it with my own eyes." Adam angrily wiped the mud smeared across his face. "Then he snuck off into the woods like a coward!"

"We must go after Flath! We must try an find him." Teo's face was twisted in worry.

Teo took a deep breath and looked up at the clearing sky. He must make a decision-the right decision.

"Ye two men," Teo pointed to the men standing on the outskirts of the clearing. "Ye go back ta the group and tell um what happ'n. Tell um ta keep moving quickly, an ta not stop til they get ta Bell. Tell um we will meet up with them as soon as we can, and they are all ta stay hidden in the forest. The four of us will go looking fer Flath." He swept his arms in a motion to encompass Jon, Bleen, and Adam. "Go now, and hurry!" The three men turned and ran back the way they had come.

"Adam, yer skills as a tracker will come in handy this night, me friend." Teo patted the older man's back. "Ye lead the way." The four men followed each other in a single file line into the densest part of the forest following a muddy, wet trail that was barely there at all.

CHAPTER FOURTEEN

Stalking across blue skies abright
Slinking through forest under moon's light

Creeping, crawling never a sound will it make
A caught one never knows 'till too late

Better to be devoured than look into haunted eyes
Go 'head, take a look for she tells no lies
Worry, worry; she reveals who lives and who dies

-Haunted Hunter; Rubi Jep

There was a soft patter of rain on the roof of her small tent. All around the forest the soft spatter of tiny droplets baptizing the earth were carried on the cool forest mist. The days had been warm, but the nights were still cool. A violent thunderstorm had lumbered across the sky that afternoon, painting the blue sky with dark streaks of wind-driven clouds. The rain was steadily getting lighter as Rhiannon lay on her cot mindlessly stroking the amber fur of the pax that slept below her. Luna was curled up at the mouth of the tent contentedly sleeping when from somewhere in the distance a lone wolf called out into the night. The forest was dense and wet, and there was no way of knowing how far the animal was from the camp.

Luna's head went up, and she cocked it to the side to better catch the mournful cry if it should once again filter through the trees. As if on cue, the forest creature's bay again floated on the mist. Luna gave a small whine, then got up and quickly left the tent. Rhiannon looked up just in time to see her bushy silver tail disappear from the tent opening. "No worry, she'll be back," Rhiannon muttered to the pax as if it was listening, or even cared. She did not hunt in the rain, preferring the warmth of Rhiannon's tent.

She turned over onto her back and pulled the rough wool blanket up under her chin. Her mind drifted to her father, and she wondered if he was cold and what he was doing at that exact moment, or if he were even still alive. Helplessness clouded her heart and crept over her cold bones. Her father's fate was far out of reach for her.

Restlessly the pax started to stir. Its coarse purring stopped, and it slowly sat up. A faint glow started burning about the cat giving the tent an eerie tint. It opened its large eyes and blinked a few times. Suddenly realizing the tent was growing lighter Rhiannon sat up and looked down at the animal who was staring up at her in a trance. She gasped, and her eyes grew wide as the amber radiance filled the tent with light and warmth. Rhiannon slid off the cot and sat on her knees in front of the pax, hands resting on her thighs. The sound of her heart pounded in her ears and thumped in her chest. The pax was quite calm as if it was unaware that it glowed like a burning fire. Finally, Rhiannon reached up to shield her eyes, for the light grew too bright.

Then, it was dark. Completely black. Rhiannon blinked,

trying to bring something, anything, into focus. The moon itself had been put out. It was as if she were floating in an abyss.

She rubbed her eyes furiously, then opened them. She was sitting in a forest. The tent, Tim, the whole camp was gone! Alone she sat on a blanket of clover, damp and cold under her legs. A huge full moon sent luminous beams through thick boughs to give just enough soft light that she could make out her surroundings. Massive rough-barked trees spiked into the heavens, farther than she could see. Their breadth was easily too large for fifty people, standing hand in hand, to ring its thick trunk. In awe, Rhiannon slowly looked around as her surroundings unfolded before her eyes. Hundreds of these mighty sentinels of the forest surrounded her. The ground was mostly bare except for tiny clovers, ferns with the most delicate lacy feathers and large gray spotted mushrooms.

From where she was sitting she could see part of a large pond. She thought she heard faint voices, but could not be sure. Slowly she got up and cautiously walked towards the pond. She stopped at the bank, ringed with clover, and looked at the water. It was as black as oil and still; so still it could have been glass.

Voices drifted on the breeze. She looked up to see a small camp across the pond. A little fire burned in the middle of a few lean-tos and a large tent. They were Beaynidan soldiers! Too afraid to move she stood perfectly still, barely breathing. From behind a massive tree, two soldiers walked into camp dragging something, or someone. They left the man sprawling on the dirt, moaning in pain. Finally, he turned towards her. Rhiannon gasped as she mouthed his name, yet silence was all that strayed from her lips.

"Rhiannon." A whisper came from the wind and drifted through her. "Rhiannon," it called again. Her heart pounded, and her breaths came in short, choppy measures. "Rhiannon." It was coming from the water! She looked down at the water as ripples began to form sending the cold, black liquid to lick her toes. The clover grew into viny tentacles encircling her toes and ankles so she could not move. It slithered up her calves turning her veins to ice. An arctic wind blew as the pond called out to her again. Black ribbons of her hair danced on the breeze like the fluttering wings of an eagle.

"Rhiannon, daughter of Sernia!" the voice called, though now she could not tell whether it was from the watery deep or from inside her very mind. It seemed to echo through her like she was a bell that had just been rung from a high tower.

"Do you deny it?" the voice whispered. "Do you deny her, daughter of Sernia?" The swells grew, sending icy water to cover her ankles. She tried to move back but was tangled.

"Do you deny her, Rhiannon of the Archigos?" She struggled, trying to move her feet, trying to get free to get away from the voice that chased her very soul. She grunted with the effort to get away, gasping as the whispers danced around her, accusing her, not waiting for a reply.

Then, all was quiet. Not a breeze or voice or even her heart could be heard. She could feel herself breathing hard, yet no sound came from her lips. Suddenly she was sucked into the black water so fast she did not have time to fill her lungs. She was swallowed whole by the blackness. The water was so cold that it shocked her as though she had been struck by lightning. Almost instantly her fingers and toes became numb. Her hair floated out around her as water filled her mouth, nose, and ears. She tried to reach for the surface, but there was nothing but cold darkness. She shut her eyes and trembled in the frigid blackness.

Finally, she felt earth beneath her and the weight of gravity. Quickly she opened her eyes to find she was lying on the dirt floor of her tent, the wide-eyed pax staring down at her.

Her heart pounded so loud she could hear nothing else. She gasped for breath and choked as tiny bits of dirt pelted the back of her throat. She turned over onto her back and stared at the ceiling of her tent trying to calm her nerves.

The pax inquisitively sniffed at her ear, then licked her cheek, curled up beside her face and went to sleep. Rhiannon lay on the cold dirt floor for a long time, just listening to the rhythm of her heart slowly return to normal. Her mind, with all its logic, was so numb it could no longer distinguish real from unreal or the truth from the imaginary.

The last vision the pax had shown her was the past. Was this vision also in the past? Tiny shreds of memory confirmed that what the pax had first shown her did, in fact, happen. So, that would mean Flath had been captured. She knew he had been captured!

Should she wake Tim and demand that he come with her? She would have to tell him why. As it was, he was already convinced that the pax was sent by some evil god to gobble them up when they least expect it. No, she could not involve Tim, he would not understand.

But how would she find this giant forest? A messenger had just returned yesterday with word that Flath and his army were still awaiting word on where Beaynid's army had gone. That being the case, he could not be more than a day's ride from camp. Though, in which direction she did not know. She did know, however, that east of the camp was just rolling hills, meadows and eventually the ocean. No big trees there. As for west, well, she was west of where the rebellion was waiting, and there were no giant trees near her. So, it was either north or south.

She tapped her fingers on her thigh mulling over her plan. All rationale was thrown out. It was inconceivable that she could even hope to find Flath in this huge, foreign land. There were enemies creeping all about the forest, yet somehow she was convinced that she could find him. Perhaps the pax would show her the way?

She sat up and looked towards the flap of the tent. Over the light rain that fell she could hear Tim's faint snoring as he slept under a small lean-to erected at the front of her tent. How frantic he will be to wake up and find her gone. Maybe she should wake him and at least give him a chance to come with her. No, he would surely wake the fighters to keep her here. She took a deep breath, then got up and started to dress very quietly.

She threw on Flath's old shirt and that pair of trousers she had stolen from one of the soldiers. Tim had also come into possession of a thick woolen coat that he gave to her that she now slipped into. Swiftly she braided her hair, secured the end with a strip of soft, oiled leather and yanked on a woven cap that matched her coat then pulled on her boots. She patted the small pouch that was hidden in a small tear in the lining of her coat and hesitated as she looked towards the tent flap. With a sigh, she slipped under the back of the tent, then held up the tent wall for the pax to follow, thankful for the companionship and maybe a clue that would lead her to Flath.

The rain had turned to a cool mist and immediately hit her in the face as she quietly started towards Zellan. Before she could go too far from her tent, however, she began to hear whispers and soggy footsteps in the mud. She quickly crouched down in the foliage and looked around. As her eyes became accustomed to the darkness, she could make out many figures emerging from the forest. A Beaynidan soldier crept from behind the tree she was crouched near. He was but inches from her! She could clearly make out the proud brightly colored crest on his uniform and his wet, glistening blond hair. She sucked in her breath, and the soldier stopped suddenly and turned to face her.

She held her breath and prayed to a nameless god that he could not hear her heart pounding in her breast. He looked around slowly and then started back towards her tent.

Quietly Rhiannon moved back towards Tim. She ducked under wet ferns, low branches, and thorny bushes. She moved around a tree and could see he was still sleeping. She wiped the rain from her eyes just as the soldier came around the corner of her tent. Tim was restfully sleeping on a pile of blankets completely unaware of the danger that loomed over him. The soldier slowly raised his broadsword ready to strike. Rhiannon burst from the bushes screaming like a banshee and leaped in front of the soldier. He stepped back and almost tripped over a tent peg. Tim sprang from his bed, sword drawn, and deftly stuck the flabbergasted soldier in the side.

Men began to yell, and the sound of steel blades rang out into the damp air. Men's strangled screams were echoing off the trees as they uttered their last breath and fell to the ground. Tim grabbed Rhiannon's hand and quickly dragged her into the darkness. They said nothing, just ran through the trees and bushes. At one point, they ran past a dead sentry's body lying motionless in the mud. When the screams grew a little fainter, they stopped and scrambled past a thorny hedge into a hollow log. Their breathing was heavy and wild, and they tried to make out who was winning the battle.

"There were too many of them," Rhiannon whispered between gulps of air. "Too many.... We must get my horse." She looked over at Tim.

Slowly he turned to her with a blank look on his face. "Milady, we must stay here, 'tis not safe to go any closer or we will inevitably end up like them."

Rhiannon grabbed Tim's cold, wet hand and gave it a small squeeze, then looked into his frightened eyes. "We can't stay here, Tim. They'll be looking for us. Our only hope of escape is to get Zellan and ride out of here as fast as we can."

He answered her after a moment of contemplative silence, "All right. I will go get your horse; you stay here."

"Tim, I-"- "

"No, milady, you will stay here, and I will not argue with you on this matter. I will go and retrieve your horse." She watched him disappear in the dappled moonlight that parted the dissipating clouds.

It seemed to take an eternity before she heard the snapping of branches heralding Tim's return with her horse. As soon as the sound got close enough, she crawled out from the log and quickly stood up.

"What took you so-," Rhiannon gasped and jumped back. She stared into the wide eyes of a startled Beaynidan soldier. He started to raise his sword, and she impulsively backed until she stepped onto the foot of another soldier, who promptly grabbed her by the arms. She whirled her upper body around to stare up at the man who held her. He drew in his breath in surprise that she was a woman. Then he smiled and laughed, saying something to the other man in a condescending voice.

Bright moonbeams showed down upon the forest as the soldier drug her back to camp. As they got closer, she could see Tim kneeling in the mud along with the cook and the surgeon. She could see the pleadingly mournful expression on Tim's mud-streaked face as she came near. She tried to smile at him reassuringly, but his expression did not change, he just looked down at the black muck swallowing his knees. The soldier threw her down next to Tim. Mud splashed up all over her and squished between her fingers.

A tall, broad-shouldered man said something to the other soldiers that were standing in the clearing, and they all looked at her, squinting through the mist and darkness. He barked out an order, his raspy voice bouncing off the trees. Tim, along with the cook and the surgeon, all jerked their heads up at this, then glanced over at Rhiannon with a look of complete pity.

"What did he say?" Rhiannon whispered to Tim.

"You do not want to know, milady."

The soldier behind her gripped her coat and hauled her up with such force that her feet left the ground. He announced something to the growing crowd of soldiers that melted out of the forest and ran a thick, wet tongue up her cheek leaving a cold trail of spittle. Disgusted, she wiped her cheek and flashed him an angry glance. Tim jumped up and yelled, but a soldier instantly punched him in the face, and he fell to the ground with a splat.

Rhiannon pushed away from the soldier and ran to Tim. "Are you okay?"

"I am all right milady," he replied, as dark rivers of blood drained from his mouth.

"How could you do this to him, he's just a boy!" Rhiannon turned around and screamed at the man.

Surprised, they returned her angry expression with bewilderment. A short, stocky man came forward. "As if an Archigos woman traveling with the rebellion is not queer enough, she speaks Jurian!"

"You should get your facts straight, soldier, before making such an audacious claim. Perhaps it would save you from making a fool of yourself."

Snickering broke out among the men as they stood listening intently. "Pardon me." He gave an overly exaggerated bow. "Tell me, then, what it is exactly you are doing here in the company of these men."

"Well, uh, first of all, I am not an Archigos." She drew herself up and looked defiantly into the man's eyes carefully wiping the moisture off her face. "My mother was an Archigos, true. But my father is a Jurian priest."

At this new revelation, the man looked surprised. "A Jurian priest?"

"Yes, that's right. And, uh, my father has sent me with these men," she waved her hand over the camp, "On a mission to Ventra."

The squatty soldier stepped closer. Kneading his stubbly chin with his fingers, he cocked an eyebrow and gave her a doubtful look. "Is that so, priestess?"

"Yes. Yes, it is. I am on a mission to find my birth mother. My father said I am old enough to know the truth."

He made a loud snorting noise. "If that is true, why are you traveling with twenty armed men?"

She quickly glanced down at Tim, then back up again to him. "My father wanted me to be safe, of course! He said it is too dangerous for a woman to travel to such a faraway place without protection, so he hired these men to protect me."

This got laughter from the assembled soldiers. "Protection? Ha! They did a fine job protecting you, did they not?"

"Well, against such highly trained and professional, fearless soldiers such as yourselves, my father's hired men would have had no chance." She smiled, thinking to herself: and they were outnumbered by almost ten to one you big, dumb animal! "My father will be furious at how you murdered all of his hired men in cold blood. But I'm sure I will be able to calm him if you allow me and what is left of my traveling party to be on our way now." Rhiannon folded her arms defiantly and stood as straight as she could.

"Humf, I am not afraid of a crazy Jurian priest!"

Rhiannon looked around at the dark figures then back at him and whispered, just loud enough for him to hear, "That may be so, soldier, but it's not *him* you need fear. It's my

Archigos mother that should cause you to think twice about your next decision."

His bushy eyebrows shot up in shock as he tried to ascertain whether or not he had just been threatened. He put one hand on his rather wide hip and scratched his damp head a few times trying to decide what to do.

Finally, he said, "You are lucky that we were temporarily separated from our commander, madam because I am quite sure he would not be so quick to let you go. But, since I am tired and do not wish to anger the northern barbarians, I will let you go." Rhiannon looked down at Tim and smiled in relief. Obviously, this soldier had no idea that his queen desperately sought both her and Flath.

"Thank you, sir. We will take our horses and be on our way."

Wasting no time, hoping the soldier would not change his mind or worse, their missing commander would show up all of the sudden, Tim and Rhiannon hastily gathered their things and saddled the horses. Under the watchful eyes of the soldiers, the cook and surgeon each gathered up a small bundle of their trade, then they all quickly disappeared into the dark forest.

Somewhere along the journey Luna appeared from the brush and followed. Rhiannon wondered where she had gone, but was grateful that she was otherwise occupied; it would have been even harder to explain why they were traveling with a wolf. Quickly they slipped into the trees and into the shelter of darkness.

"Dotted throughout the continent that is Beaynid and Ventra are the ancient Sash-nah Forests that host massive trees that are said to have been created by the Goyor God, Pom-Nih. The true origins of the trees are not known. These colossal conifers are substantially bigger both in breadth and height than any other tree found in either Beaynid or Ventra. These trees are seldom if ever seen for it is believed they are violently protected by sìochair."
-Field Guide of Beaynid; Myrin Zantroc

"Do you know where there is a grove of massively big trees?" Tim gave Rhiannon an odd look, and she thought she heard a funny sound coming from one of the men behind her as they picked their way through the wet forest. "Tim, it's very important."

"Yes, Lady Kossi, I do know of such a place," he finally answered with much trepidation.

Rhiannon took a deep breath, moved Zellan closer to Tim's gray mount. "Good. We must go there now."

"We cannot go in there!" the surgeon protested.

Rhiannon looked back at the thin, pale-faced man. "We

do not have time for this. Flath was captured, and they have taken him there." She turned back to Tim.

"Flath has been captured?"

"Yes. We must go to him now."

"How did you find this out?" He looked suspiciously at her.

"You won't believe me," she replied as Zellan snorted and sidestepped.

"Lady Kossi, this information is of the utmost importance," he pried.

"Tim, I cannot tell you right now, but I am certain that he has been captured and he is being held in a spot where there are huge trees." She leaned closer to him. "And a large pond with black water."

The surgeon gasped. "I am not going anywhere near the Sash-nah Forest!" "Do you hear that Cook? That woman wants to drag us into Sash-nah, right up to the sìochair!"

Rhiannon turned back around to face the surgeon. "If you don't want to come with us, you are welcome to go back to the camp and stay with the queen's men!"

"Those men who took the captain would have to be mad. No one goes into the Sash-nah Forest. No one!" Tim shook his head in disbelief.

"Exactly! If you were looking for a good place to hide, wouldn't you head for a place where you knew no one would be looking for you?" Rhiannon tried to reason with the men.

"This is nonsense! Will you men let a woman lead you?" asked the surgeon, his long greasy hair was plastered to his narrow skull making him look like a jungle pigmy's most prized shrunken head.

"You pompous, old windbag—," she started.

"If Lady Kossi says that they are holding the captain in Sash-nah," the cook tactfully cut in, "then it is our duty to do what we can to free him. I will go with you, Lady Kossi."

"Thank you, Cook," she said and turned to face Tim. "Now, are you with us Tim?"

He sighed, knowing he had no other choice. "Yes, milady, I will come with you."

"Good! Lead the way, Tim." She heard the surgeon make a rude sound, then sigh as he followed along.

With less than an hour left of darkness, they eventually reached their destination: the ancient forest of Sash-nah. The clouds were long gone, leaving a clear sky and a warmer wind blowing from the east. The thick canopy blocked almost all of the moonlight making it hard to see.

"We will all die for coming into this place," the surgeon whispered. "You will see how foolish it was to follow a woman to your death."

"Shut up you constipated 'ol badger!" the cook said as he led his horse around the surgeon, catching up to Tim and Rhiannon.

"Do you know where there's a large pond?" Rhiannon regarded Tim seriously.

Abruptly Tim pulled his horse to a stop and slid off. "I need to speak with you, milady." She sighed and impatiently slipped off Zellan's back. Quickly, they walked a short distance away from the cook and surgeon who were engaged in a conversation that involved questioning each other's sanity. Tim stopped and grabbed Rhiannon's arms, looking deeply into her eyes, trying his best to convey the graveness of the situation. "You must tell me how you came to know of the captain's capture and his whereabouts."

"That's not important, Tim. It's important that we save him!"

"Milady, this is a very dangerous place, and I must know if this information came from a reliable source or if we are just being fooled into blindly following a path to our deaths." Rhiannon studied his eyes in the scant light and could see that he was quite serious. She had a sudden feeling of apprehension. She paused, not wanting to divulge the source of her information. "Milady?"

She exhaled in defeat. "I saw a vision." She felt, rather than saw, his shock.

"A vision?" He let go of Rhiannon's arms. "You are a Seer?"

"Well, no, not exactly."

"Then what do you mean?"

"The pax."

He stepped back and threw his arms in the air. "Gods! You brought us here because of a vision spawned by a creature of the underworld?" Rhiannon glanced over to see that both the cook and the surgeon stopped their conversation and were now looking over at them.

She looked back at Tim and grabbed his shoulders. "Tim, listen to me. I know it was real. I was there; I saw Flath being brought into their camp just on the other side of a pond. You must believe me; I know it's true."

"Do you not know of the Sash-nah forests?" he asked slowly.

"I don't know anything about this place," she answered, clearly out of patience.

Tim shook his head and started to explain. "Small Sash-nah forests are dotted across both Beaynid and Ventra. The area they take up is not a great amount of land any longer. Legend says that all of Beaynid and Ventra were once filled with the giant trees. When man came into the forest, he started cutting down the great trees until there were but a few small forests left across the whole land.

"It was then that Pom-Nih, the god of earth and elements, formed a pond in the middle of each of these great forests and put there, in the water, sìochair to watch over the trees and protect them from all men."

"That's interesting, Tim, but we are not here to chop

down trees, we are here to retrieve Flath. So, what does all that have to do with us?"

"Milady, this place is guarded by sìochair. They will kill any who enter this forest, regardless of their original intent. We are in grave danger as we speak."

"Then point me in the direction of the pond, and I will go alone." Her face was very solemn and though she did not want to go alone, she would.

Tim shook his head. "Milady, I swore to Flath that I would go anywhere you did and that I would protect you with my own life. I will go with you if you feel you must go further."

She smiled, genuinely touched by his valor and bravery. She gently kissed him on the cheek. "Thank you, Tim. Now, where's that pond?"

As they cautiously approached the pond, the thick darkness of night slowly began to hint at losing its grip on the forest. They quickly tethered their horses, and the surgeon whispered in a shaky voice that he would stay with their mounts.

Very slowly they crept to the bank of the black water. Rhiannon looked at the pond warily, recalling her vision. A chill went down her back, feathering her spine and covering her body with gooseflesh. She glanced over to see Tim and the cook giving the water much the same guarded expression. Rhiannon took in a deep, uneasy breath.

It was just as she saw in the pax's vision. Somewhere in the back of her mind, a questioning voice echoed its doubt of the reality of the whole situation. It was quickly quelled, however, for Rhiannon knew that this was very real. No amount of denying the plausibility or sheer magnitude of this world would bring her father back to her and bring her back home to Montana.

No, she somehow knew she would never again see the

cabin she grew up in or the ranch that she and Matthew were to someday run together. She just hoped she would see her father again.

Voices drifted over the still water, pulling their attention from the pond. They squatted behind a few reeds that were growing out of the water. "Do you see Flath?" she whispered.

"I bet they are holding him in that tent." The cook pointed across the pond through the long slender leaves. They had no weapons, so the only chance they had was to use the waning darkness and stealth.

Suddenly she thought she felt the prick of something sharp in her back. Yes, she definitely felt something very sharp, biting into her back right through the heavy wool coat. She sucked in a breath and turned to Tim.

"Be very quiet, and I will not run you through." A voice whispered from behind her. Tim started moving toward the dark figure but was stopped by Rhiannon's muffled gasp of pain. "I warn you; I'll slice him open if you move a muscle."

Tim looked at the cook, then back at the dark figure. "Who are you?"

"*Who are you?*" it echoed. Just then Luna launched out of a nearby bush and sank her teeth just deep enough into the figure's arm to cause him to drop his sword. They all looked over at the camp, but evidently the soldiers had heard nothing. Tim wasted no time in grabbing the fallen weapon. Rhiannon whirled around and tried to see who the dark figure was.

She reached down and gently stroked Luna's head. "Good girl," she whispered. "Let go, let go Luna." She coaxed the wolf from the young man's arm.

As soon as Luna let go, Tim stuck the sword to his throat. "Who are you?" he asked again.

"A-are you with the rebellion?" he asked guardedly.

"Yes. Now, who are *you*?" Rhiannon persisted.

His eyes widened at the realization that Rhiannon was a woman. "I am Ian. I fight for the rebellion also."

"He looks Seun to me." The cook observed and then cautioned Tim not to remove the sword from where it rested on Ian's throat.

"I am Seun, as a quarter of the rebellion is also. Like them, I fight for freedom. I fight with Captain Flath."

Rhiannon leaned in closer towards the young man. "Where are the rest of the soldiers who fight with you?"

"We were ambushed. They took the captain, so I followed. They have him over there, in that tent." He pointed.

Rhiannon looked over the water, then back at Ian. "Where's Teo? Is he alive?"

"I do not know if he lives or is dead."

Rhiannon sighed and looked over at Tim, "I think he's all right." Slowly Tim lowered the sword but kept a keen eye on him.

"Do you have any more weapons?" Tim asked Ian.

He shook his head. "Only my sword." Covetously he eyed his sword in Tim's hand.

"We need a plan..." Rhiannon mumbled, as much to herself as anyone else. She crouched down and stared at the black mud in concentration. After a short while, she looked up at Tim. "Okay, we need a diversion. Maybe if Cook and the surgeon take a few of the horses and ride through the camp, whooping and hollering, and get most of the soldiers to follow them, then Tim, Ian and I could swim across the pond—,"

"Swim across the pond?" Ian tried to stifle his exclamation in an agitated whisper. "The woman is clearly mad, and why are you taking orders from a woman, anyway? Who is the commander of your party?"

"Hold your tongue. This is Lady Kossi of the Archigos. She is due your respect as royalty," Tim reprimanded.

Rhiannon was impressed by his sudden show of authority. Ian seemed taken aback by this declaration.

"Thank you, Tim, but I am not royalty. I am, however, the only one at this moment who has a plan." Ian's eyes shifted from Tim to Rhiannon and back to Tim, not knowing what to think.

They were bought out of their debate by a sharp gasp. All three looked towards the large, round shadow that was the cook. "The w-water..." He started backing up very slowly.

Rhiannon whirled around to see the black water start to glow. She clenched her fists and held her breath as ripples began forming causing tiny waves to wash up on the muddy bank. Bits of the vision started playing across her memory. She recalled how cold and dead that black water felt and became very frightened.

Emerging from the water, a large amber colored ball slipped from the surface and slowly hovered above the pond. A strong smell of dirt, grass, murky water, and reedy leaves filled the air and dropped down upon them like a thick blanket. Abruptly, the light then split into three smaller balls and flitted around, encircling them, casting an amber glow onto their faces.

Slowly the tiny globes started melding into shapes until three tiny winged creatures in the form of hauntingly beautiful women hovered around them.

"Sìochair," Ian whispered, his eyes wide and round.

The three men immediately fell to their knees, bowing their heads. Rhiannon looked down at them but could not move. One of the sìochair came closer to Rhiannon so that she could make out her tiny features. She wore a remarkably detailed dress that was painted with all the colors of a rainbow, soft and flowing and so delicate. Her hair was long and equally fluid and light green in color. She had the most absurd impulse to reach out and touch the sìochair.

"So, you will deny her, Rhiannon Kossi?" Rhiannon jumped at the sound of the sìochair's voice, much harsher than it should have been coming from such an elegant, creature. The three men slowly raised their heads watching the sìochair float on the frigid air.

"Deny who?" Rhiannon finally found her voice.

"The goddess of your people, the Archigos," the sìochair explained.

"The Archigos are not my people." Rhiannon followed the sìochair as it slowly floated about her head. A cool wind whistled through the trees and toyed at wisps of her hair that had pulled loose from her braid.

"Ah, but they are, Rhiannon Kossi. Just as they were your mother's people."

"I don't remember my mother. She died when I was very young." Her voice trailed off on a forlorn note.

"You have memories; you just need to awaken them." The sìochair said in a softened tone. "You were chosen by the goddess Verna to lead your people, just as your mother was chosen before you and your daughter after you. You are the Empress of Ventra."

Ian let out a gasp of surprise. Rhiannon looked to the three men, still kneeling in the mud. Their faces were awash in just enough of the light for her to see the shock in their expressions.

"I am not the Empress of Ventra!" She protested with a little more force than she planned. "I-I am no one of importance. I am here to save my father and go home." She added a little softer.

"Oh, but you are, Rhiannon Kossi. Your importance will change this land and goes far beyond the boundaries of Ventra, or even Beaynid."

"I don't care about Ventra or Beaynid. I'm here to retrieve

my father, then go home." Stubbornness and defiance seasoned her words.

Just then Ian jumped to his feet. "Are you mad, woman? Do not speak to a sìochair in that manner!"

One of the other sìochair, who up until that moment had been silently hovering, started glowing a little brighter. "Careful, young Ian. Your heart is pure, but your youth betrays you. Do not be so quick to condemn this woman, for she will be your queen someday." Ian looked, wide-eyed from the sìochair to Rhiannon.

"I-I'm sorry, milady," he murmured to Rhiannon then sunk back to the ground in a deep bow of respect and fear.

"I will not be his queen or the Archigos empress! I—,"

"Enough Rhiannon Kossi. If you will deny your goddess and your people, then there is little we can do. However, this matter with the leader of the rebellion must be taken care of now before it is too late. Go now and retrieve this man, Flath. Your wolf and cat have been asked to help." The sìochair swept her tiny arm towards the camp where a commotion was starting. "May your heart soften, Rhiannon Kossi." Then, as suddenly as they were there, the sìochair were gone.

Tim and the cook stood up next to Ian, who quickly jumped to his feet when he heard the disturbance in the camp. Everyone was staring at Rhiannon, not knowing what to say. The silence was broken with a loud howl. They all looked toward the camp. The sun was just starting to push the darkness away. Luna ran through the camp barking, and snarling, then grabbed a large leather pouch and ran into the forest with several men chasing after her. Just as they disappeared into the gray brush, a screech and the sound of beating wings echoed off the huge trees. More yelling from the men who were left in the camp could be heard. The pax swooped down and clawed one of the men. He screamed in pain and ducked under a lean-to. Three other men drew their swords and tried in vain to slash the creature out of the dim air. A man appeared from the flap of the tent and yelled something that Rhiannon could not understand. He unsheathed his sword and joined the attempt to down the cat.

"Okay, we must go now. We need to get Flath out of there as quickly and quietly as we can. Tim, have that sword ready. Let's go." Rhiannon quickly waded into and across the waist deep water towards the tent. The three men quickly waded in after her, suddenly willing to follow her into the pits of the underworld.

CHAPTER SIXTEEN

Will you deny her? Will you deny her, daughter of Ventra?
Red diamond blazes upon your breast,
Daughter of Sernia; warrioress of Verna.
Can you deny any longer that which flows in blood and bone?
Reborn in the sìochair's black water.
Daughter of empresses.
Blessed by goddesses.
Claim your birthright.
-Daughter of Sernia; Kyia Kossi

Three dark forms crawled from the still pond, leaving shiny black trails of slimy mud behind them. The earth smelled of water, dirt and cool grass. The cold air, much colder than a summer's dawn should be, immediately wrapped its frosty tentacles around them, turning their nervous breath to mist, but all were too lost in the moment to realize.

Rhiannon's heart pounded loudly in an anxious rhythm as blood rushed noisily through her ears so that she could not hear anything around her. Adrenaline drowned her sense of fear, pushing her closer to the rear of the tent. Suddenly there was a sound of a blade cutting through the thick forest air. Tim jumped back and held up the sword just in time to deflect another blow. His sword went flying and landed on the damp earth with a thud. A Sona Tuathan Royal Guard held his sword to Tim's throat.

"Now what do we have here?" he hissed. "Intruders?" No one dared to say a word. "Who could these brave souls be who sneak through the Sash-nah Forest?" He sneered at them. Rhiannon moved closer to the man, but he quickly dug his sword tip into Tim's tender throat. "Do not come any further or your comrade will die!"

Ian inched toward his sword that lay several feet away. His slow movements went undetected by the distracted guard. He crept closer to his weapon and silently picked it up. Like the lethal spring of a hungry panther, Ian brought the blade down upon the man's arm. He screamed and let his sword drop to his feet. The guard fell holding his bleeding arm. Ian was quickly on the man, his sword hovering at the man's chest. Suddenly Ian's eyes grew wide. "Father?"

The man looked closer at the boy. "Ian?" he asked, clearly shocked. "What is this madness, boy?" Ian said nothing, but let his sword falter. "You betray your country and queen to fight for this rabble?" His angry voice rung out across the camp.

"I know what is wrong and what is right," Ian finally said with force and gripped his sword tightly.

"You know nothing! I should have sent you right back to your mother when you showed up at my doorstep!" He shook his head. "The filthy whore! You are most likely not even from my seed!" The guard started to rise, careful of his injured arm. Ian stuck his blade tip to his father's chest. Ian was strong enough to push the sharp blade through the chain mail, and his father knew it. "Will you run me through then?" he asked jokingly.

"You will not move," Ian stated. Rhiannon watched the men stare at each other and wondered how this came to pass. A father and his son pitted against each other-separated by much more than the angry length of a sword.

The man forcefully brushed Ian's sword away and quickly stood up. "Then you have made your choice and will die like the rest of these gypsy lead rebels." He lunged toward Ian, but the younger man was quicker and so spitted his father onto the gleaming blade he had been so proud of.

His father's body fell heavy on the ground, and his blood ran black in the dimness of a forest dawn. Ian wiped the blade on his father's pants and returned it to its sheath at his hip. His movements were mechanical and deliberate as though he were in shock. "Are you all right Ian?" Rhiannon asked quietly.

"Aye, I am finally all right," he solemnly answered. Then he looked up at her and straightened to his full height. "I have proven my loyalty to the captain and the cause," he stated boldly.

"That you have, Ian," Tim answered.

Shouts from returning men began to move closer, so Rhiannon quickly grabbed the guard's forgotten sword and sliced through the thin tent wall. She stuck her head in the tent, and when her eyes adjusted to the darkness, she could see a body crumpled on the floor. Other than that, the tent was empty of people.

"Take this and stand guard by the tent entrance. Don't let anything come in until I have him out of here." She handed Tim the sword, then quietly slipped into the tent.

The newborn sunlight outside had yet to brighten the tent within so she took a few seconds, blinking her eyes into focus. The tent was sparsely furnished with a small cot on one side and a pile of blankets lying carelessly on the floor. A small writing desk and chair were near the entrance, on top rested an unlit oil lamp and a small stack of papers. A sheathed knife lay forgotten on the seat of the wooden chair.

A moan broke the eerie silence, and the crumpled form moved slightly. Rhiannon ran to Flath and gently turned him over. The sun was quickly reclaiming the cold morning, revealing fresh bruises and a split lip across a stubbled, sleeping face.

"Flath," she whispered and gently shook him. "Flath, wake up."

Slowly, swollen eyes opened. "Rhiannon?"

"You're alive! I was so worried." She clumsily hugged him evoking a loud protest.

"God's woman, you will kill me for sure!"

"I'm so glad we found you in time."

"Where are Teo and Adam?"

Rhiannon sat back on her heels. "Who's Adam?"

Flath tried to sit up, but pain took him back to the floor. "Where are my men?" he asked through clenched teeth, eyes clamped shut against pain.

"I don't know." Rhiannon quickly surveyed his body for injuries. She sucked in her breath when she spotted the large dark circle of blood staining his breeches. "What happened to your leg?"

Flath reached out and grabbed her arm. "Rhiannon, where are my men?"

"I don't know," she quietly repeated.

"Are you here alone, woman?" His eyes widened.

"Of course not!" she answered, in an exasperated tone. Flath let out an audible sigh of relief. "Tim, Ian and Cook are standing guard outside of the tent." She pointed her thumb toward the entrance of the tent. "Oh, and that cowardly surgeon stayed with the horses."

"They are the only ones with you?" Flath's voice rang with alarm.

"Well, I'm sorry, but they were the only ones I could get on such short notice." Rhiannon folded her arms across her chest and frowned down at him. "We're here to rescue you, and you're complaining?"

"Aye, I am complaining! Do you know how dangerous this is for you to be here?" His harsh whispered voice sounded like furious steam rushing from a cracked pipe. "This is not a rescue; it is a slaughter!"

"Well then, maybe we should have just let you rot here by yourself." Just then they heard muffled voices and the sound of swords clashing, ringing out into the forest.

"We must go, hurry." Rhiannon got behind Flath and with much effort started dragging him towards the back of the tent.

A tall, thin man ducked through the entrance of the tent, then asked them a question-Rhiannon did not understand the language. He held his sword tightly in his left hand, the cold steel, perfectly visible in the dim light. With much effort and a little help from Rhiannon, Flath slowly stood, biting his lip against the burning pain he must surely be feeling in his thigh.

He stood, wobbling slightly, shielding Rhiannon with his body. He reached around his back and pushed her towards the hole in the back of the tent only a few feet from where they stood. Defiantly, she kept her place behind Flath refusing to leave him. "Your hospitality leaves much to be desired, commander. I thought I might try a more reputable establishment," he said in Jurian. She watched the man come a bit closer and then recalled the knife, still innocently sitting on the seat of the chair near the entrance. She cursed herself for not grabbing it when she had the chance.

"And who is your friend?" The man slowly walked closer, trying to look beyond Flath's shoulder at Rhiannon. "We do not supply whores, did you bring one of your own, then?"

Flath clumsily backed into Rhiannon forcing her to step back. Once again, he motioned for her to make her escape out the back of the tent. Once again, she stubbornly refused to leave him.

The tent was now bathed in the morning sun, and Rhiannon could clearly see the man's arrogant sneer. His blond hair was neatly tied back in a queue at his neck. The shimmering white castle, red water, and bright blue sky of his the Sona Tuathan Royal Guard uniform were a little less sunny, though, stained with blood, dirt, and sweat. His face was haggard and creased with exhaustion. His piercing ice blue eyes lewdly raked Rhiannon up and down setting her temper to boil. "Much too big to be a bar whore, men do not like such savage women." He walked closer.

"She's of no consequence, just an Archigos who was expelled from her homeland. She fights for the rebellion only as long as I can keep paying her well enough." Flath shifted his weight to better shield Rhiannon from the man's roving eyes. The man laughed a small, dry chuckle. "I think not, gypsy. I know Queen Baobh is searching for an Archigos woman who travels with you. In fact, my queen has offered a chest full of gold to the one who brings her in. Imagine my luck to have you both here at my disposal."

"I would not quite say we are at your disposal, Commander. My men are surrounding you now and are just waiting to hear a call from me." Taking them both by surprise, the man drew back his right hand and delivered a vicious punch to the side of Flath's head sending him flying across the tent then limply falling to the floor completely unconscious.

Shocked and too frightened to move, Rhiannon stood staring down at Flath who was sprawled on the floor. She started to go to him, but the man sheathed his sword and grabbed Rhiannon from the back so tight she could hardly breathe. Frantic, she started batting at the air, trying to connect with anything but could not reach him. He dragged her across the tent and roughly threw her down on a pile of blankets lying on the floor. Rhiannon turned and sat up watching in disbelief as the man quickly unbuckled his breeches. She looked over to Flath, who remained lifeless, crumpled on the floor. Without warning the man threw himself on top of her, clumsily ripping her shirt open and groping her breasts.

"We should have some fun before I must return you to the queen, no?" The man's breath smelled like stale wine and decaying flesh and churned her stomach. She screamed and tried to fight him off as he fumbled with the clasp on her pants.

"Get off of me, you stinking fool!" she ordered. But her voice fell on deaf ears, and he roughly took her mouth in his. Suddenly, the man cried out in pain and quickly rolled off Rhiannon. Flath stood over them, swaying as if on the verge of falling over, the once forgotten knife she had spotted earlier now firmly grasped in his hand.

"You miserable gypsy filth!" the man called out as he unsheathed his sword, its point glistening in the filtered sunlight.

"Leave her be, and you will be spared," Flath said, his voice wavering as he fought off the blackness that slowly began to swallow him. Rhiannon scrambled to her feet trying to reach Flath before he fell. He turned towards her; his look stopped her from moving any further. "Leave now, hurry!" he ordered, leaving no room for debate.

"I will not leave you here to die!" she stated firmly.

The man laughed in hysteria. "You are breaking my heart!" he said smoothly as he pointed his sword at Rhiannon sticking the tip into her bared left breast, just below the ruby colored diamond marking her empress. A bead of dark blood welled at the point. Rhiannon did not move, she just stared at him defiantly, not giving him the pleasure of seeing her wince in pain.

"*Her*, the queen wants alive," the man stated, then removed the sword tip from Rhiannon's breast, "*You*, however, I need only to bring in your head." He quickly jerked his sword up high and then brought it down in a curving arc to swiftly remove his opponent's head.

As if sitting somewhere in a safe, dark corner of the tent, Rhiannon watched the scene unfolding in the slowest of motions. She felt a scream ripped from the depths of her soul. It escaped her mouth like a flock of birds bouncing across the roof of the tent frantically escaping the tent only to slam against unyielding trees. She leapt from the floor, throwing herself against the unsuspecting man causing his sword to miss its intended mark.

Missing his neck, the cold steel blade cut deep into Flath's side as if he was nothing more than melted butter. Iron smashed bone, severed sinew, muscle, and even organ. Flath's breath left him in a gush sounding like a popped balloon or a sudden gust of wind. He fell to the floor drowning in a pool of his own blood.

The man fell with a thud, his bloodied sword sticking obscenely into the cold air. Rhiannon smashed his face with her balled-up fist, then quickly crawled across the floor. "Flath!" Rhiannon screamed. Quickly she removed her coat and held it tightly to his wound. "Flath!" she cried again. Sobs wracked her body, and she held him tightly. Lost in a sorrow so deep it threatened to take her life as well; she did not see Teo quietly enter the back of the tent, sword drawn, ready for retribution.

When the man's lifeless body hit the floor with a thud behind her, she did not even notice. Nor did she see Adam and Tim enter the tent. Lost in a world of agony, she was unreachable.

Teo sheathed his sword and bent down at Flath's side. Tim collapsed on the tent floor in a prayer to any god that would listen. Adam was too shocked to move, just watched as the blood thickened and devoured the floor.

Lost to a primitive call, Rhiannon fumbled for the leather pouch in the slit of her torn coat. She shook the pouch until the single, red stone fell into her blood-soaked palm. She placed the stone into the gash in his pale flesh. Coughing away a tearful voice she began to hum a tune which filled her senses. It grew louder within her body as her humming gave birth to words. The tune spilled forth from the stone as it began to bathe the tent in a blood red light.

Rhiannon sang louder and louder as the light grew more intense filling the tent with radiance and a cool mist. The words twisted from her mouth in quick secession, each verse faster than its predecessor, pouring from her soul and floating up into the forest in a hopeful, desperate song to an ancient goddess. She poured all her emotion, all her desperation, into the unknown words.

All three men were helpless to deny the power that soothed each one, sucking them into a force both foreign and wonderful. Their faces were glowing with the hot light of Rhiannon's healing stone. The twisty words were like a poem spoken by a river, never to be understood by men. It spoke to their souls, quieting all discontent, fondling harsh thought and memory.

When Rhiannon's song was done, and all the words were sung aloud, the stone's light and energy slowly started to sleep. Rhiannon removed the hot stone from Flath's wound that had already started to heal. She replaced it into the pouch and then shoved it to back into the rip in her coat. Tenderly she smoothed the hair from Flath's face and kissed his cheek, keeping her forehead to his.

Breaking the silence, the surgeon rushed into the tent

holding his little bag of implements. "What have you done to him, woman?"

Calmly Rhiannon got up and looked at Teo, his face wearing a serene, yet befuddled look. "Do not let that man touch him," she muttered, then left the tent.

The air outside was cold and crisp, free from the coppery taint of blood. She tilted her face up towards the healing sun closing her eyes against the warmth. She filled her lungs almost to the point of choking, thankful to be feeling the sun once more.

She finally walked down to the pond whose waters were still as they were in the dead of night. She dropped to her knees and washed Flath's blood from her hands. As she brought them up from the water, she saw they were still stained, unable to be washed clean.

Like the waves of the sea, unbiddable and undeniable her tears crashed upon the shores of her face. Frustration, fury, exhaustion, worry, love, and hate, washed over her like strong tides under a full moon. She tried in vain to wash the blood from her body, only to have it continue to stain. She jumped to her feet and waded into the middle of the black pond, mournful sobs echoing across massive trees. The water was bitter cold, but she did not feel it, for her skin burned like fire and ice together. The slimy mud that rested on the pond's floor was deep and pulled at the soles of her boots making it hard to walk. She continued to trudge through deep, murky waters and thick, sticky mud.

She stopped in the middle of the pond, water to her waist, and tried to wash her blistering tears away, drowning them in the sìochair's water. Still, her tears could not be washed away, they too stained, hot and salty upon her cheek.

Slowly she began to sink deeper into the mud and mire that held the pond. Without even a struggle she slipped beneath the waters of the sìochair's black pond. A cool blackness surrounded her as she continued to sink as if she were a heavy stone. Suddenly aware of what was going on she looked up only to see the whiteness of the dancing sunlight growing dimmer as the surface of the water ebbed away from her.

Rhiannon began to thrash and tried to stop her quick descent. She kicked her feet and waved her arms in a desperate attempt to reach the life-giving air just atop the now invisible surface. Her lungs ached to breathe; her body started to shake from its primal need for oxygen. With her last breath, she screamed out, the sound stopped by dead, black water, leaving only bubbles rushing to the surface as a witness to her drowning.

She wept tears for a father she would never see again, for a man she would not love any longer and a land she would never go home to.

"Giving up so easily, Rhiannon Kossi?" She felt the sìochair's commanding, yet soothing voice as it reverberated in her soul.

"I am already dead, what is there to fight against?" Rhiannon formed the question in her mind then sent it to the sìochair.

"The daughter of the Great Empress of Ventra gives up so easily?" Rhiannon stubbornly did not respond.

"Will you deny her?" the sìochair asked.

"Deny who?"

"Her." The statement was harsh and absolute, and Rhiannon knew at once who the sìochair spoke of.

"My mother is long dead. She's nothing to me."

"Oh, but she is, Rhiannon Kossi. For it is her legacy you must continue, and it is she that calls to you at night."

"My mother is dead, and she left me nothing! No legacy, no past, no future-nothing!" Rhiannon opened her eyes to the inky blackness but was not surprised to find the three sìochair floating next to her in the void.

"She left you a kingdom, Empress Kossi." Suddenly their tiny bright images disappeared and turned the blackness into a memory long forgotten.

She ran through the cool, lush grass of a park where the sun never quit shining, and the flowers always bloomed. Leaves of giant trees swayed in the warm, sweet breezes and beautiful birds called to her from the branches. She and her best friend Shih 'Ni ran through the huge, glossy, marble halls of Màrrach, laughing and screaming with joy.

Finally, they reached the Throne Room, filled with throngs of people all talking and laughing. With childish abandon, they quickly weaved their way through the crowd and carefully climbed the hard, cold marble steps up to where her mother sat, so beautiful and elegant on her golden throne.

"Mommy!" Rhiannon cried as she climbed up on to her mother's lap. She touched her mother's hair; it was so soft and almost shiny enough that she might see her reflection if she looked hard enough. Then she touched her mother's beautiful necklace of dark red stones embedded into gleaming silver. It was warm and benevolent, sparkling in a gentle shaft of sunlight. It made her mother glow with power and courage-it made her even more beautiful.

"Are you and Shih 'Ni having fun?" her mother asked, smiling down at Rhiannon.

"Yes, mommy! We went to the stables and rode our ponies. But I want a big horse like Xorn—like your mighty horse."

"One day you will have a horse just like mine, Rhiannon. When you're old enough, you will have all of this." She swept a tanned, silk draped arm across the throne room in the Royal Palace of Màrrach.

"I don't want all of it mommy, I just want a big, shiny black horse like Xorn."

"In time, my sweet child, in time." She tenderly kissed Rhiannon's chubby cheek and hugged her until she squealed.

The memory faded until there was nothing but blackness once again. Rhiannon's body shook as she cried empty tears in cold darkness. "Mommy," she whispered into the dead water.

"Stand up, Rhiannon!" her mother commanded.

"I can't!" she wailed

"Stand up, now!" Sernia ordered, more firmly.

Rhiannon did as she was bid; forcing her legs to straighten as they once again hit the murky bottom of the pond. She came up from the black water, and her body shook violently as she took in the cold, living air as if taking her first breath all over again-she had been reborn.

There was no rejecting who or what she was born to do. There were no more excuses she could use or lies she could tell herself that would make it all go away. She was who she was, plain and simple. Rhiannon brushed her wet hair back and wiped the birthing water from her face. Slowly she started to emerge from the womb of the earth that had held her until she could no longer disavow her existence. The gestation was over, the fetus now birthed to this land and to a destiny she now accepted.

Still dripping from the sìochair's pond, Rhiannon walked up to Tim and took the sword from his hand. All were quiet as they stared at Rhiannon standing near to two captured Beaynidan soldiers, her breasts bared; her birthmark lain open for all to see. She read the soldier's eyes as if a book: disdain, arrogance, and fear.

She grabbed the sword tight in her hand and ran one of the men through without a thought. He fell to the ground still wearing his arrogant sneer as shocked gasps filled the air. She turned to the soldier left standing that was now looking at her in horror-a single tear rolled down a pale cheek. Long, greasy, blond hair fell around his shoulders. Large blue eyes stared back at her with so much fear she thought she might laugh at him. Roughly she jabbed the tip of the sword into his chest. He whimpered as blood welled up onto his tunic around the sword.

"What is your name, soldier?" she asked, coolly.

"D-Don, son of Kreel Jent of Sona Tuath, milady," he stuttered.

"Don, son of Kreel Jent, I have a mission for you. If you do not complete it, I will hunt you down and slice your ugly head from your shoulders and feed it to the swine." Don swallowed hard and shook uncontrollably.

Rhiannon dug the sword tip a little deeper into his pale flesh, causing his blood to run down the cold, steel blade. "I want you to go back to Sona Tuath and deliver a message to your queen." She leaned in closer and looked deep into his eyes. "Tell your queen that Sernia's daughter-the Empress of Ventra-has returned and will shortly cut the black heart from her chest and take vengeance for all the innocent blood that she has spilled."

Don flinched and started backing away. "Y-yes milady,' he stammered.

"Go now you fool before I change my mind and deliver the message myself!" she screamed, her shrill voice bouncing off the trees. He turned and ran with his hands still bound behind his back, and disappeared into the thick brush. She turned and walked back over to Tim and gave him the sword. "We must leave now," she said and walked back to the tent to collect Flath.

CHAPTER SEVENTEEN

The gypsy and his lover so exotic.
The gypsy and his lover with the dark, dark hair.
He is a son of the South and she a daughter of the North.
Still, he takes her hand in his.

A great warrioress and her lover so common.
A great warrioress and her lover with his light, light hair.
She is the daughter of an empress and he the son of a gypsy.
Still, she takes his hand in hers.

-The gypsy and his lover; O.G Yellon

Flath writhed as fever bathed his body in flame. He had not awakened and in fact seemed to slip further away. Rhiannon did not leave his side. She stubbornly poured cool water or warm broth down his throat. He grew pale and thin and looked almost transparent in the stifling, mid-August heat. A nagging doubt stirred within Rhiannon and whispered to her that perhaps she had not used the stone in time or that maybe she had used it incorrectly. She looked on helplessly as a silent witness to a war that was raging within his mind and body. She did not talk nor did she eat, but sat and held Flath's nearly lifeless hands in hers.

They traveled on by day and camped at night under the concealing protection of the trees. They pulled a wagon, and their progress had been agonizingly slow. Finally, at the close of the fourth day, they reached the remote clearing where the rest of the men, battered and defeated, had been waiting for Flath's return.

Flath was taken from the wagon and placed in a large tent on a pile of soft pelts and blankets. Rhiannon had a cauldron hung above a small fire under a smoke hole in the tent's roof. She asked for clean clothes and bandages and soothing poultices. She bathed his body, then cleaned and wrapped his wounds. Periodically Luna entered the tent and licked Flath's hand in encouragement. Rhiannon had seen the pax circling above as they traveled, but it never approached her, and it had not been seen around the camp.

She sat quietly by Flath's side on a blanket watching dust motes whirl in the stale air of the tent. The summer sun beat down upon Sorrel Valley, and a soft, warm breeze blew through the camp. The constant fire and bubble of the cauldron kept it hot and humid within the confines of the tent. She wiped the sweat from her brow and wondered how much longer he would languish in the flames of a fevered sleep.

She heard someone approaching and knew it was Teo by his short, fast stride. He scooted through the tent flap carrying a bowl of stew in one hand and a skin of ale in the other. He sat down beside her and put the bowl and ale skin by her folded legs.

"Ye must eat, lass, 'tis no good fer ye ta continue this way," he finally said.

"Thank you, Teo." She touched his hand, so dry and hard under her fingers. "I'm fine, really."

"Ye haven't eaten in a week's time, Rhiannon. 'Tis only water that ye'll take." He shook his red head. "Ye'll soon replace the lad, and then there'll be two of ye ta care fer."

"What if he never wakes up?" Tears streamed down hollowed cheeks, food forgotten.

"Yer wee stone has more power than ye ken, lass. Our lad will recover."

She looked down and brushed his blond hair from his fevered face. "I don't know what I'd do if he doesn't..."

"None of us would ken what ta do," he said poignantly.

Flath woke in the small hours of the morning. He was met by only a still, deadly silence. His mouth was as dry as the crackled, spent leaves of fall. Thirst clung to him like heavy mud, and hunger pains rolled through his body as thunder does across an stormy sky. A bright, white-hot pain throbbed in his belly and leg. He flexed his fingers to make sure they were all there and then moved his aching jaw. With concentration, he moved one of his legs a bit, but dared not move the other. He closed his eyes and let himself get lost in the burn of exquisite pain and then the darkness of haunted dreams.

The next morning Flath pried his eyes open thinking he must be dead, or close to it. Hot sunlight filtered down into the tent. The minutes passed as he stared at the thin ceiling and tried to remember what had happened. His mind was slow and rusty as he coaxed his thoughts back out into the light. He thought he must have been asleep for years to be so stiff.

His mind slowly formed thoughts, then shadows of memory. The small trickle of memory became a slick river of blood as bright images of ambush, and fighting sparked in his mind and then washed him towards a face hidden in the darkness. Suddenly he was drowning in the recollections of what had happened to him. He tried to form her name on his cracked lips, but no sound would come out of his constricted throat.

He moved against the white-hot agony as he forced himself up on an elbow, squeezing swollen eyes shut against the pain. The pierced muscles and sinew of his belly stretched like fraying cords of decaying rope taking his breath away and threatening to plunge him into darkness. He forced himself up further, through the dense fog of gruesome torture, and finally, he swayed upon one weak elbow, and he saw her. Her dark skin had gone pale, and hollowed cheeks clung to high, proud bones. He was mortified at the sight of her dead body lying in the sleep of death.

His voice crackled from a dry throat, and her name hung ion the warm air. He spoke it again, this time with force and emotion. A single tear fell from his cheek as he reached through the pain to touch her cold flesh. Suddenly she moved and then opened her eyes. Quickly she sat up and whispered something, but he could not hear. She moved towards him and took him into her arms. Now he could hear her speak his name. In hushed sobs, she was calling to him.

Much later, Flath sat in the warm sunlight in a clearing carved from the woods skirting Sorrel Valley. He watched birds silently float by on a hot wind and fuzzy red squirrels jump from tree to tree, busily storing away their fodder for the winter.

Teo approached him and sat next to him on a felled log. "'Tis a nice day ta sit in the sun."

"Aye," Flath answered quietly.

"The men grow restless."

"There are so few of them, what is left for them to do?" Flath asked, but Teo remained silent. "Have them return to their homes. The war is over." Teo nodded. "How many are left?" Flath turned to his best friend.

"Mayhap five hundred," his voice trailed off on the breeze.

"Thousands of lives have been spent in this futile war." Flath looked away again. "What was it all for?"

"Fer freedom an what's right."

Flath looked at Teo once again. "It was all for naught."

The older man shook his head. "'Tis not over, lad. We can keep them soldiers busy wi attacks here 'n there. An ye are ta ask the Archigos fer their help, are ye not?"

Flath sighed and mindlessly rubbed his mending leg. "I suppose I will, though I am not optimistic that their response will be to our benefit." He shook his head. "There is nothing more that I can do."

"Don't discount the Archigos yet. Ye hold a special place in their empress' heart, laddie. She'll see that ye are not forgotten."

"She might not have a choice. They might not accept her as their empress."

"They can't deny her. She wears the mark!"

"You know as well as I do that they are a stubborn people." Teo did not answer. "In any case, we leave at dawn tomorrow for Ventra."

"Tomorrow? Ye have barely joined the liv'n but a week ago. Ye can't travel yet!" Teo was shocked.

"We leave tomorrow," Flath stated firmly. "There is no reason to put this off any longer. The outcome will be what it may, but Rhiannon needs to be with her people."

"What shall I tell the men?"

Flath thought for a long while and then finally let out a long sigh. "Tell them to go to their homes, but to come back here in two month's time." He looked at his friend. "We will do what we can to keep the queen's men occupied until winter hits. Hopefully, over winter I can come up with a better plan."

Teo nodded in approval. "I will be com'n wi ye, then?"

"No my friend," he shook his head. "You will go home to your family."

"I can't let ye go by yer self!" he argued.

"It is not up for discussion. You will return to your family and meet me back here after two months have passed."

Teo took a deep breath. "It will be nice ta stay wi me family for more than a few days at a time." He smiled and then walked away.

* * *

The young man nervously waited in a sunny room in the great castle of Sona Tuath. He had returned days before but had delayed his visit with the queen. He, like everyone in Sona Tuath, and beyond, was petrified of the woman. The queen and her mate were the only Forest Folk that he had ever seen, and he wondered if they all had such evil dispositions. He paced back and forth across a beautiful woven carpet that he was sure was worth more than his family could make in a lifetime. He wondered if he would get a promotion, or perhaps a reward to send home to his ailing father to care for his nine brothers and sisters. His mood lightened at the prospect. So involved with his thoughts, he did not see the queen enter the room.

"You wanted to see me?" a voice asked coolly.

The boy's eyes widened as Baobh strolled towards him. He was completely taken aback by the sheer beauty of his queen. It was the first time he had seen her up close and could clearly make out her delicate, Forest Folk features, though not as pronounced as that of her consort, Eagle.

"Your Highness, I have word for you," he said, trying his best to sound confident. She looked up at him and raised a perfectly shaped brow. She was clearly impatient and annoyed. He decided to not waste any more time and just tell her what he saw. He did not like being in her presence, and all thought of a reward or promotion was lost. "I have found the stone you have sought."

Baobh's eyes widened, and a smile formed on plump red lips. "Then give me the stone!" She held out her hand.

Involuntarily he stepped back. "I-I do not have the stone, my Queen. Rather, I know where it is," he stuttered, suddenly very frightened.

"Where is it then?" she demanded.

"You know of the escape of the gypsy leader of the common people? I was told that the messenger had arrived two days ago. I was there, hiding in the trees watching them. The gypsy was gravely injured and was dying in the commander's tent. I heard a woman crying, and I crawled to the tent. I peered in and saw that she held a blood red stone in her hand and it started glowing right in front of my eyes!" He stopped just long enough to take a breath and started talking again, "The stone grew brighter and brighter until I had to shield my eyes from its light. Suddenly it began to hum and seem to be playing the most beautiful music." He took a quick breath. "Then the stone became dark, just as it was before, and the woman put it away in a pouch she kept in her coat." He lowered his voice a bit and leaned in as if to relate a secret. "I heard them planning to go to Bell, my Queen."

Baobh turned away and clenched her fists. "The woman has it!" she howled. "She has the stone!" Her screams were shrill and ran through the huge room and out into the hall. In terror, the young man ran from the room and from the castle and even from his post as a Royal Guardsman. He left Sona Tuath-never to return.

CHAPTER EIGHTEEN

"The life of a Sona Tuathan Royal Guardsman is a life of both hardship and leisure. In times of war, the Royal Guard has many responsibilities, protecting the royal family, being the most important. In times of peace, however, guardsmen need to take care against laziness and slovenly behavior."
-Sona Tuath; Thomas Ulln

Sunlight lazily peeked through yielding trees branches. Sweet melodies of bright red birds serenaded them as they passed through the scrubby wood that would eventually take them to the Vel' Kur Mountains and beyond-to the legendary land of the Archigos: Ventra.

They had been traveling north for a week's time and had another three weeks before they would reach Rhiannon's new home. Her new home-she thought the words sounded so ludicrous. It had been a little over three months since she had come to this land in search of her father, and now, after so much had happened, she was traveling towards a destiny she did not want.

Suddenly the wood opened to reveal a large sun-drenched meadow. Elk bolted for the cover of the trees as large white birds flew up from the tall grass and were lost in the deep blue of the summer sky. Flath led the way across the lush meadow, followed by Rhiannon, Tim, Jon, and Bleen. Teo, Adam, and Ian had been left behind to gather what men they had left and make plans for when Flath had returned.

Soon they would part. She doubted that she would see him again and it left her with a hollow, dark feeling. They both knew that the time would come when they would each go their separate ways, so what good would come from yielding to foolish emotions. There was something much greater at stake than love-much more could be lost if the rebellion was not successful in ousting Baobh.

Flath slowed his horse and pulled up next to Rhiannon. "What is it you are thinking, Greannmhor?" he asked.

"How beautiful the day is," she replied smoothly.

"'Tis too hot if you ask me." He swatted at a fly. She looked over at him as he rode tall on his horse. A gypsy he might be, but a leader, he was also. His men would follow him to their death if they had to, in fact, most of them had. The golden serpent that hung from his ear winked in the light as a breeze ruffled his blonde hair. She continued to watch him, trying to analyze just how she felt. That she had fallen in love with him did not seem a possibility; though she knew she had. She studied his skin, darkening in the summer sun, and his straight posture and solid build that made him an intimidating opponent. His panther-headed sword with its ruby red eyes had tasted much blood. He was not a bloodthirsty man; she knew that, but a realist just the same. *Can I leave him when the time comes?* The question echoed through a pained heart. She sighed and looked away.

"Is it meeting the Archigos that disquiets your thoughts?"

"I guess so," she answered, not wanting to speak of

anything so inconsequential as love when so much more was at stake.

"Is it the arriving or the staying that burdens you so?"

"Both, I suppose," she shrugged. The harsh afternoon sun started to slip behind wide oaks and thin conifers. "If they are as steel-hearted and bloodthirsty as everyone says, what makes you think they won't just kill us all as soon as we set foot in Ventra?"

Flath snorted and looked over to her with a lopsided grin. "Greannmhor, are you afraid of your own people?"

"Maybe," she admitted.

"When they see the mark of the empress, they will not bar you from Màrrach." He mindlessly rubbed his side, his healing wound, still pink and tender. "There has been word that the proxy empress, Shankee, is not well suited for her role and so would be happy to step down."

"And I'm sure she would be more than happy to hand over her kingdom to an outlander who has no knowledge of their ways or customs."

"You are the rightful Empress of Ventra, Rhiannon; she will have no choice. You will be schooled in their ways and groomed to be a leader and then take your place as Sernia's successor."

"I'm not so sure it will be that easy," she said doubtfully.

"Easy? No." He shook his head. "It will be very hard work for you. However, when the time comes you will be a fear-inspiring Empress of the Archigos, of that I am sure."

"What if I'm not any better than Shankee?"

"You are the heir to the throne. You are the prodigy of warriors and leaders born to the Archigos nation for a thou-sand years. You will be very different than your cousin, Greannmhor. You will do fine," he reassured her.

"My cousin?" Rhiannon asked, suddenly interested.

"Yes. Teo has told me that it is Sernia's niece that sits on the throne-your first cousin."

"I've never had family besides my father," she whispered, her words dying away on the hot wind.

The night was crisp and cloudless, and nocturnal birds sang into the blackness and owls screeched from overhead. Rhiannon lay quietly on her back and looked up at the stars. She knew none of the constellations, for all the familiar ones of her world, were now replaced with new ones, sparkling in a myriad of colors far above this new world. In shades of rose, citrine, and violet they were tiny dancers in a huge midnight sky-the world and its inhabitants, their audience.

Thoughts of her father drifted into her mind, and she wondered if he could see the same stars that burned above her. She wondered if he were hurt, or sick, or even if he were still alive. Tears welled in her eyes and rolled down her cheeks. She felt so far away from him-so helpless to free him. She was uncertain about what would be expected of her when they reached Ventra and was not convinced that they would help her retrieve him.

She knew Flath had planned on asking the Archigos for their help in ridding Beaynid of Baobh but was not entirely sure they would render such help. If they refused, the cause was lost for sure. The five or six hundred men that were left were no match for the thousands of Beaynidan and Yellow Island soldiers that fought for Baobh. She hoped the men that were left behind would be safe until Flath's return.

Over the next week, the sweltering days of September started losing its relentless grip as the woods slowly grew into the start of a forest. Their pace was leisurely, and Rhiannon was happy for it-she was not in a hurry to arrive in Ventra and then her home city of Màrrach. Flath had grown increasingly despondent and taciturn.

They had reached a long, narrow path that cut across the mountain for about a mile, and then continued to zigzag up the treeless slope. A mighty fire had ravished this part of the mountain, leaving a naked blanket of long burned out logs, gray under years of sun and snow. Now that they had left the shelter of the cooling trees, the hot sun burned down upon them once again.

Rhiannon wiped the sweat from her face and took a long drink from her water skin. Zellan was getting agitated and wanted to rest, but the narrow path was cut from the steep mountain and did not offer a resting place. As they rhythmically moved along, Rhiannon's eyes grew heavy with sleepiness. Her thoughts began drifting as the huge white clouds did across a blue sky.

"Jump baby girl, jump!" Her mother's happy voice echoed in the huge marble hall. She stood on the edge of a great pool-her chubby toes curled over the side. "Come on honey; I will catch you." Her mother's arms stretched out to her. Rhiannon reached out and could almost touch her mother's fingers. Afraid of the deep water, but trusting her mother, she squatted down and sprung into the pool with a splash.

The water was warm and sweet. Her mother's protective arms hugged her tight as she whirled her around in the pool. Rhiannon's childish laughter filled the hall, bouncing off huge amber colored marble walls and floors. Giant planters held tall green trees with huge round leaves and the juicy red fruit that Rhiannon loved. Massive windows carved out of the walls let in golden sunshine to bathe the hall in warmth and light. "I love you, mommy! I love you!" Rhiannon laughed as her mother pulled her through the blue water.

The sudden jarring of hitting the harsh ground woke Rhiannon. She looked up to find Zellan staring back at her with a confused look on his equine face. Tim had reigned in his horse just before it had stepped on her. "Are you all right, milady?" Tim excitedly asked as he dropped from his mount and helped her to her feet.

"I'm fine Tim," she said as her cheeks grew red with embarrassment. She dusted off the seat of her pants and climbed up onto Zellan's back again. "I fell asleep," she told Flath, answering his questioning gaze.

"You need to take care, Greannmhor, or you will find yourself rolling to the bottom of the mountain." He smiled at her, and they continued to climb. She thought for a long time about the napping dream that seemed so vivid. She knew it must have happened, for the dream was too intense to have not been a memory long forgotten.

When they finally reached a more level area with a wide, friendly path, Rhiannon dismounted to give her aching back a rest. They walked ahead of Flath who had lingered behind to talk to Tim. Her pace quickened as she turned each corner taking them into the heart of the forest. The pine-covered hills grew green and cool. Long beards of lichen hung from moss-covered branches and blue jays could be heard squawking through the thick trees. She breathed in the mountain air and could smell the scent of pine, wild herbs and the sweet scent of honey wafting towards her. She heard the low, busy hum of bees high up in a tree.

The men could not be heard any longer, and she gave a fleeting thought that maybe she should wait for them, but the forest path was too inviting. The sense of discovery was too much of a draw to her, so she quickened her pace even more.

All of a sudden a rabbit burst from a large bush and scampered across the trail and disappeared on the other side. Rhiannon jumped as she watched the small speckled varmint scurry past her boots. Zellan stopped short and shook his large, black head. Luna whined and took off after the fleeing bunny.

Rhiannon took a deep breath, trying to calm her nerves

and slow her heartbeat. She felt foolish to have been scared by a little rabbit and continued. Suddenly she was overcome by an urgent sense of dread. She looked into the trees but saw nothing. Her skin bloomed with gooseflesh and her hair stood on end. Zellan let out a low, throaty warning as his ears folded down to his head. She felt she was being watched and became afraid. Her heart started pounding in her chest again, and her senses heightened. "Flath!" she called out. But there was no answer.

Suddenly several men burst forth from the concealment of the forest. They quickly surround her and slowly started to approach. Instinctively she backed up against Zellan and drew a small sword that she had convinced Flath into giving her. She was not skilled in using it-though she knew she could run a man through-for she already had. But as far as actually fighting with it, she lacked the skill.

The men stared back at her with evil grins. They all wore the bright yellow tunics of the Sona Tuathan Royal Guard. Finally, one of the men put his arm out signaling the others to stop. Zellan whinnied loudly and stomped the unyielding path.

"Put your sword down, woman, and we will not hurt you," he ordered, his greasy face turned up into a lurid smile.

"I will not put it down and just what do you want with me?" She tried hard not to shake as all the blood drained from her face. She knew what they wanted: to take her back to Baobh.

"'Tis not what I want with you, 'tis what the queen wants with you, Lady Kossi. Now release your sword, and you will not be harmed," he ordered as he inched closer.

A familiar feeling crept through her soul as her vision turned red and the men's faces started to blur. She was no longer afraid-but hungry. The uncertainty of her skills and lack of instruction was long forgotten as a new reality boiled up from deep within her soul. She screamed her mother's name, taking the men off guard and charged forward. The men jumped out of the way and whirled around. One man quickly came after her, and she effortlessly ran him through. As he fell, another was on top of her, but she swung around and cut him down.

Suddenly the first man was standing in front of her again. He laughed and lunged at her. With a mighty ark, he smacked her sword with his, sending waves of pain running up her arms. He skillfully twisted his sword around and pried the weapon from her fingers, flinging it into the bushes.

From behind her, she could hear Zellan's screams and turned just in time to see two men fall beneath his sharp hooves. A young guard quickly produced a small bow and shot an arrow into the mighty horse's side. Zellan cried out and quickly ran back down the path.

Finally, the man sheathed his sword and smugly folded his arms across his chest. "Are you quite done playing around, milady?"

Rhiannon huffed and let out a roar and jumped on top of the man knocking him to the ground. She screamed and pummeled him as hard as she could. With one hard knock, she broke his nose with a loud, stomach-churning pop. A spray of blood splashed across her chest and face as two men quickly lifted her off the injured man. She screamed and kicked, and it took four men to finally subdue her.

The man jumped up from the ground, his pride severely wounded, and quickly walked over to her. He balled up a wide fist and smashed her jaw. She fell to the earth with a dull thump. Her head exploded in pain, and she could taste blood from a split lip. She rolled over and spat in the dirt, making a bloody mud puddle.

"I have had quite enough of you," the man said in a high

nasally voice, his eyes still watering. "Give me the stone, now!" he ordered.

Her mind was fuzzy with pain as she kept spitting blood to the ground. "What stone?" she finally replied.

"You bloody well know which stone I refer to, you heathen bitch, now give it to me!" the man's voice reverberated across the mountain bouncing off the trees and causing her head to bloom in renewed pain.

"I don't have a clue what you're talking about." Panicking, she wondered how they knew she had the stone from her mother's necklace.

"Bring the boy," he called to someone in the bush.

Rhiannon looked up and sucked in a deep breath when Tim appeared all battered and bloody. Two men drug him from the forest, his blood leaving a small crimson trail.

"Milady, are you all right?" His was speech barely comprehensible. His face was so bruised and swollen she did not know how he could even see her.

She slowly got to her feet, swaying in the breezeless forest. "I'm all right, Tim." The man drew his sword and stuck Tim in the chest. Tim let out a hiss as a small spot of blood formed on his shirt around the sword tip. "Stop it!" she screamed.

"Then give me the stone now, or he dies!" Quickly Rhiannon fumbled for the pouch at her waist. Her fingers were cut and swollen, and she found it almost impossible to untie the leather strip holding the pouch to her breeches.

Finally, she got it loose and threw it to the man. He removed the sword tip from Tim's chest, sheathed it, and then very carefully poured out the contents of the tiny leather pouch into his open palm. The blood-red stone winked in the sunlight, sending a small shaft of light to fall directly on Rhiannon. "I'm sorry, Mother," she muttered under her breath, hoping her mother could hear. Quickly the man bagged up his little treasure.

"Now milady, you will come with us," he said.

"I will not!" she answered.

"You will, or the boy will die. It's as simple as that, Lady Kossi. You have no choice but to comply."

Suddenly Luna burst from the trees. She launched at the man who had been holding Tim. He tried to scream, but Luna clamped down on his throat, and then he was gone. The great she-wolf turned and jumped on another guard who quickly suffered the same fate.

With a sharp thwack, a large arrow shot from the trees and one more man went down. The four men who were left standing drew their swords as Flath, Jon and Bleen emerged from the forest. Three men charged with a loud cry, while the man who had stolen Rhiannon's stone, quietly melted into the trees and was lost.

Rhiannon ran to Tim and took him into her arms. "Tim, I'm so sorry!" she cried.

"I am all right m-m..." Tim staggered in her arms and his world slipped away.

"Flath!" she screamed, holding his lifeless body.

CHAPTER NINETEEN

"The haunted mountain range known as Vel' Kur should be
avoided at all costs as many a hapless traveler has disappeared into
its northern regions never to be seen again. Of course, on the other
side of those steep, treacherous mountains live a blood-thirsty race
of giants known as the Archigos."
-Field Guide of Beaynid; Myrin Zantroc

The air was much colder high up in the steep Vel' Kur Mountains. Birthed from the earth's rocky core, they soared above the Alba Forest, and when the sun was low in the sky, they cast shadows into the deep crevices slashed from rock and hard earth. Like the jagged claws of a giant beast, they pointed into the heavens and cleanly separated North from South.

Men feared the Vel' Kur Mountains, and none but the bravest ever ventured very far up onto its thick forest let alone over the steep mountain pass. Any who had business with the Archigos arrived by ship through Turr'ah, a shipping town on the western tip of the Ver' Sol Isthmus, or one of the military outposts situated on the north and east coasts of Ventra. A wider, more used road snaked its way from Ventra, over the mountain, and into Beaynid. It is used by large Archigos trading parties in the spring and fall every year.

Flath had kept to a smaller, rarely traveled path, hoping to go undetected. Now, however, they had forsaken even the slightest path to hide amongst the primeval trees of the Vel' Kur Mountains. They had quickly crossed the naked opening of the Pass of Koslyn and then rode back up into the cover of the trees.

They now camped on the southern edge of Tem Lake. The placid waters mirrored the deep red and pink sky of the setting sun as it slipped behind pointed treetops. They built no fire for fear of being seen and ate a cold supper. Rhiannon looked over at Tim, who slept peacefully on his bedroll. His freckled face was so swollen and bruised that he was hard to even recognize. He had regained consciousness hours after the fight with Baobh's Royal Guard but had slept most of the two days that they had been at Tem Lake.

"He will recover, Greannmhor, do not worry so," Flath said sitting beside her. The ferocious heat of summer could not penetrate the forest, so days were chilly and the nights much cooler. Rhiannon pulled her coat tight around her body and slipped cold fingers into her pockets.

"I know he will recover, but will he be the same?" she lamented.

"Nay, he will not be the boy he was," Flath sighed. "Perhaps a man will emerge from ruined flesh and a haunted mind."

Rhiannon wiped a tear from her eye. "I will hunt them down, one by one, and end their miserable lives." She looked up at him and spoke in low, serious tones.

"I know you will. And I should not expect any less from an Archigos Warrioress seeking vengeance," he answered with equal seriousness. The name sounded foreign on his lips, and she was not quite sure how she felt about the designation. "You have barely spoken since we left Baobh's men. Something very heavy is weighing you down. I can see it in the reflection of your eyes, but you do not speak about it with me." He spoke with emotion and sadness. "Rhiannon, do you still not trust me?"

The pain in his voice crushed her heart and constricted her throat. She pulled her hands from her pockets and took his hands in hers. She looked into his eyes that had turned dark in the approaching night. "I would trust you with my life," she spoke said softly. "I've been sad and hopeless and didn't want to talk about it before now." She took in a deep breath and tasted the pine and the wetness of the lake. "They took my stone," she whispered.

"The healing stone you found? Why would they take that?"

She let go of his hands, the cold air immediately froze her palms. "I wasn't completely truthful when I told you that I found the stone," she said hesitantly.

He clamped his mouth shut tightly and frowned at her. "Who did you steal it from? Hepin?"

"No, no." She shook her head. "I *did* find it, but it was more like I remembered where I had put it from when I was a child." She searched the lake's black waters and then looked back at him. "My mother gave me that stone the night she died."

Flath took in a quick breath, and his brows rose. "The stone was from the Necklace of Verna?"

"Yes, it was from my mother's necklace." She confirmed.

"Gods! She has been looking for that stone for years. 'Tis the missing stone of the necklace." He ran his hand through his hair and looked up into the dim sky. "Her power will be complete then. She cannot be defeated," his voice trailed off.

"Don't say that Flath, she will be defeated! She will lose Beaynid."

He shook his head. "Nay! Not with the whole necklace at her disposal. It holds more power than either of us know," he said mournfully.

"Don't you remember the prophecy? Suddenly you don't believe in it?"

"Suddenly you *do* believe it?" he retorted.

"We have no choice but to believe. It's our only hope to save Beaynid. It's our only hope to get my father and the necklace back."

Over the next week, they slowly climbed higher up into the Vel' Kur. Tim's wounds began to heal, though he remained stoic. Rhiannon rode or walked next to him most of their journey. She said nothing but stayed close to the young man she had grown so close to. A few times he looked up at her, and when she smiled at him, he would quickly turn away.

Almost four weeks since their departure from Sorrel Valley near the small village of Bell, they reached the crest of the trail that they had been forced to follow once again due to the steep, rocky terrain. The trees thinned and then finally gave way to sheer, rocky cliffs and the sharp spines of the mountain. The air was cold and thin, making travel slow and tedious. It would be easy to drift off into a sleepy daydream and find yourself hurtling down the mountain.

The chilly October wind bit into exposed flesh as they descended further down into Loach Valley. Rhiannon put her scarf over her head to warm her ears and neck. Zellan happily picked his way down the rocky path as if he knew they were going home. Everyone was quiet on the long journey down the rugged slopes as it gracefully turned to forest once again and then into a vast meadow of browning grasses and bushes.

The small traveling party carefully started descending back down the Vel' Kur Mountains and slipped back into the cover of giant conifers as the day started to grow old. They stayed in a small, flat area sheltered by a huge boulder that had split in half centuries ago and now lay open like an enormous cracked egg. Knowing that no one would follow them this far up into Vel' Kur, so near to Ventra, they built a large fire and roasted a mountain goat that had met its demise at the end of Bleen's arrow.

The day ebbed and a frosty night covered the land. Tim had eaten to his full and lay sleeping next to the brothers. Flath and Rhiannon huddled together near the large fire. It crackled and popped and spit out bright orange embers that were swiftly carried away on the early October wind. Flath did not bring his lute but started to sing a lonely, sad song without its accompaniment. His voice sounded weak in the ever-blowing wind, but the sound of it was sweet warmth to Rhiannon. His face was expressionless as he stared into the flames and told his sad story with melody.

Three days later they reached the floor of Laoch Valley and the outer fringes of Ventra. The sun began to set, as lazy white clouds blushed pink, then red, and finally disappeared from the naked eye. They could have reached Màrrach by nightfall, but Flath wanted to approach during daylight, lest the Archigos believe they were under attack and kill them before they had a chance to announce themselves.

A blackened kettle sat in the middle of erratic, orange flames. The water frantically boiled as Rhiannon carefully removed it from the fire and poured it over black tea leaves in the bottom of two waiting cups. Jon and Bleen had taken young Tim out to hunt for food and Flath mindlessly cleaned the gleaming blade of his sword.

She sat a cup of tea on a rock next to Flath and then sat down on her bedroll with her steaming cup.

"What did you do before the rebellion?" she asked, shattering the silence.

"I was a mercenary," he finally replied.

"Really?" Her eyes widened. "What kind of things did you do?"

"Whatever anyone needed, providing they had enough coin," he smiled at that.

"Did you kill people?"

"Sometimes," he said matter-of-factly

"You killed people for money?" she asked, shocked.

"I have never taken a life hastily or without reason," he replied quickly.

"You murdered men for money?"

"No, I assassinated them-and only for good reason." He looked at her very seriously. "Is it any different to kill a man in war, then to exact vengeance on a man who is far more blood guilty than a young soldier?"

She opened her mouth and then closed it again. "I guess not," she finally admitted. Content with his answer she changed the subject. "How did you meet Teo?"

He chuckled, "I was hired to kill him."

So much for changing the subject. "So, why didn't you?"

"I told you, I only killed those who deserved to die, and he did not." He took a drink of his tea, letting the soft wisps of steam curl around his nose. "I was hired by a pirate. He told me that this man they called Red Man was a dangerous thief and on more than one occasion made off with their stolen booty". Rhiannon laughed, and he looked over at her with an amused smile. "The pirate recounted how this single man, blessed with the strength of The One God, Ak, killed his whole crew then jumped into the frigid sea and swam to shore."

Rhiannon raised a brow with an unconvinced look. "Well, that is what the pirate told me." He shrugged and started to speak again. "That night I found him drinking and causing a ruckus with his loud joking and drunken singing. I decided to wait until he left the tavern so that I could dispatch him with not much interference. Finally, Red Man, as he was known throughout town, left the establishment. I waited for the opportune time and called out to the man as he stumbled home. To make the story short, we wrestled and punched and kicked in the mud until we were suddenly drenched with ice cold water."

Flath took another drink of his tea and stared into the fire as it stretched orange tongues to the heavens. "Well?" Rhiannon prodded when he did not go on.

Flath blinked and looked over at her as if he had forgotten she was there. "Aye," he said and nodded his head. "Well, we sat up very quickly, and I found a stout little woman holding an empty pail and a pack of little red-headed kids staring at me through the darkness like a nest full of little ruddy barn owls. I could not kill the man in front of his family, of course, so I extended my hand and pulled Red Man from the mud.

"Then I found myself sitting in front of a plate piled high with food, a full mug of beer and a roaring fire." Flath smiled and shook his head. "I thought it was prudent to ask some questions and get the straight of the matter, at that point. I found out that Red Man, who I was introduced to as Teo, did, in fact, in fact, dispatch the pirate's crew. But of course, he had the help of other townsmen from Perth. However, these men were protecting their shipments of food and supplies that the pirate had been absconding with."

"I'm surprised you would even take the word of a pirate in the first place," Rhiannon commented.

"Well Greannmhor, I did not know he was a pirate at that time. He passed himself off as a respectable commander of a fleet of supply ships from the east," Flath took a deep breath.

"I ended up staying with Teo and his family for quite a while, and it was Teo that convinced me to gather supporters for a rebellion against Queen Baobh.

"So what did you do about the pirate?" she asked.

"We snuck aboard his ship and tried to bring him into the magistrate, but he had other plans, and while trying to get away, he slipped and fell from the ship into the red waters," he explained, "It turns out the man could not swim!"

"A pirate that couldn't swim?" Rhiannon laughed and then as if suddenly finding the humor in the situation Flath laughed too. The fired roared up in a sudden chilling breeze; his earring glinted in the firelight as did the gold torque around his neck, its ruby eyes twinkled in a red light.

"Aye. We hauled him out of the water with a large hook before he sunk into the depths of the sea and handed him over to the city magistrate." Flath chuckled to himself, probably recalling the experience.

"Tell me about your family," she finally asked after a period of reflective silence.

He looked at her, and his expression turned solemn. "You know my family are gypsies," he stated flatly.

"Yes, you've told me that," she said with a nonchalant wave of her hand, "Tell me about them, and about your childhood."

A strange look passed over his face but was quickly gone. "My parents were good parents and always had an abundance of love to share." He looked into the fire as if trying to conjure up long forgotten memories. "We traveled with family; aunts, uncles, cousins, and the old man who was just about everyone's grandfather or great-grandfather," he smiled, remembering.

"Sounds wonderful to be so close to so many relatives," she said wistfully.

"Aye, most of the time, but not much privacy, you know.

We traveled around from town to town, from village to village singing and entertaining, selling herbal remedies, charms, sweet cakes, and candy and doing the odd job here and there. I got to see a great many places, Greannmhor, and a great many people. Not all of them so nice."

"How many brothers and sisters do you have," she asked, moving closer to the fire as the night grew colder. "I have one brother and two sisters," he said proudly.

Rhiannon nodded her head and smiled into the fire, then looked back up at him. "What are your parents' names?"

"My father's name is Toby, and my mother's name is Caroline." From far off a wolf offered up a howl to the moon. Luna quickly got up and ran off into the night.

"Why aren't you with them and have a pack of your own kids?" She saw him stiffen and he did not answer right away. She looked away. "You don't have to answer that," she quickly interjected.

"I was accused of stealing and was banished…," he said without emotion.

"I'm so sorry." She took his hand in hers.

"No worry Greannmhor, it was a very long time ago," he smiled and softly kissed the palm of her hand. "It has turned out for the better. Look, I have even found the Archigos' long sought-after empress!"

Later, Rhiannon stared through skinny pine needles into the endless night. She wondered once again if she was indeed, the Archigos' missing Empress. And for the first time, she hoped she was.

CHAPTER TWENTY

"Brutal warriors are the barbarians of the land called Ventra,
known as the Archigos. They are renowned for their ferocious
battle prowess that is most often accompanied by a lengthy state of
madness in which the warrior is possessed by their vulgar gods and
induced to perform unspeakable acts against mankind."
-The Teachings of Ak; Volume II

The lazy sun slowly rose out of the east to spill its warming rays into the valley. A large flock of brown and white geese flew overhead, their loud calls breaking the gentle quiet of a newborn day. They followed a winding dirt path through dry grass that had started to bow to the creeping fall. No human voices could be heard-only the clattering jabber of hundreds of birds hiding in tall meadow grass. A bull elk screamed out to his herd, but his call was quickly carrie,d away on the wind. Luna stayed close to Zellan's side as the horse's ears remained erect and his attention focused on something unseen.

The group remained quiet, lost in their own thoughts, and perhaps, fears of what the day would bring. They crossed a busy stream that broke off from the East Fork River that meandered past Màrrach and disappeared at the foot of the Vel' Kur Mountains. Laoch Valley, (which meant The Valley of Warriors in the tongue of the Archigos) was long and relatively narrow, running from east to west, its floor gently rising up to a hill that prevented them from seeing any further in the distance. Scores of camouflaged pheasants suddenly burst from the grass and took flight into the cold morning. Almost bare, gnarled trees stood on a hill in dark, ghostly shapes in brightening sunlight.

As they approached the other side of the valley and began winding their way into the trees, two riders appeared. Flath held up his hand in a gesture to stop his party as the riders slowly approached. "Do not arm yourselves," Flath said but rested his hand on the hilt of his sword, the snarling panther head peeking out from gloved fingers. "If the gods are with us, we will not have to take up arms."

Rhiannon took in a slow, deep breath as time seemed to stop. The two riders gradually made their way down the sloping hill; their horses were in an unhurried, even pace as they came closer. Rhiannon studied them with wary curiosity. Their long black hair was worn in a single tight braid that disappeared down their backs. Their skin was dark, like hers and they wore leather tunics and breeches. Long fingers of beaded fringe swayed in time with hoof beats. She could see sword hilts peeking over their left shoulders, and each had a set of small axes strapped across their chest with leather harnesses as well as sheathed daggers strapped to each thigh. Their horses had brightly colored beaded fringe hanging from bridle, saddle blanket and even from bands of leather bindings wrapped from knee to fetlock.

Rhiannon's heart pounded in her chest, and the blood rushing in her ears drowned out almost all other sound.

There was no doubt that these two men were Archigos warriors in all their brutal, savage beauty.

Flath said something to Rhiannon, but she did not hear-she was too absorbed in the sight of the approaching men. Jon and Bleen came up from behind her and reined in their mounts, surrounding Rhiannon. Suddenly she was in a cocoon of edgy horses and sweaty, anxious men. Zellan lifted his head and gave out an ear-piercing scream that was quickly answered by the approaching horses. All the horses apprehensively danced in place and stomped thick hooves as their irritated riders tried to keep them under control. Zellan was severely offended by having been unceremoniously swallowed whole by horse rumps. His glossy black ears stood pointing to the heavens as his deep black eyes intelligently watched the warriors approach.

Finally, the men pulled their mounts to a halt in front of Flath, and his party and one man spoke as if asking a question. Flath quickly replied, keeping his hand resting upon his hilt. Zellan lowered his big head and made a low growling neigh, causing Rhiannon to tighten her hold on the reins. They were speaking a language that Rhiannon did not understand, so she tried to read expressions. She looked at Jon who was in front of her, but she could only see the back of his head. Looking to her right, Bleen sat tall on the back of his mount-his face giving away nothing of the conversation.

Flath and one of the warriors continued their terse, tight-lipped exchange. She could see Flath was getting angry. Zellan stomped the ground and lashed his tail around. She tried to peer past Bleen and Jon, who had completely closed off her vision of the warriors, but she could not see past horse and men. She glanced over her shoulder at Tim, tiny beads of sweat dotted his upper lip and forehead, and his hand tightly gripped the hilt of his sword. His healing bruises looked darker purple in the northern light.

Suddenly Zellan nipped the rear of Jon's horse and the poor beast let out a funny screeching noise and gave a wicked kick, missing Zellan altogether, but connecting with the side of Bleen's horse. Bleen's mount reared up with an indignant roar and moved away from Zellan, thus parting the way for him to push his way through surprised horses that angrily danced aside for the raven stallion.

Rhiannon yanked the reins up tightly, but Zellan violently pulled back, almost pulling her from his back. He reared and screamed, lashing sharp hooves into the air. Rhiannon clung tightly to him knowing she had lost all control. He charged up to the warriors, and they quickly drew their swords. Their mounts did not move but watched intently as Zellan stopped suddenly in front of them. Zellan shook himself, then quieted down, sniffed and gently nudged one of the warrior's mounts.

The men gasped as they looked upon Rhiannon. She felt small and so out of place next to the powerful Archigos warriors. As she tried to back Zellan away, one of the men grabbed her reins preventing her from leaving. Flath was quickly beside her with his sword shining in the sunlight. He shouted at the man as Rhiannon tried to pull the reins from his grasp, but she could not get away.

The shouting rose as she looked around for an escape-on foot if necessary. She began to tremble when she heard the clashing of swords. The man finally let go of her horse, and Rhiannon pulled him away. Luna began to snarl, and her fur bristled. Jon and Bleen rushed towards the fighting, quickly lashing out with their swords. Tim suddenly appeared at Rhiannon's side his sword drawn and ready to defend.

An angry, frozen wind started howling from the north through twisted, hibernating branches and calling to dead half-decomposed leaves that were rotting on the cold ground, sending them whirling and dancing into the air.

Zellan reared up and gave a high, loud shriek that echoed off the trees and was carried on the wind into the valley. She tightened her long legs around her mount and held onto reins as the twisted thong that bound her hair broke loose, sending long, wisps of midnight silk reaching to the heavens.

From somewhere above them a low whining grumble that ended in an ear-piercing high-pitched scream echoed out across the land. So loud and unearthly it stopped the men where they were. Cold steel glinted in the sunlight as time seemed to stop. Dark and light heads alike looked up towards the sky. The only sound was ringing of horse bit and bridle and the loud beating of huge, tawny wings. The pax dropped from the sky and landed in the middle of the fight. She let out a low, throaty growl as her furry feet hit the ground and sent the horses backing away nervously. Luna's ears once again stood erect, and she quietly sat down next to the pax.

One of the warriors had yanked a small axe lose and held it in his hand, menacingly looking down at the large winged cat. Rhiannon hastily jumped from Zellan and ran to the pax. She knelt down and gently ran her hand down the pax's silky fur. The cat tenderly licked Rhiannon's arm, then contentedly began to purr.

She then looked at the warriors and stood tall; her dark hair blowing in the wind and slowly unsheathed her sword, not as an expression of hostility, but as a demand to be shown honor. She stared at the warriors, her warriors, she thought with irony. "I am

Rhiannon, the daughter of Sernia and we are here to speak with proxy empress, Shankee."

She saw comprehension on the faces of the warriors, so she knew they understood her. Slowly they sheathed their swords as the men Rhiannon was with did the same. One of the warriors said something to Flath, and they turned their horses and began to leave. Rhiannon quickly jumped back onto Zellan and, with much apprehension, followed them.

Less than an hour later Màrrach slowly unfolded before them. Behind them laid vast fields, orchards, and large vineyards, all mostly harvested for the season. In the distance to the southeast lay plains of livestock. They had passed a large settlement of quaint thatched roof houses neatly nestled into small foothills that divided the agricultural area from the livestock. All were tended by short, stocky people with the whitest hair and palest skin Rhiannon had ever seen. Their features were all very similar to each other; even the children looked like tiny versions of the adults as they played in the dirt with small toys or a puppy.

Now, however, Màrrach lay looming before them. To say that the Archigos city was a colossal structure would be incredibly inadequate. Huge, sleek walls abruptly rose up from a landscape that was turning from fertile green to winter browns. Gleaming marbled hues of amber, coral, pinks, oranges, and rusty browns were accented with intricately carved moldings, cornices, and ornaments made of snow-white ivory and studded with sparkling gems. Against the backdrop of a clear blue sky were soaring towers topped with smooth, curving domes that came to a point with a high finial in the middle. A massive pennant whipped in the wind picturing a black horse with a single silver horn protruding from its forehead on a cinnamon colored background.

Rising above them all, however, was a crystal-clear dome of shimmering glass that looked like it covered the entire inner structure. Arches were carved in the walls in the same curved dome shape that came to a point at the top. A huge statue of a woman that looked as if it were made of gold stood tall at the entrance. She was so ornately molded that Rhiannon had no problem making out her facial features. Huge onyx eyes gazed down at the courtyard and all its residents. Her golden clothing was covered in glimmering jewels. She held a sword encrusted with diamonds, and her long, flowing hair was of glossy onyx. Rhiannon could do nothing but stare at the image she knew must be the goddess, Verna.

Just past the palace were a long line of massive bowl-like altars. A few of them flared and smoked into the blue sky filling the air with the smell of burnt herbs and flesh. Dispersed around the altars were stone statues of various gods and goddess'-none as grand as the image of Verna, however.

As they came closer, Rhiannon could see soft pink sandstone steps leading up the large arched entrance with tall, scrolling letters carved above. Rhiannon wondered if it was a welcome or a warning. A darker colored pink sandstone parapet decorated with complex designs of flowers, animals, and strange twisty shapes ran the entire length of the building meandering out of sight at either end as it rounded the corner of the massive mosque-like structure. The large size and scale of Màrrach made it seem more suitable to giants than for mere humans.

A large group of people had gathered when they spotted them riding up. Proud, Archigos warriors and warrioress watched as the group stopped and dismounted. Several small, blond-haired boys came running up to take the horses. Rhiannon looked up at Flath who wore no expression. Her hands were trembling slightly, and sweat trickled down the small of her back as they slowly climbed the sandy pink stairway to the Grand Palace of Màrrach.

Rhiannon's eyes grew wide, and she heard Tim's indrawn breath as they entered the inner courtyard. Covered completely by an enormous curving glass dome hundreds of feet tall, large green trees, still in full leaf, grew up from a thick carpet of cool green grass. An assortment of bushes in colorful blooms dotted the park-like setting. The air was cool and sweet, and the sound of a stream could be heard. Drifts of flowers exploded into wisps of color offering passersby a vivid display of texture and relaxing aromas. Peahens mewed loudly to each other while large peacocks shivered into brilliant displays of grace and beauty. A small flock of squawking parrots gathered in a nearby treetop. Their long, glossy feathers of red, blue, yellow, and green were of the crispest colors Rhiannon had ever seen. Smaller birds darted around the trees singing their bouncy, cheerful songs, not caring that the rest of the land would soon be under a cold blanket of snow.

One of the warriors spoke, breaking the stunned silence and it was only then that Rhiannon realized that they all had stopped. They followed the warriors into another arched entry, then down a long, deeply veined hall made of the same amber hewed marble, its long domed ceiling was also of translucent glass. A large glass walkway stretched across the expanse of the park connecting the upper stories above. The gleaming walkways threw rainbow colored light across the marbled floors and walls. Huge planters made of marble, stone, ivory and hard gems were home to an assortment of broadleaved trees, small flowers, feathery ferns and mossy green clumps of clover.

A small group of dark-haired children ran past them, laughing and screaming as they disappeared down the hall. A spark of memory passed through Rhiannon's eyes. An almost overwhelming feeling of yearning developed in the pit of her stomach. Pictures of small white ponies with long, silky manes and tales adorned with braids and tiny bells standing next to her best friend Shih 'Ni and her older cousin Shankee slowly waltzed across her mind spilling forth memories long forgotten.

"Are you all right, Greannmhor?" Flath asked in a low voice.

Her mind was reeling, and she found it hard to answer. Then finally: "Yes, I'll be okay as soon as this is over."

Flath reached over and took her hand. He smiled and pulled her closer. "You are not ready to be empress yet?" he whispered, jokingly.

"I don't know if I'll ever be." They walked the rest of the way in silence.

Finally, they stopped in a large room with towering ceilings, made of marble and honey-colored wooden beams. Across one wall, enormous windows were flanked with voluminous, shimmering, golden colored draperies that pooled on the cool floor. More smooth planters overflowing with lush plants spilled out onto the thick, brightly colored carpet. Ornately carved dark wood furniture sat in small groups. A fire danced in a massive fireplace, sending warmth into the room. The mouth of the fireplace was sandwiched between two large, twisting pillars of creamy ivory, studded with tiny gemstones and capped with a huge slab of lapis that served as a mantel. A picture of Màrrach that was painted upon a substantial piece of bleached leather and encased in a gilded frame hung above the fireplace. More statues of gods and goddess were carefully placed about the room as if intently observing their subjects. Vividly colored tapestries, (likely from Bell, Rhiannon thought) hung around the walls, giving the large room a relaxing, comfortable feeling.

One of the warriors said something to Flath then disappeared back into the hallway, leaving the other warrior to keep watch over them. Rhiannon walked over to one of the great windows. Outside, the grass gently slopped down to a massive livery with thousands of horses. Large, corded muscles flexed with ease as they gracefully pranced in spacious stables and pastures. The small, white-headed people were quite a contrast to the large warhorses of Màrrach.

Far in the distance were towering purple mountains that looked like a lethal stone fence had been thrown down by an ancient goddess to divide Ventra from Beaynid. Rhiannon knew, however, that more than vast mountains separated the two cultures-something much more impassible: hate.

Turning away from the window Rhiannon saw Tim looking up at one of the more cheerful tapestries. Sadness dulled his features and a forlorn look burned in his eyes. She came up from behind him and draped an arm around his drooping shoulders.

"My mother made that tapestry," he said softly.

Rhiannon had guessed as much. "Your mother was a wonderfully talented artist; I bet you're proud. It's absolutely beautiful."

"She was one of the best in the whole village," he said with a little more enthusiasm. "Warriors would often come into Bell looking to trade for or buy our tapestries. They always picked more of my family's tapestries than anyone else's."

"You trade with the Archigos?" Rhiannon asked in surprise.

"Yes, twice a year a group of warriors comes through our village. They usually stay for a few days, then they are off to Tel' Rhia. They are not well thought of further east, but from about Bell to Sach then westward, people are not so harsh to them." Tim looked up at Rhiannon. "That is how I know how to speak their language."

Tim and Rhiannon were interrupted by voices and turned towards the entrance of the room. Flath was talking to a tall woman wearing a bright orange tunic trimmed in pearls and lace with a silk ribbon and matching silk, wide legged pants. A low swoop of neckline showed bronzed skin, small ropes of gold hung around her long neck and her thick black hair was pinned up in a series of tiny braids and plaits with a petite diadem encrusted with amber and diamonds sparkling on her head. She exchanged a few words with Flath, and then he pointed over at Rhiannon.

The woman quickly crossed the room and stood before Rhiannon. She was taller than the woman by a few inches, but they shared so many features it was obvious they were related. The woman said something in a questioning tone and Rhiannon looked over at Tim, arching her brows in a request to translate. "She asked if you are truly Rhiannon Kossi, the daughter of Sernia."

Rhiannon turned back to the woman. "I am," she stated and straightened up to her full height. Suddenly the woman reached out and ripped open the front of Rhiannon's cloth shirt. She sucked in a breath as the cold air hit her bared breasts. The woman gasped and pulled her hand away as if she had been burned. She stared at the blood red diamond shape birthmark on Rhiannon's chest and whispered something as her eyes traveled up and held Rhiannon's gaze. "It is true…" Tim whispered in translation.

CHAPTER TWENTY-ONE

"That the empress would someday come home
was told about in an ancient tome.
Ride into Màrrach she did, one day;
where she had been, no one could say.
The mark upon her breast could not be denied;
Though for the fair-haired gypsy, she cried."
-Empress Come Home; Kyia Kossi

Rhiannon jumped back and quickly pulled her shirt closed. She frowned at the woman, but then let her expression fade into resignation. A small group of people had entered the room and were curiously watching, a few keeping an eye on the pax who had jumped up on to the jewel-toned lounge. Two more men hastily entered the room and quickly walked up to the woman. One of the men's tunic and breeches were more colorful and ornamented than the other warriors, and Rhiannon wondered if that meant some kind of rank distinction. Small, beaded braids hung with unbound sleek black hair that reached to the middle of his back. He had bronzed skin, high cheekbones, and a straight nose, which seemed to be typical Archigos features. He looked at her as if seeing an apparition. His keen eyes bore into her and tried to speak of something she did not know. She weakened to his hardened, accusing face and looked away.

She cautiously observed the other man who was clearly not an Archigos. Shorter and of a slighter build, his shoulder-length light brown hair and bright green eyes were nothing like the dark features of the Archigos. He dressed in saffron-colored clothing, and a golden circlet with an intricately molded gold medallion hung from his neck. He stood close to the woman, nodding as she talked to him in hushed tones.

"What are they talking about," she whispered to Tim.

"The man asked if you had the mark and the proxy empress told him that you do. Now they are apparently trying to figure out what to do with you."

Rhiannon shifted her weight and looked at the woman with a renewed interest-a cousin she never knew she had. She took a deep breath and looked away under the icy glare of the proxy empress. She tried to picture the serene pastures of the Montana ranch she had called home, but like a whisper on the wind, it had faded so much she could hardly remember what home looked like.

Flath walked over, still limping from his injury, and stood next to her. She knew he would soon be gone. In the pit of her stomach fear sparked and started to burn. She did not want to be left alone with these strange people who she could not even communicate with. However, what alternative was there, really?

Later that night Flath and Rhiannon sat in Màrrach's great indoor park. Hundreds of torches burned, bathing the lower levels of the massive atrium in faint, golden light. Most of the birds had roosted for the night, the lonely melody of a whippoorwill occasionally floated on the sweet air.

While the others slept, Flath and Rhiannon sat in

awkward silence on a warm stone bench amongst a small stand of gleaming aspen. Vines of moonflower and night jasmine twisted around trellises and host bushes, perfuming the air. A small fountain sang a soothing song of peace. A single warrior loomed off in the distance, an ever-present shadow.

"Tim has asked to stay with you," Flath said, breaking the silence.

"He wants to stay?" she asked in surprise. "What did you tell him?"

"He pleaded his case quite articulately, telling me that you needed a translator and if he did not stay you would be lost, not knowing the language. These stubborn people refuse to use the tongue of the Priests," he sighed. "At first I was uncertain. However, I concluded that this is the safest place for him."

So, did you tell him yes?" Rhiannon hesitantly asked.

He smiled. "I will miss the boy."

"Oh, thank you, Flath! I'm glad I won't be all alone now." She finished the last part of the sentence very quietly. A tension grew between them and threatened to choke out the fragrant air. They did not speak, just looked out over the lush gardens watching the firelight dance and play over grass, tree, and flower.

"When will you leave?" she asked, after a while.

"Tomorrow, after I speak to Empress Shankee," he replied.

She nodded, looking off in the direction that Luna had gone. "So you will ask her to send warriors to help in the rebellion?"

"Aye, but I am not sure my request will be granted."

"She doesn't seem like a real friendly empress, does she?" Rhiannon smiled.

"No, Greannmhor, she is not. However, I am not sure any

rulers are very amicable." He smiled and looked over at her. "Present company excluded, of course."

"I'm not feeling so empressy at the moment, and I'm not sure I ever will," she said, looking down at her dark green, silk pants and colorfully embroidered tunic. She wore her hair loose; shiny tussocks fell over her shoulders as she buried bare feet in the cool, green clover.

"Ah, well, you have much to learn about your people's ways. Knowledge and confidence will come in time."

"Maybe not. Maybe I'm not the empress type." She shrugged. "I don't know anything about running a kingdom or leading an army."

"It is something one has to learn, Greannmhor. You will do fine and become a great empress someday."

She took a deep breath. "So much has happened and I'm not who I once was." She shook her head. "I'm not talking about who my parents are, or where I came from. I'm talking about the person I've been my whole life-the thing that makes me, me. I don't know that person anymore, Flath."

He reached over and took her hand. She looked up at him, studying his eyes that looked orange in the firelight. "You will find your true self again, Rhiannon, do not worry. It will be a hard journey, for you have many things to learn, but those things will become a part of you, like muscle and bone, and will mold you into someone you will recognize, but at the same time, someone new."

"What if I don't like who I become?"

"Having power is not always easy, Greannmhor. Sometimes you will have to wield it in ways that are not so merciful, and those decisions will not come easy. The Archigos say that each empress is chosen by the goddess Verna and given that mark you bear. If that is true, you were born for this. Thus, you will succeed."

Finally, she looked back up at him and said, "I wish you could stay. I mean, for a little while, at least."

Flath took a deep breath and let it out slowly. "You know I cannot, Greannmhor. I must get back. It is going to be a long, hard winter and if I do not receive help from Empress Shankee, there will be a lot of planning that we will need to do to get us through the months ahead."

Rhiannon looked away and nodded, knowing she could not change his mind. He was loyal to his men and would die before abandoning them. After a while she looked back up at him, holding his eyes in hers. "I'm not going to see you again, am I?" The bubbling sound of the fountain that was once so serene and welcoming was now loud and obtrusive.

"I do not know," he finally replied.

Her chest tightened, and she swallowed painfully, trying to keep her throat from closing off completely. She could feel warm tears trailing down her cheeks.

"I will miss you, Greannmhor," he whispered into the night.

* * *

The next morning Flath stood before the proxy empress in her private sitting room. Bright sunlight spilled through large windows. A small, black and white dog lay curled in the warmth of dusty sunbeams.

"I know you wish to ask me something, Seun, ask it, for I am a very busy woman." She made no attempt to be polite- her words were icy and hateful.

Flath clenched his jaw and looked at her. "I want to make sure the woman will be taken care of before I depart."

She made a funny, impatient sound with her lips. "Of course she will be taken care of! She is the empress."

Flath took a deep breath. "Please forgive me Empress Shankee, but I would like your word that Rhiannon will be taken care of and protected."

At that, Shankee did look surprised. "What would a gypsy-like you care about this woman?" Flath stiffened, and his color deepened. "Do not look so surprised! I keep informed of what is happening, even in such an inconsequential place such as Beaynid. I know you are leading a rebellion against the Queen of the Seuns."

"Then you are aware of the prophecy and how important Rhiannon is for our cause."

"Is that the only reason you wish to secure her safety?" Her full lips curled into a cruel smile, and she arched a black brow.

Flath clenched his fists, trying to control his anger. "Can I have your word, Empress Shankee?"

Shankee sighed. "You have my word, gypsy, she will be protected, now leave me." She dismissed him with the flip of a hand, then walked over to a large table and poured herself a glass of wine as the sunlight sparkled off the fine, crystal decanter.

Flath stood and watched her, not moving a muscle. Finally, she turned around. "Is there something more you wish to discuss with me?" she asked impatiently.

"I would ask for your help, Empress."

"My help?"

"I would like to request that you send some of your warriors back with me to aid in the rebellion, milady." Flath's heart pounded, he knew that her answer could very well decide the outcome of the rebellion. She did not reply, just strolled to the window and gazed out as if she had not heard him.

Finally, she replied, "No."

Quickly he walked over and stood mere inches from her. "We fight to dethrone the queen that killed your empress!" She turned to look at him, yet she still did not speak. "We cannot defeat her without the help of the Archigos," he stated, more quietly.

"Then you will not defeat her." Her expression was cold and detached.

"Her power and cruel tyranny grow every day." Flath swept his hands in the air trying to make her understand. "She will soon pose a threat to Ventra itself. She continues to seek Rhiannon, to destroy her and even holds her father, a Kossi, in her dungeon."

She did look genuinely surprised at that, but her expression soon faded into its customary cool haughtiness. "I gave you my word that the woman will be protected. As for the wretched souls of Beaynid, I do not care about what they suffer, nor do I care about your weak, insignificant rebellion lead by nothing more than a dirty gypsy." Her hateful words bit into his flesh, but he would not bend. She turned and started to walk from the room.

"She has the missing stone from the necklace now!" he yelled after her. She stopped but did not turn around. After a few seconds, she quickly left the room.

* * *

Rhiannon walked over to a large mirror that stood near her dressing quarters. Her clothing was so unexpected and foreign. Her top and pants were both of silk and heavily embroidered with golden thread. One beaded strap was slung over her bare shoulder, and her neckline plunged to reveal the proud mark of an empress. Her top was cut short with small glass beads along the hem and sewn onto the waist of her low-cut pants were tiny bells that musically chimed when she moved.

Tiny blonde servant girls had come in and slowly dressed her and molded her hair into ropes of ribbon threaded braids. They had placed earrings in her ears, a circle of gold around her neck and a sparkling ruby into her navel. She took a deep breath and forlornly let it out, for she did not recognize herself and realized that the new had completely replaced the old.

She planned on speaking to Shankee this morning and waited for Tim to arrive. Her pulse quickened, and her stomach fluttered when she thought of her task: to ask the empress to grant Flath's request. Anxiously she walked over to one of the massive windows that bathed her room in warm light. She looked out and saw Flath hastily heading towards the stables, his limp still pronounced. Jon and Bleen quickly trailed behind him. Several fair-haired boys were bringing their horses out to meet them. She turned and ran from her room.

Her bare feet slapped against cool marble as she raced down the glass-domed hall, sending children, servants, and warriors scrambling to get out of her way. She descended a great, curved staircase and ran out of the palace afraid that she would not be in time to catch Flath before he left. Her breath came hard, and the deafening sound of rushing blood drowned out all other sounds as she wondered why he had not come to say goodbye. She could see them riding towards her in the distance.

When they were but feet apart Flath dismounted, and Rhiannon ran into his arms. She held him tight, but was too out of breath to say a word. After a few long moments, she looked up into his mismatched eyes. "Why didn't you come to say goodbye?" she was finally able to ask.

He smiled down at her. "I thought it would be easier if we parted without farewells."

"It would be easier if you would just take me with you," she answered.

"You have much to do here. And I have much to do in Beaynid. This is as it has to be, Greannmhor."

Tears spilled from wet eyes, leaving shiny little trails

streaking down her face. "I can't do this without you," she breathed, resting her head on his chest. She could hear the beat of his heart.

"You must be strong, Rhiannon. You have a nation of warriors that you must lead. This is where you belong," he said softly into her hair, holding her tightly. Slowly he bent to meet her lips and then pulled away. "I will never forget you, Greannmhor," he whispered into her ear.

"I will find you, Flath," she cried. Her throat was so tight the words could barely slip out. He let her go, mounted his horse and swiftly rode away; his tears were hidden from her face.

EPILOGUE

The elliptical red stone lay unobtrusively on a square of black velvet. So gentle and smooth were its lines and so soothing its color that nothing about this stone would reveal its true use-a weapon of terrible power. Next to it rested the Necklace of Verna. Cool silver gleaming in a shaft of sunlight. Smaller red stones nestled into delicate prongs fused into a stream of pure, sparkling silver.

Baobh paced around her bedchamber lost in deep thought. She had not slept or eaten much for the whole week since that bumbling soldier brought the stone to her. She recalled how his dirty hand dropped the tattered leather pouch into her open palm. She had been searching for that stone for over twenty-four years, and now it lay in her hand!

However, now her bones were filled with dread. Apprehension and uncertainness orchestrated her every move. She knew the time had come to replace the missing center stone into the necklace. The raw power of that necklace could easily burn flesh and consume organs, leaving only charred bones as a witness to its wild power. She knew only the basics of how to wield the energy of the necklace but not nearly enough to be sure that she would not be killed by returning the largest of the stones back to its empty socket. Would her will be sufficient to constrain and channel the enormous power of the necklace or would it consume and extinguish her?

She could agonize of this no longer. With a new breath of purpose, she crossed the room, and with a silent prayer to the Goyor god, Pom-Ni, she picked up the stone. It was frozen to the touch, and she had to fight not to drop it. Hastily she placed the blood-colored stone into its empty socket of silver. Immediately the small prongs curled around the brilliant gem as if welcoming it home. The necklace began to hum, and a mist rolled from the stones. The humming grew louder like a buzz and then a roar as the room filled with the color of death and violence. The honeyed scent of passionflower and orchid whirled in the room, threatening to steal Baobh's breath completely. A blood-red glow radiated out from the necklace; its light so bright that she shielded her eyes and slowly backed away.

Her heart pounded in her chest so violently she could feel every throb. She was overcome with fear thinking it would demand her blood and she knew she would be powerless to prevent it from exacting its revenge. The heavy fragrant smell turned caustic, and she began to gag. Her chest heaved as she tried to force the acid-laced air into her lungs, but they were closed off. She fell to her knees gasping for air; black tears painted her cheeks as her world faded into nothing.

As the sun crested the treetops, it sent inquisitive tendrils of warm light through undraped windows. Gently it caressed Baobh's face calling her back to consciousness. She stirred and moaned, feeling like she had broken all the bones in her body. The brightness of the sunlight rushed in as she opened crusty eyes sending pain exploding through her head. Weakly she rolled over onto her back and out of the light.

She lay for a long time, breathing slowly, listening to the gentle beat of her heart. Gradually, the throbbing in her head eased, and her muscles relaxed into a dull ache. Finally, she could bask in the knowledge that she was alive and had not been killed by the Necklace of Verna.

Baobh carefully pulled herself up from the floor and drug herself to where she had left the necklace. A smile formed across her face when she found the necklace resting peacefully, gleaming in the light and completely whole. With shaky hands, she took up the necklace and warily laid it around her neck fastening the clasp at the back under a blanket of black hair.

Denying the ache and stiffness in her muscles, she walked across her bedchamber to her long, oval mirror encased in a carved mahogany frame. She stood quietly, taking in the reflection of the necklace as if she were seeing it for the first time and slowly stroked the red stone; smooth and cool under her long fingers. It sat like royalty surrounded by its lesser subjects. Her black eyes narrowed to slits, and her faced split in a wide sneer. "I did it," she murmured. "I hold all the power now," she said to her reflection. She tilted her face to the ceiling and, despite the pounding in her head, choked out howling laughter that echoed across painted walls.

She walked to the open window and looked out over the choppy Carnaid Sea. A school of dolphin playfully leaped from the cold, crimson water as a flock of determined seabirds fought against the salty wind to reach the shore. The sea breeze whipped her hair and left a salty taste in her dry mouth. She shut her eyes and took in a deep breath. The air was cool and crisp and so relaxing that the quaking in her bones finally ceased.

Her mind drifted to Màrrach and to the Archigos' new raven-haired empress. She knew Rhiannon would come for her father, and suspected it would be with the whole of the Archigos' army. "Let them come," she whispered with a smile. "Now I will finally end you, Rhiannon Kossi."

ACKNOWLEDGMENTS

There were many people involved in helping me get this book finally published. I would like to take this opportunity to thank everyone, from the bottom of my heart, for helping me realize this lifelong dream. Thank you!

First, I'd like to thank my very first beta-readers from all those years ago: my beloved sister, Amy Marshall-Waddell, and my friend, Shawna Fernley. Amy, you gave me some wonderfully creative ideas and encouragement, and Shawna you gave me invaluable constructive feedback.

I want to extend a hearty thank you to my hard-working editor, Courtney Cannon, from http://fiction-atlas.com/ who is also responsible for my beautiful cover design and making this book look fabulous with her formatting skills.

A huge thank you to my copy editor, Amy, who is also my sister. She did a great job at tenaciously hunting down ALL my typos of which I am the typo queen. Here is her editing service:
https://www.facebook.com/WaddellEditingServices/

Thank you to my extraordinarily talented cover artist, Jackie Felix. She brought my characters to life in her breathtaking cover art! https://jackiefelixart.deviantart.com/

I'd also like to thank the very talented Cornelia Yoder for my magnificent map of Ventra and Beaynid and her seas. It was so exciting to see my world take shape! You can find her at: http://www.corneliayoder.com/

A big thank you to the fun and accomplished Charles Renne from Under Production Multimedia at http://underproduction.tv/ for making me look so good in my professional headshot.

Thank you, Annie Beatty, from Mirrors and Chairs Salon for doing a terrific job on taming my tresses and making me look so spectacular for my photo! You can find her here: www.facebook.com/annieatmandc

I'd like to give a huge thank you to all the ladies from the group, Women Fiction Writers on Facebook, for all your help and advice and patiently answering all my questions along this publishing journey of mine.

Lastly, I'd like to thank you, my loyal reader, for coming along with me on this epic adventure into the lives of Rhiannon and Flath and I hope you continue with me into book two of the series: *The War of the Gypsy*, out now!

Come explore my website at www.melissaebeckwith.com. While you're there you can check out my calendar for book signings and release dates and read some of my short stories and poetry. Don't forget to sign up to get updates!

Melissa E. Beckwith

Fantasy Author

Melissa has been writing books since before she learned to read, in the form of picture books, and planned to be an author at age four. She spent her youth penning short stories, poems and writing in her diary. At nineteen she married her high school sweetheart and started her family. Born and raised in beautiful Southern California, she and her husband now live along the Ohio River in Indiana to be near their beloved grandson, Bryar.

Melissa enjoys the outdoors and nature, especially camping. She has an interest in the natural world, particularly the wonder of birds and bugs. She can't grow plants to save her life, though she likes to try. She loves art and paints a little herself. She has a great interest in history and plans on trying her hand at historical fiction in the future. Someday she hopes to travel the world starting with Scotland, Ireland, Africa and Australia.

Melissa loves to listen to heavy metal, Irish rock, and Celtic music…well, anything Celtic really. She loves renaissance fairs, crystals, dangly earrings, bright clothes, the color red, yellow roses, orange cats, and little dogs, like her fuzzy Shih Tzu, Abby.

Most days you will find her tapping away at her keyboard, doing research for her next great novel, or catch her with her nose stuck in an Epic Fantasy or Historical Fiction story.

Please feel free to look me up on my official website or any of these social media sites.

www.melissaebeckwith.com

facebook.com/AuthorMelissaEBeckwith

twitter.com/M_E_Beckwith

instagram.com/author_melissa_e_beckwith

pinterest.com/M_E_Beckwith

goodreads.com/MelissaEBeckwithFantasyAuthor

Printed in Great Britain
by Amazon